THE DE[...]

Barefooting stealthil[...] the strange noises, Ber[...] was doing a very brave or foolish thing. He had seen so many TV shows and movies, and had identified with the bold hero so thoroughly, that it had never occurred to him that he was not himself brave, resourceful, strong, young, and a demon fighter.

Belatedly hesitating at the foot of the stair, he reflected nervously that there was no director making sure he won.

"Hyaw Raw Yaw!"

He jumped and looked around. Someone was coming at him from the kitchen! It came into the light from the window.

"No! you're dead!"

Uncle Albert's face gleamed waxily, pulled back and fixed into a scowl, teeth gleaming. His eyes were swelling, popping out, despite the embalming. He cawed and croaked, no longer able to speak intelligibly—but hatred still animated him enough to send him shambling toward Bernie. His best suit was incongruously festive.

"Harr Yaw!" It came on, not fast, not slow, like some wind-up machine, clumsily, powerful, unsophisticated.

Bernie was frightened, but despite that he had a sudden flood of unreality. It was too absurd a picture, himself confronting this tenacious dead thing from which all rationality had departed. What would the neighbors think? A flash of anger shook him. He fell back to the fireplace and wasted time fumbling for the poker because he couldn't bear to look away from the corpse stumbling toward him.

"Dirty rotting scoundrel!" he screamed and swung the poker again and again . . .

ROB CHILSON

BLACK AS BLOOD

Copyright © 1998 by Rob Chilson. First appeared in *Tomorrow Magazine*, 1997.

A Baen Books Original

Baen Publishing Enterprises
P.O. Box 1403
Riverdale, NY 10471

ISBN: 0-671-87883-2

Cover art by Charles Keegan

First printing, July 1998

Distributed by Simon & Schuster
1230 Avenue of the Americas
New York, NY 10020

Printed in the United States of America

Prospero: A freckled whelp hag-born—not honour'd with
A human shape.
Ariel: Yes, Caliban, her son.
Prospero: A creature compounded of wormwood, bitter gall, and humours Black as blood.
THE TEMPEST, Act I Scene II

This book is dedicated
to the memory of
MISS FOWLER
and to all other staff, past, present, and
future, of the St. Clair County Library

CONTENTS

Chapter One:

Peg O' My Heart

1

Bernie McKay coughed hollowly. Other coughs echoed, here and there, in the hollow room.

"Ah-men," the Reverend Hallowell intoned, and a relieved rustle went through the mourners. Bernie raised his head. Taking a breath and steeling himself, he looked toward the gleaming, solid copper coffin— no, "casket"—on the trestle. Beside him, Angie pretended to dab at her eyes, sniffed perfunctorily.

The first row filed out for the Viewing of the Remains; Uncle Albert's brothers and sisters.

Bernie felt his stomach tighten with tension, and hoped he wouldn't start having cramps or something. He wished he'd applied double deodorant. He wished it weren't so hot in here.

Murmuring, shuffling, the mourners filed forward. "Sir?" The discreet usher. "If you will, sir." The second row now; nephews and nieces, including Angie.

1

Bernie stood, taking a breath, and led Angie slowly out between the damned uncomfortable pews and up the aisle. Slowly, slowly, to give those behind them time. The casket grew before him, a gleaming copper trap with a satiny bed in its maw, a terribly strange bed. On this bed, incongruously dressed in a black suit, white shirtfront, wink of diamond from his tie, lay a dead man.

Uncle Albert, a fringe of gray hair around a polished dome across which a few errant strands straggled; Uncle Albert, shriveled and dried and shrunken in death as in life; Uncle Albert, his scrawny hands folded hypocritically on a shiny new briefcase; Uncle Albert, his mouth drawn down in a censorious scowl, only the cold, dead eyes now closed. An unrepentant Scrooge, dead at last in the midst of his Scrooging.

Near the head of the casket was a stand with an open Bible. On the Bible was a silver letter opener in the shape of a dagger, pointing to a line highlighted in gold: *I am the Resurrection and the Life.* I hope to hell not, Bernie thought.

He paused before the casket, calculating the minimum time he need wait without exhibiting unseemly haste. And then his stomach lurched.

Uncle Albert's eyelids flickered.

Oh, no.

Uncle Albert's eyes blinked. They opened, cold and dead. They focused on him, Bernie. Cold and deadly.

Angie squeaked, clutching Bernie's arm. He stood frozen in shocked horror. They all stared.

Expression came to the dead features, the stiff mouth opened, contorted in anger. The whole corpse convulsed as if electrified. Uncle Albert croaked, gasped; his left arm jerked up stiffly. The corpse came up on the right elbow, each motion easier than the previous.

Uncle Albert gave him the finger, glaring. "*Up yours,* **Bernie!**" he rasped hoarsely.

Bernie recoiled, flushing with fear and anger. Angie stared at him, horrified, embarrassed. Reverend Hallowell wrung his hands and bleated in dismay. The other mourners gaped in shock. Recovering, Bernie stabbed his finger at the corpse. "Shut up and lie down, you swindling old fart!"

But Uncle Albert had never been easy to shut up. "*Don't you call me a swindler, you lying thief!*"

A deliciously shocked murmur was already starting behind the chief mourners. Bernie started to sweat in earnest.

The corpse made as if to climb out of the coffin, bringing its left leg up stiffly. It probably couldn't walk—though with Uncle Albert you never knew— but Bernie, alarmed, leaped forward and shoved the cold, jerkily moving thing back, his hands on its slablike chest. Its left arm flailed aimlessly about his head, the other hand gripped the edge of the casket.

"*I know all about you—I know the truth—*" Uncle Albert was muttering in his hoarse rasp, struggling like a wind-up toy entangled in the carpet. "*You little shit—*"

Revolted, sweating and desperate with fear of what the corpse might say, Bernie cried, "Help, police! Cessation! I demand cessation!" He struggled to hold the grisly thing in its coffin, drowning out its words with his cries.

The bored cop at the back of the room had brightened at the beginning of the fracas. He filed forward along the wall of the room, eager but pretending to be deadpan official. Bernie turned a sweating, desperate look on him.

"Cessation! This man is legally dead. Please!"

"You got a death certificate?" the cop said, as if this happened every day. He had the blank expression of a man chewing gum, but wasn't.

"Yeah—Mr. Culter, quick, show him the death certificate—you have it, don't you?"

"Officer—arrest this man—"

"Oh, shut up! Officer, please, this is very embarrassing."

"We gotta do things by the book, sir," said the cop.

Mr. Culter, the mortician, did not alter his sad expression. With mournful dignity he pulled the death certificate out of his inside coat pocket and extended it.

Uncle Bill jostled forward, peering at his dead brother with the pleasantly horrified expression of a man relieved that a dull ceremony has been enlivened. There was a certain recognition in the relative's expression. Just what you'd expect of Albert, William Smithers as good as said: Never could shut *him* up.

"I'll get you—I'll haunt *you—little bastard—"*

Still struggling with the thing, Bernie cried, "You heard that! A threat, a threat, harassment! I'll have you exorcised—Reverend Hallowell, you heard that—"

Reverend Hallowell shook his head, spread his hands: Not without a warrant.

The cop pushed the certificate aside. "Yeah, right, so Albert Smithers is dead. You there, in the coffin. You Albert Smithers?"

"Officer—arrest him—he's Bernie McKay—the thief—"

"You Albert Smithers?"

The corpse's expression changed, its glittering dry eyes shifted. Alarmed, Bernie cried, "Hell yes it's Albert Smithers! Who the hell else could it be? Ask us! We're just the next of kin, you know!"

"Gotta go by the book. You could all be in it together."

Bernie shoved the cold thing back viciously again. "So go ahead, tell him you're not Uncle Albert, tell him you're Dracula, you're Frankenstein, you're the Ghost of Christmas Past!"

The cop leaned forward. "Albert Smithers!"

The corpse's head turned sharply toward him—then froze. Too late. Its withered features revealed its dismay; its reflexes had deprived it of the chance to muddy the waters.

"Right, it's him." The cop pulled his pistol slowly.

"I'll do it!" snapped Bernie, furious, impatient.

Holding it back with his left, he reached across and snatched up the blunt dagger that pointed to the Resurrection and the Life. He brought the weapon back.

"Be *careful* with that thing, sir," the cop grumbled, ducking away and holstering his pistol. "We ain't *all* dead, you know."

"For the third time, die!" Bernie said, and slammed the blunt point into Uncle Albert's gleaming white shirt front.

The corpse jolted. There was no blood. Then it was as if the toy's spring had run down. Its joints loosened and it began to relax, subsiding into the coffin. Not waiting, Bernie shoved it back. It was like shoving a door with an automatic closer. Feverishly he started prying at the fingers on the edge of the coffin, before instant rigor froze them in place.

"*You—haven't—seen—the last—of me—*" it said, its hoarse rasp also unwinding.

Frantically Bernie tore the gray pinkie loose and reached for the lid of the coffin. He had to push down the left hand, its middle finger still stiffly extended, to lower the lid. Viciously he snapped the latch shut.

He blew out his breath, straightened his coat, patted his face with his handkerchief. No sound came from within.

The cop was fading, looking back with an expression of concealed amusement. He'd have tales to tell—this didn't happen at every funeral—and the upper crust, yet. Bernie's relatives looked at him with embarrassment and dismay; some shuffled their feet; some coughed. The other mourners were more pleased; they murmured together in subdued delight.

That social climber, Mrs. Whatshername, was equally pleased, despite her disdainful exclamation: "Shocking! Absolutely shocking! I thought them a refined, *genteel* family—"

Someone else was saying, "Old reprobate, you know, black sheep."

"Nothing like this ever happened in our family before," came another murmur.

Reverend Hallowell, trying to bring order out of chaos, was saying, "Mr. McKay—Mr. McKay—"

"For the *third* time?" a woman said quietly.

Hearing that, Bernie turned, met Angie's gaze. It was questioning, dismayed. Mutely shocked.

"When people die, I wish they would just plain die and be done with it," he grumbled, taking her arm and tugging, to start the procession moving.

No one seemed to have any desire to re-open the coffin.

2

"There he is," said Deputy Rod Parker, pointing and frowning officiously. White Bird Hadley, spiff in his blue uniform—and the officer who had witnessed events in the funeral parlor—was just entering the Bus Stop Cafe on the east side of the town square. How do these skinny guys do it, Parker wondered. He himself was short and squat, like a troll.

Hadley sat down in the booth with Parker and his boss. He looked like he had something interesting to tell, all right.

Evelyn Anderson, perennial sheriff of St. Claude County, Missouri, raised his eyebrows in expectation. "What did the corpse say?"

"Called McKay a thief. McKay's his partner—*was* his partner. Think it means anything?"

Evelyn Anderson laughed. Parker laughed too, not so loud. "Hell, Smithers hisself was the biggest cheat and liar in the county," Evelyn said. "No, I don't reckon it means anything. What a dead man says ain't evidence anyway."

"Maybe McKay was cheating him in the business, taking loot outta the till," said Parker. From what he'd heard—

"That's for the accountants to find out," said the sheriff to Hadley, good-humoredly. "And prefer charges or file suit, as they've a mind to."

White Bird grinned back. "Guess who the accountants are? Smithers and Waley."

Parker chimed in with their laugh.

"Less trouble for us," said Evelyn. "You ceased the corpse?"

"McKay didn't give me time. He stabbed it with Culter's sterling silver letter opener. Smithers still has it, in the coffin." He grinned. "I heard Culter calling him a damned old thief." Sobering, he looked from Anderson to Parker, who tried to look alert. "Anything going on?"

"I'm lookin' at Brad Schiereck for that cornfield deal,"

said the sheriff. Parker nodded, ignored. "Somebody drove up and down old man Hatterson's east cornfield, row by row, and knocked about half his crop down."

White Bird nodded. "Figured it for one of the Lesslies or Watsons," he said. There were about a dozen of these cousins, some pretty wild.

"Could be, but I'm gonna want to talk to young Schiereck one day soon," Anderson said deliberately.

"Better be soon," said Parker. "That old nigger Hatterson's a mean jay."

White Bird gave him a look. "Yeah, well, I gotta be goin'. Don't look good for one third of the city cops to be sittin' around jawin' with one fifth of the county law."

What'd I say? Parker thought, aggrieved.

3

Bernie McKay tore off the black jacket and tie with relief. Thank God it's over, he thought. Jesus, what a thing to have happen. Be just like the old bastard to haunt me. Angie slipped her dress off her shoulders and let it fall. He watched approvingly in the mirror. She'd kept her figure well, and her face was practically unlined.

"You're not going back to the office this afternoon," she said. "It wouldn't look right."

"I didn't mean to *open* it," he grumbled. "There's all kinds of paperwork we got to go through. Uncle Albert's will—"

"By the way, what did you mean at the funeral, the third time? He had only been killed once before, from what I heard."

"Well, I meant die, you know. I said, for the third

time, *die*," Bernie said uncomfortably. "He *died* three times, we had to kill him twice. Anyway, before the will can be probated—"

"That reminds me. You'll be changing the name of the agency?" She pulled on a fresh slip and turned to face him. Pink face, blue eyes, alluring womanly figure—suddenly Bernie realized how tired he was of her. If she'd only keep her mouth shut, she'd be the sexiest woman her age in St. Claude County.

"I hadn't thought about it," he said, looking away.

"Don't lie to me," she said without rancor. "I can always tell. Listen, don't be in a hurry to rename it 'The McKay Agency' or whatever you had in mind. For one thing, the Smithers name counts for a lot. For another, you'll be needing a partner, you can't handle it all yourself. That associate of yours, Gibson—"

"Assistant," he mumbled.

"Assistant, associate, what the hell. You're gonna have to make him partner, or he'll go elsewhere. He's already had an offer from Gunderson."

Bernie looked at her sharply. "How do you know that?"

"I play bingo with Lottie Gunderson." She looked calmly back at him, then raised her arms and lowered a loose white dress over her head.

Selecting a summer shirt, he considered that. Paul Gibson was a young fellow with an irritatingly smug attitude which he'd been able to turn into smarmy obsequiousness in the presence of the senior partner. Damn him, he'd urged Bernie not to propose retirement to Uncle Albert. Had said it would make the old man more stubborn, which it had.

Fortunately, he'd found an answer. He wondered if Gibson knew.

He wondered if Uncle Albert knew.

"Kind of leaves me at a loose end for the afternoon," he said, pulling his thoughts away from that.

Angie gave him a cool glance, drawing a brush through her thick brown hair. "I'm seeing Lena and Jennie. We set it up at church. I'm sure you can find plenty to do around the house."

Bernie grimaced. "It's the paperwork I really need to get done," he said. As she left the room, he added, "I could go down and appraise that land for the County Court. Been putting that off long enough."

"Do as you please," her voice came distantly back.

"Yeah," he said bitterly, unheard.

He waited uneasily till he heard her car pull out, then drove out to Ross's Amoco station on Highway 13, where he had the maroon Cadillac fueled. From the booth he called Nona Martens. After his morning, he needed a pick-me-up, and since Angie had rarely been in the mood, despite her looks, for some years—

"Hey, Nona, it's me, Bernie. You free this afternoon?"

"Don't you have your uncle's funeral today?" suspiciously.

"It's over, baby. I'm loose. My wife's off to see her friends, and she's forbidden me to go to the office."

"Oh. Well, you know I don't go to work till six."

He knew it well. Nona was a waitress on the night shift at the Night Owl, out here on the highway. And she lived in a trailer in the country, a discreet half-mile from her nearest neighbor.

Five miles by blacktop on Highway B and two by gravel county road would bring him to her place. As he drove with the air conditioning cranked up full, Bernie thought back on Uncle Albert. He hadn't said a thing at the funeral, not a thing about it.

Bernie had been in the habit of stopping by Uncle Albert's place on Hoover Street every evening, during his final illness. And for three weeks prior to the old man's death, he'd administered his heart medicine. Or rather, he'd given him aspirin and thrown the heart medicine away. Tough old bastard. Took weeks for him to croak.

Wonder if he knows? Wonder what he said to Culter when he came alive during embalming?

Oh well. Uncle Albert was dead, and nothing he said could be used in evidence. He had lost all property and all but a few civil rights. More important, that coffin was locked down with a big thick latch and buried six feet under. Four feet was the legal minimum in Missouri, but when Bernie'd heard that the corpse had come to life, he'd told Culter to make it a full six feet, and the fellow had done so. Even a strong, live young man couldn't break that latch, and an animated corpse had little strength. Nor did they remain animate long. Not long enough to dig up through clay soil.

Thus reassured, Bernie punched in a tape and hummed along. Outside, spiky oak leaves of the impenetrable forest glittered in the hot sunlight. Nona's trailer was a hundred winding yards back from the county road, and he'd park the Cad behind heavy bushes. The cicadas were trilling in a rising, falling chorus. Mating-minded quail called hopefully. He was protected from the heat by tinted glass and air conditioning, and on his way to a good fuck.

And he was about to inherit the agency, at last. He went from humming to singing.

4

"Hey, Hat!"

The Night Owl was jumping, but the shout came clear. Jody Stetson looked around from where he sat at the bar, and waved. He'd been "Hat" to his friends since the fourth grade, and his father before him. Billy Martens, Bob "Poochie" Dubret, and Orlin Deutscher waved back and scurried through the throng toward him.

Hat stood up and hollered, "It's all off! It's all off!"

Deutscher grinned and hollered back, "What's all off?"

"The hair on his head!"

They all laughed at the bald-headed old coot at the nearest table, who gave them a sour glower.

"Hey, look, guys, let's get a booth," said Hat, grabbing his beer and carefully picking up his trademark; a cheap white cowboy hat. He waved to Nona Martens and led them to an empty booth at the back.

Hat leered as Nona took their orders. She was a shapely imitation redhead in her thirties who returned his leer with a cool look. To her son, Billy, she said sharply, "Why are you hanging around these losers? Why don't you hang out with your old high school friends anymore?" Martens ignored her, sullenly.

Hat glanced at them quickly and spoke up. "Who's a loser?" he asked. "Gimme a try. It's *your* loss if you don't!"

She turned away without answering. Victorious, Hat laughed loudly, seconded by haw-haws from Poochie and Deutscher. He slapped at her ass as she left, missing. She had sidestepped in anticipation.

"Hey, she's a great horse," Hat said to Billy. "Anybody ridin' her these days?"

Billy Martens gave him an irritated glance and shrugged, embarrassed.

Hat leaned forward and said, "Hey, what happened at the funeral?"

The gravediggers looked at each other. "We heard he sat up and called his pardner names," said Deutscher.

"Ole McKay," Poochie Dubret said, pushing out his lips.

"We wasn't there," Deutscher added.

"Oh. Well, how about at the grave service?"

"Nothin'."

"Reverend Hallowell was sure nervous, though."

"Yeah, and the audience was whisperin'. We heard all about it."

Hat laughed. "Jeez, what a sensation. Figure it'd be ole Smithers'd sit up and jaw at his funeral. I fixed his eaves for him once. I bet ole Hallowell had a hell of a time writing up a brief for *his* soul, to put in his damn funeral briefcase! Damndest old bastard that ever farted."

The others laughed dutifully.

Hat passed for good looking, despite his big nose, and among his friends for a wit, despite his lack of it. He was by five years the oldest of them, ten years older than Billy Martens's eighteen. He'd served a hitch in the army, with two years in Europe, where he'd learned two furrin words: "*Bitte*" and "*Schnell*." They both meant, so far as he knew, "Get your ass in gear." He'd also fucked an Arabian woman in Hamburg. It was in the Reeperbahn, she was older than he'd thought at first, and tired; and he'd had to pay for the privilege— details he'd never told his friends. But he qualified as a traveled cosmopolite to them.

Especially Martens. Hat jerked a thumb at him. "He okay?" he said to Deutscher, who nodded.

Martens looked from one to the other. "Sure I am," he said protestingly, and picked up his beer. He chug-a-lugged the last half of it to prove it.

Hat said, "Okay, okay, Orlin says you're okay. Sorry about what I said about your mom. So: what about the coffin?"

They all looked at each other, and glanced around, on pretense of looking for the waitress. Nobody near enough to hear.

"Solid copper," Deutscher said, dropping his voice.

"Solid," said Poochie Dubret. He pursed his lips.

"And what does it weigh?"

The gravediggers looked at each other. Poochie said, "Four hunnerd, five hunnerd pounds. What coffins usually weigh."

"That Judy Lammers tell you that?"

"It's Luh-moor, like in Dorothy Luhmoor," Poochie said, pushing out his lips in irritation. "Hell, everybody knows what a coffin weighs."

"Five hundred pounds," Hat said. "And number one grade copper's bringin' damn near a dollar a pound."

Martens looked at him uneasily. "Jeez, Hat, you really mean it? I mean, the ole man sat up and cussed out his nephew, fa cry sake. Think he'd like bein' dug up?"

"Hey, it's just a stiff. They ain't got no stren'th. You ask Poochie. Tell 'im, Poochie."

Dubret swallowed beer and nodded. " 'Cordin' to what Judith tole me, they don't move around for long, and they ain't got no stren'th, like Hat says. You heard 'em say that McKay stopped this stiff just by stabbin' 'im through the heart. He gives us any lip, we bash him and that's it."

Martens looked unconvinced. Deutscher said, "C'mon, man, we need a fourth. Bastard's heavy."

Martens still hesitated, and Deutscher added, "Pal, we're splittin' maybe four hundred four ways."

Hat pushed a hand at him and Deutscher shut up. "Hey, it's up to you, man," he said easily to the boy. "We prob'ly can't do it without you, but if you don't want no part of it, just say so."

The boy thought it over for a few moments, then nodded. He looked up and managed a grin. "Be somethin' to tell about, if we was able to."

Hat grinned back at him. "Yeah. If we was ever able to."

5

Justin Waley passed a hand over his balding head, brought it down over his beak of a nose. He hoped his thin pale features didn't reveal the flush he'd worn, he felt, since those boys had jeered at him. Damn that Hat Stetson anyway, he thought miserably. Those boys, he had called them—he was only four years older than Stetson. He felt twenty years older.

Nona Martens had laughed with the rest at his balding head, and when she went over to take their orders, Hat had joshed with her and slapped her backside. Justin sighed, swallowed ice water. Damn his inhibitions and general shyness! He could imagine himself joshing with Nona, but he could never do it. Why do the worthless bastards like Stetson get everything that's good, throw it away, and still flourish?

No point in hanging around here and trying to talk to Nona, he thought glumly. Might as well go home and read a book. The new Stephen King comedy, perhaps that would cheer him up.

Tomorrow he and his partner, William Smithers,

would be going through Albert Smithers's books. Albert's brother, checking out Albert. Justin shook his head.

6

Hat Stetson shushed the others and looked around, listening.

It was well before midnight, but most of the houses near Mount Pisgah Baptist Cemetery were dark. Only a couple of ghastly green-yellow yard lights flickered through the heavy belt of cedars along two sides of the cemetery. The third side was beyond a hill, and the fourth faced the church itself across a narrow blacktop road. Hat's pickup and Poochie's mother's cast-off station wagon were hidden behind the shed that housed the tractors.

"Okay, everything's quiet."

"Maybe we should come back later, when everybody's for sure asleep," whispered Deutscher.

"Don't be a sap; anybody hears the tractor, he'll figure somebody's workin'. After midnight, he might be curious." Hat gave him a shove. "Go start it up."

As Deutscher was struggling with the lock in the weak moonlight, Hat had a thought. "Hey, how come ole man Smithers is buried out here? Don't the Smitherses go to the Methodist church in town?"

"Yeah, but I guess he bought a plot when he was younger, and naturally he wouldn't buy another." Poochie Dubret sounded strained.

"Figures," Hat mused, tugging nervously at the bill of his John Deere cap. He'd left his cowboy hat behind; too easy to see in the dark. "Hurry up, Dutchies!"

"God damn it t' hell," Hat heard the other mutter

hoarsely, and there was the rattle of a chain. "Okay, ouch, dammit!"

There was the flicker of a flashlight from inside, and just then headlights glowed along the road. Hat and the others ducked behind the shed. A pickup rattled by with a blast of rock music indistinguishable from the half-muffled engine roar, went over the other hill, and was gone. Deutscher backed a tractor with a mowing machine on it out of the shed, and, cursing, went back for the backhoe.

"C'mon, we're gonna need shovels," Poochie said.

They fumbled shovels out of the shed, Hat barking his shin and cursing, and threw them into the back of Hat's pickup. Smithers's grave was well to the back; that was good. Hat followed the backhoe slowly, and finally parked under a big walnut on a couple of graves close to the fresh mound of yellow-red clayey earth.

He opened the tailgate while Poochie kicked plastic flowers off the grave and pulled up the wooden marker. The tombstone wasn't set yet, so it wasn't in the way. Deutscher went to work, chunking the backhoe's toothy scoop through the packed earth and throwing the dirt down in a neat pile, like a damn professional gravedigger. Several cars went by and even Hat became uneasy. The backhoe made too much noise; he couldn't tell if anybody was hanging around, like maybe from one of the nearer houses.

"At least we don't have to worry about roots and rocks," said Poochie nervously, watching the backhoe bite into the ground.

At last there came a clunking sound from the grave. It was repeated on the next two scoops, and Deutscher peered carefully into the hole. "Hold the light," he said. He performed a long slow scrape along the top of the coffin that set Hat's teeth on edge and sent shivers down the spines of the others, by the way they winced.

Deutscher killed the engine. "Right, that's it with the backhoe. We'll have to dig down the sides with shovels to git the handles. Git the lead out, Billy-boy." He shoved Martens toward the pickup.

Hat took a shovel and slid down into the dark hole. It was damp, and smelled cool and earthy, like worms. The others followed him, the copper coffin thudding under their feet. In the dim light, it was black as dried blood, with the same hint of red. Hat drove his shovel into the soil on one side. Unaccustomed though they were to work, this went quickly, despite the darkness.

"Th'ow your dirt right onto the pile," Poochie said to Hat. "Don't fling it just anywhere."

"We gotta leave it lookin' the same as it was before," Deutscher explained. "Not a lot of dirt scattered around."

"Right," Hat said, seeing the wisdom of that, and trying to comply. It wasn't as easy as it looked.

"We gonna cut it up t'night?" Martens asked nervously.

"Whassa matta, Billy-boy, you afraid of stickin' it out?" Deutscher jeered. He nearly dropped his shovel as it hit the bank; there were too many of them in the grave.

"Naw, I figure we better hide it and lay low for a few days, see if anybody notices," Hat said pacifically. "I know a place we can stash it."

"Maybe we should bury it," Poochie suggested, with a shaky laugh.

At length they had uncovered the rails. With Deutscher directing, they squatted, gripping the rails, and hoisted it up, hampered by standing almost on top of it. Once they had it waist high, their backs pushed against the side of the hole, it got easier; then they pressed it up over their heads.

"Out on your side, Hat," Deutscher grunted, heaving, and Hat ducked under it. "Heave, Billy-boy! You ain't bakin' a cherry pie now."

"Aw, lay off, Dutchies," Martens grumbled.

When they had it braced on the edge of the hole, Hat asked, gasping for breath, "Why this side?"

" 'Cause the latch's on this side," Deutscher gasped. "It wants to go up with the latch side facin' the hole. Then we open the lid and dump the stiff back down in, an' cover it up. See?"

"Yeah."

They stood for a long moment in the grave, in the dark under the walnut's thick leaves. Hat saw their eyes gleaming in the gloom. "Not long now," he said, his voice raspy. All the beer had evaporated out of him. In fact, now he thought about it, he'd give his soul for a beer.

"I'd sell my soul for a beer," he said. But nobody laughed.

"We c'n git a drink soon," said Deutscher. "Okay, look, me an' Billy-boy will stay down here an' brace it, if the kid don't faint from fear. Hat, you an' Poochie git up there and haul 'er up, okay?"

Assenting, Hat and Poochie eased the load onto the others and ducked carefully out from under. In their exhausted state, arms and legs quivering from the strain of lifting that thing over their heads, they had a little difficulty scrambling out. Mount Pisgah Baptist Church's windows winked reproachfully across the road at them.

"Make sure you wash up good t'night and hide your clothes or wash 'em," Hat said. "Don't want no evidence."

He and Poochie grabbed the rail on the top side and, half lifting, half dragging, tussled the thing back onto the thin turf. Deutscher and Martens couldn't help much from inside the grave. But they didn't need to go far.

"Aw right, how do we open this thing?" Hat asked.

They looked at each other, faces dim in the shade of the walnut.

"Gimme the flashlight," Deutscher said, giving Martens a shove.

Martens walked resentfully to the pickup and then to the backhoe, where Deutscher had left it. Hat realized that the gravediggers' expertise did not extend to the actual coffin. He peered over Deutscher's shoulder, heard Poochie and Martens breathing across the coffin.

But the latch was simple enough, and clicked back easily.

"Okay, let us git around an' we'll raise—"

"*Yaaah!*"

The lid flew up and a big dark spidery thing scrambled out. Hat's hair stood up and he yelled too. It fell out of the coffin at his end, rasping unintelligible words in a harsh parody of a voice. Then it *sprang* at him!

Hat yelled again and shoved, feeling a cold solid Thing in a formal three-piece suit vibrating against his palms, its tie flapping despite the diamond tie tack. It exuded a sickly chemical breath that didn't cover a darker taint. Cawing harshly, it pawed at his head, tearing off his John Deere cap. Close to him, its face gleamed waxily in the freckles of moonlight through the leaves. Eyes, teeth—

"*Help—*"

Deutscher, bug-eyed, had fallen over backward; the other two were yelling on the other side of the coffin.

He was all alone and the Thing was all over him. He couldn't hold it—

"Help me—hit it, git it back in the—"

The world crumbled beneath his feet and he fell, scrambling, into darkness.

For a moment Hat cowered panting in the grave, having caught himself on his left hand, his feet still up in the air. With a sudden rush of panic he righted himself, stood up. He could see nothing, hear nothing but a gasped cry or two and the multiple sound of running feet, fading fast.

Those bastards—! They've run off and left me with it—

Hat stood dazed, looked from side to side for It to appear above the rim of his world. Then he had a sudden fear of Its cranking up the backhoe and burying him. Fearfully he scrambled out of the grave, expecting It to materialize and shove him back at every moment.

Panting, he stood looking around. No sign of It, and no sign of life. Nothing. Yes! The sound of Poochie's wagon coughing to life in the distance. He heard a car door slam, and the engine raced, the tires burred as they kicked dirt.

There in the shadows— Something moved!

Hat was halfway inside his pickup before he realized it, scrambling for his keys. He rolled the windows up as he started up and backed around; his teeth rattled as the pickup jolted into a tombstone. His heart was pounding like a tom-tom. Then he was in motion, looking in all directions.

Nothing moved, living or dead.

The copper coffin lay forlorn, gaping open, beside the gaping grave.

7

Bernie McKay awoke with a start, feeling as if he'd swallowed a snore. Was it a sound, a snore, a dream? He sat up in the still night, looked around muzzily. Angie was a satin-covered hump in the other bed.

Tinkle of glass from below, some obscure sounds, and a dull floppy thud. More glass.

Burglar!

Bernie's heart thudded. Call the cops now, or go check first? His first reaction was to go check, but then he hesitated. The only gun in the house was downstairs. He reached for the phone.

"Yeah, police here. What can I do?" Sleepily.

"This is Bernie McKay, Twelve-fifteen Coolidge," he said rapidly. "I hear somebody moving around downstairs; sounds like they broke a window."

"What! Right, I'll git somebody there right away— Twelve-fifteen what?"

Angie sat up and snapped on the light as Bernie repeated himself. "Bernie McKay, what are you doing? Who are you calling at *this* time of night? I— No, I will not shush, Bernie Mc—"

A clatter from below stopped her; her face paled, her eyes standing out. "A burglar!" she whispered. "Bernie, do something!—there's a burglar—"

"Police will be here soon. Listen, I'm going to see if I can get down and get hold of the gun."

She opened her mouth, closed it, and he heard her shoot the bolt when he was in the hall. Barefooting stealthily down the front stair, Bernie gradually realized that he was doing a very brave or foolish thing. He had seen so many TV shows and movies in which the hero acted thus boldly, and had identified with the hero so thoroughly, that it had never occurred to him that he was not himself brave, resourceful, strong, young, and a demon fighter.

Belatedly hesitating at the foot of the stair, he reflected nervously that there was no director making sure he won.

"Hyaw Raw Yaw!"

He jumped and looked around. Someone was coming at him from the kitchen! He had stumbled away from the stair, so he ran and ducked behind the couches around the coffee table, heart beating quickly. It came into the light from the window.

"No! You're dead!"

Uncle Albert's face gleamed waxily, pulled back and fixed into a scowl, teeth gleaming. His eyes were swelling, popping out, despite the embalming. He cawed and croaked, no longer able to speak intelligibly—but hatred still animated him enough to send him shambling around the coffee table and its couches. His best suit was incongruously festive, the diamond winking from his tie, shirt sleeves open where he'd lost his studs, black shoes scuffed.

"Harr Yaw!"

"Back—get back—" Bernie danced sideways, spun a chair into the thing's way.

It patiently fumbled the fallen chair aside, never taking its gaze off him. *"Raw Raw Rawrr."* It came on, not fast, not slow, more than ever like some wind-up machine, clumsy, powerful, unsophisticated.

Bernie was frightened, but despite that he had a sudden flood of unreality. It was too absurd a picture, himself confronting this tenacious dead thing from which all rationality had departed. What would the neighbors think? A flash of anger shook him.

"You stupid asshole!" he barked. "You can't come in here like this—"

Ignoring him, it got close enough to lunge. Sweating, Bernie danced around again, brief anger gone and choky fear back. It wouldn't ever stop coming— He gripped the smaller of the couches. When it turned and started for him again, he aimed the couch like a pool cue and thrust with panicky strength.

It was too slow to dodge and was bowled over backward. Shrieking *you old bastard*, Bernie was running for it even as it fell. He grabbed a chair and made a full overhand sweep with it, staggering as its legs bounced off the ceiling. It came down with diminished force on Uncle Albert's unprotected head.

Wood or bone crunched, and Bernie raised the chair again, panting, glaring. This time he swept it around in a lower arc, but the corpse let itself fall backward to raise its arms. The chair crashed into them and did little harm. Before he could pull it back, Uncle Albert, cawing, had seized it. For a moment there was a nightmarish tug-of-war over the chair, then Bernie released it, falling back to the fireplace.

The corpse struggled slowly to its feet; Bernie wasted time fumbling for the poker because he couldn't bear to look away from it. When he finally had it, the corpse was upright and swinging the chair back over its head, stumbling toward him.

Quickly Bernie ran at it, taking advantage of its slow clumsiness, to shove it. But that brought him face to face with it, and into its evil putrid chemical odor. He almost panicked, eyeball to eyeball with Death.

Hysterically he shoved it away, screaming, "Die! Die! Die!" and swinging the poker again and again, smashing the face, the head, the chair it finally brought forward, following it up as it staggered backward, as it fell, striking and striking and striking, screaming and screaming. *"Dirty rotting scoundrel!"* His fear was gone, leaving only rage. The smashed skull leaked hideous fluids over the carpet, and finally he realized that it had stopped moving. He stood sobbing for breath, gripping the beslimed poker; then he flung it away.

"Do I have to drive a stake through your damned black heart?" he gasped. Stumbling, looking back at it, he walked sideways to the light switch. In the glare of light, it seemed more unreal than ever, more dreamlike, and more hideously dead—yet with a grin on its fractured features that sent a superstitious shiver down his back.

Red lights flashed as the cop car pulled into his driveway. Late, as usual, Bernie thought. I'll put a flea in their ears. And that damned Culter, too. He said he'd never be able to dig out. By God I'll have him cremated this time, will or no.

What the hell's that on its chest? Oh my God. It's that letter opener.

Chapter Two:

In the Good Old Summertime

1

"Flashlight," said Deputy Rod Parker. He squatted on his thick short legs and looked at the extinguished light, lying on thin grass dotted with clods of clay. The light was old and cheap and battered and looked as if it had been rolled in the clay. "Button's still on, but," he cupped his hand over the end and peered at the bulb, "batteries is run down." He picked it up carefully and took it to the hood of the sheriff's car, laying it next to the John Deere "gimme" cap.

Evelyn Anderson was dusting the coffin latch with light gray powder. "Good," he said abstractedly. "Anything else you find, let me know."

White Bird Hadley was making casts of the pickup tire marks. Parker got out the camera and walked around importantly, trying not to get in their way. He took pictures of the tire marks—the treads didn't match, and one was worn more than the others. He looked at the controls of the backhoe, observed that it hadn't been hot-wired, that the ignition was off, and no key in it. He took a picture of that, and looked around.

The others were busy, and intent.

Parker walked back to the shed, where he found tire marks on the grass. A car had spun out from behind it. He took a picture of that, but the marks were too vague to be worth anything. He looked at the mowing tractor. Key off, not hot-wired. He looked at the padlock on the shed. Not forced.

As he walked back, he saw White Bird Hadley silhouetted against the cornfield beyond, elegantly slim in his blue uniform. Parker thought sadly about White Bird and his brother Red Bud. It wasn't fair, he thought. They were tall and slim and good looking, and friendly and likeable and all. And he was short and fat and nobody liked him, not really. Anderson was always friendly, but he never invited Parker over to his house.

How come them two got all the charm and he got none?

God knows he'd tried to be like them. He used aftershave and mouthwash and deodorant, because he sweated and stunk like a pig if he didn't. Bad as Ma, his stepmother. He watched the TV for products like that, and tried lots of them. Didn't work. And he watched how people dressed and talked and acted, and tried to do that, too, but somehow he always looked and acted different.

When he got back to the grave, he sighed and wiped his brow, though it was early yet and wasn't really hot. Evelyn Anderson looked up from where he and Hadley were working on the shovels.

"What do you boys make of it?" he said.

Hadley shook his head and looked at Parker.

Surprised at being asked for his opinion, Parker said, "A pickup and a car. Four or five guys. Po' boys. They had keys."

"A car?" the Sheriff asked.

"Yeah." Parker explained and patted the camera. "We gotta check into who all had keys to the shed and tractors."

"Poor boys?" White Bird asked.

"Their tires was all worn; one pretty bad."

"But what did they want with ole Smithers' body?" Hadley asked.

Parker shook his head. "Not knowing, I can't say."

"Could just be an asshole redneck joke," said Anderson, looking up from a shovel handle and shaking his head disgustedly. "Nobody liked the old skinflint. Well, hell, we got five-six prints we can maybe match up, some day."

Parker looked at the desecrated grave and laughed. "Bet they looked surprised when it come to life," he said. Walking corpses held no terror for him. "Like to've seen their faces."

Hadley grinned back at him, and that pleased him too.

2

Justin Waley dropped a dollop of vanilla iced milk onto his popcorn and poured reconstituted skim milk over all. As he munched this inexpensive whole-grain breakfast, he tuned in to KBKB in Clinchfield, the Voice of the Valley. The top news item got his full attention:

"The body of Albert Smithers, of Oswego, St. Claude County, was found last night at the home of Bernard and Angela McKay in Oswego, apparently having walked from the cemetery, where it had been exhumed illegally by persons unknown. Mr. McKay ceased the corpse with a poker and called police. Our information is that this is the third time the corpse of the former real estate agent has been ceased, it having begun to move and speak during the funeral yesterday. Mr. Smithers died of heart failure on April eighteenth. The Sheriff's department of St. Claude County is investigating the incident."

Justin ate his popcorn, not hearing the rest of the newscast. When he had finished breakfast, he called the senior partner, William Smithers. "I just heard about the corpse," he said.

"Oh, yes, Bernie's furious. We have no idea who dug him up, and that stupid Culter—"

"Is this likely to happen again? I mean, it's been days, but the corpse was embalmed—"

"Never," said Smithers, determined. "Bernie's getting a court order for a cremation, despite the deceased's expressed desire for burial. Where it's a matter of public interest, the court'll overrule that."

Justin nodded. "Yes," he said. Especially if the Smithers family asked. "Anyway: I wanted to convey my shock, and my support. Of course, life goes on and business won't wait. We begin the examination of the partnership books today?" He knew they would rush the will through probate, but the court couldn't do a thing without a listing of the partnership assets, just for a start.

"Oh, uh, well, don't worry about the audit, I'll take care of it. You just open our office and hold the fort, okay?"

Justin lifted his eyebrows. Smithers was semi-retired; he hadn't examined books for two years. After a moment Justin said, "Of course, sir."

Replacing the phone, he sat sipping his second cup
of tea reflectively. The old farmhouse creaked around
him comfortably. Something, he concluded, is rotten
in the Smithers family. Corpses don't walk without
compelling reason; reason based in powerful feelings
during life. Something rotten that they want covered
up.

He looked around the old house.

God knew he didn't make a lot of money, but it didn't
take much to live well in St. Claude County, Missouri.
Especially if you knew, as he did, how to eliminate
everything unnecessary from life. So: he owned free
and clear a big house and forty acres, and he wasn't
yet middle-aged. All it wanted was a wife and kids to
complete the picture of the good life. All in good time,
he had long thought. But his infernal shyness, he was
beginning to understand, had more to do with his lack
of wife or even girl friend than his determination to
put all that off till he could afford it.

Till he could afford it.

Justin Waley looked around at his comfortable
situation. He hoped to hell that whatever was going
down in the Smithers family didn't take him down with
it.

3

"Damn ole Albert Smithers anyway," said Jody "Hat"
Stetson. He shifted the 12-pack of Bud Light to his
other hand and started the descent of the wooded hill.

"Yeah," said Poochie Dubret sullenly, pushing out
his lips.

"We're gonna wind up hidin' out in Monny-go Cave
like the Jameses."

"Yeah."

They descended the hill silently except when Poochie slipped and cursed. The hillside was steep, split into a wooded gorge. At the bottom of this vast crack the soil opened in a raw wound where a wet-weather stream occasionally trickled out of the hillside. Rocks and boulders erupted from the soil, framing a hole: Monegaw Cave, once haunt of the James Gang, legend said.

"Dead people should lay down and stay still," Hat added, aggrieved.

It was very hot here just outside the cave, the sun slamming down where the trees had fallen back. They ducked quickly through a humming haze of mosquitoes and found themselves in a narrow, mud-floored passage. Grateful coolness surrounded them.

They pushed on back to the Bat Cave, a wide spot into which dim light leaked from the opening. Its roof went up into darkness and it was paved with beer cans. With twin sighs of relief, they set down their 12-packs, each of which had nine or ten cans left in it, and each opened a can.

"Damn ole bastard," Hat muttered, blowing out his breath.

"Yeah."

They drank in brooding silence for a while.

"You think they'll git us for that graveyard deal?" Poochie asked, pooching his lips anxiously.

Hat looked at him in the dimness. Their eyes had adjusted, and he could see the other's nervous expression. He had felt more than a few twinges of fear himself.

"I dunno. I mean, we prob'ly left fingerprints all over, and footprints and all that shit. An' Dutchies still has the keys to that shed, an' the tractors," he added.

"Not'ny more," Poochie said. "He snuck 'em back into Culter's box first thing this morning."

Hat looked at him in surprise, and some admiration. "That was smart! Anybody ask, you say you boys turned 'em in yestidee after the funeral."

In their relief at this escape, they drank for a good while, forgetting their worries about money. They were aroused by a muttering voice and a giggling laugh, both muffled. Brogans crashed down the slope to the cave mouth, and the voice continued to half-whisper, half mutter, giggling at its own wit.

"Whuzzat?" Poochie asked.

Hat sat up, holding his can suspended. After a moment he recognized the voice. "Aw, it's only ole Joe Bumgardner."

The cave mouth darkened and a spry, wiry, elderly little man fumbled his shadowy way toward them along the narrow passage, then paused. "Hullo? Who's there?"

"It's just us, Joe. C'mon in."

"Who is it?"

"Stetson and Dubret," said Poochie, pronouncing his name Missouri fashion: Doo-brett. "Have a beer."

"Oh, *you* boys," said Joe. "Didn't reckonnize you in the dark. Beer? Sure, thanks, boys."

Joe lived mostly on his pension as a disabled vet. His habit was to pay all his debts when his check arrived, then drink the rest of it up in one binge. For the rest of the month he subsisted on odd jobs and credit at small country stores. When he was more than usually short, he had been known to camp out in the cave.

He accepted a beer and offered cigarettes.

"What're you doin' here, boys?"

"Oh, just dodgin' work," said Poochie, pursing his lips.

Joe laughed his characteristic giggling laugh, louder since he was not talking to himself. "Me too. Abner Mazarofsky wants me to fix his hog fence again. Tole 'im I'd think about it. He ain't payin' but ten bucks fer it."

Abner owned the only remaining store in Monegaw Springs.

"Maybe he's got some job we could do," Poochie said.

Hat didn't get along with Mazarofsky, or with the Baptist Church of the town, or in fact with anyone or anything in Monegaw Springs. He'd been raised there. "Only thing I wanta do in Monny-go is piss in the spring," he said sullenly.

Joe laughed. "Wha's that? Piss in the spring?"

Monegaw Springs was named for an evil-tasting sulfur spring, world famous in Missouri.

Sullenly Hat said, "Me an' my cousins useta go down 'n' piss in the spring whenever we knew anybody like from the church was gonna go down there for sulfur water."

Joe's giggling laugh went on and on, interrupted by delighted cries of "Pissin' in the spring!" Poochie joined in, laughing hysterically and pounding his fist into the damp clay.

Realizing he'd been funny, Hat started to laugh also.

"Hey, Stetson, you boys hear about ole Smithers bein' dug up las' night and runnin' off?" Joe giggled. "Ole Bernie McKay found 'im in his house and caved his head in. He must 'a' been mighty supprised when he opened the door! Ain't never heerd tell of bodies walkin' like that around here, not in years and years."

"Smithers would be the one," Hat said swiftly, glancing at the alarmed expression on Poochie's face.

"They say hanged men useta walk a lot. With their heads hangin' down. Hey, you boys know how to tie a hangman's noose?"

"No," said Poochie, evidently having recovered. "You know?"

"Sure, I'll show you."

There was a length of old but still strong light rope in the cave, left by previous explorers. The older man got it down and shakily knotted a hangman's noose for them. Fascinated, they took it apart and re-tied it several times, till both Hat and Poochie had mastered it.

The conversation rambled around from the effects of hanging to trying the noose out. Hat earnestly offered Joe a fifth of whiskey if he would let them hang him. Questions about getting the fifth, he pushed to the back of his fuzzy mind.

Next thing Hat knew, they were outside, blinking and squinting in the blast of light, tying the rope to a limb and standing Joe on a rock nearby.

"Remember to choke and kick around," Poochie told him, blearily trying to drape the noose over the older man's head.

"Sure, boys."

"An' then play dead," Hat said. "Ready?"

"Gimme one more swaller," said Joe, tipping a nearly empty beer can. He flung it down. "Okay, boys, let 'er go."

They pushed him off the rock, leaving him swinging and dangling beneath the limb, his heavy brogans five or six inches above the dirt. He put on a good show.

"Way t' go, Joe!" Poochie cried.

"Yeah, man!" Hat said.

"Uuurrrk," Joe said. He kicked enthusiastically.

Gripping the rope, he tried to pull himself up. "Urk urk harrrk!"

"Cut 'im down, you assholes!" someone else cried. "He's chokin' to death!"

Hat staggered around in a half circle, but was pushed almost off his feet by Billy Martens. He heard a click as Billy whipped out his knife. As Hat was just coming to grips with the realization that Martens was ruining their fun, Joe dropped onto the hillside with a thud and tore weakly at his neck. Martens bent over him, and in a moment turned on them wrathfully, holding the noose. Joe fell over backward, gasping.

"You assholes! You could 'a' killed 'im."

"Aw, man," said Poochie. With grave deliberation he sat down, pursing his lips in irritation.

Hat stumbled toward the kid. "Hell, kid, we was just havin' a little fun. Joe agreed t' do it."

"The least you can do is give 'im a beer," Martens said angrily.

"We ain't got none left," said Poochie mournfully.

"Who asked *you* to jump in, Billy-boy?" Hat roared, suddenly angry. He didn't know why he kept the stupid kid in the gang. Time he showed the brat who was the man here. He stumbled toward the kid, but his feet got tangled up somehow and he fell over.

Instantly he threw up, heard Poochie throwing up, and repeated.

"What a buncha losers," he heard Martens mutter. "C'mon, Joe."

"You boys owe me a fifth," Joe's voice came weakly.

Hat retched again.

4

"What's that you say?" Bernie McKay pocketed the mortician's check for the refund for the copper coffin— about the price of a new, mid-size car. He looked sharply at the mortician, who'd muttered something suspiciously like "Son of a bitch."

"Nothing," Culter said, his face a bland mask. "Now, you have the court order for the cremation?"

"Right here," said Bernie, flourishing it. "And I'm staying here till I see it done."

Culter gave him a cool look. "Very well."

Bernie had a thought. "Hey, wait a minute, you got the corpse?"

"The Remains were returned to us by the police department this morning," the mortician said. "You want to watch the cremation?"

"You bet," Bernie said grimly.

Culter put the court order for cremation in a filing cabinet and, gesturing Bernie after him, led the way back into the shop.

"At least we got the casket back," a pretty young woman said. "Eddie's hosing it down outside."

"Good," Culter said. "Bernie McKay—Judith Lamour."

Bernie offered his hand.

"Oh, you got the court order already?" she said, taking it. She looked brightly at him.

"Hell, yes," said Bernie grimly. "The Smitherses were pretty embarrassed, and they have a lot of influence. I got stuck with the job of following up, though," he added glumly.

Culter went over to the crematorium and turned on the gas oven. It caught with a *Fflooom* like a jet engine. A blunt-looking young man, whom Judith addressed as "Eddie," came in wearing old clothes spattered with dirt and clay. He was pushing a truck with a dripping copper coffin that Bernie remembered from the funeral. He wheeled it into a corner and picked up a large sloppy barbecue sandwich in a green napkin.

"You want the stiff, boss?" he said to Culter, around a mouthful.

"Yeah," Culter said.

Bernie stepped back nervously when the other took down the cessation spear. This was a boar spear, two meters long, with a cross brace about a foot back from the point.

Eddie took another large bite, laid down his sandwich, and, chewing hugely, opened the door to a small cold room. He slid open a drawer, snatching up a big club. Culter braced himself in the cold room's doorway with the spear, and Judith fell back next to Bernie, catching her breath. Bernie also caught his breath, but craned his neck, as the two men glared, ready, down at the occupant of the drawer.

After a moment Eddie lowered his club, and Culter also relaxed.

Bernie drifted over to the door and looked past the mortician. The corpse lay stiffly, its smashed head still leaking a little. Its hands and feet were tied tightly, without regard for nonexistent circulation, with nylon piggins from the hank on the wall. Culter had recovered his sterling silver letter opener from its chest, Bernie saw. Despite the cold, a faint hideous odor leaked out.

"Don't put the spear away yet, Mr. Culter," said Eddie. He picked up his sandwich and took a monster bite, causing Bernie's stomach to lurch. Brushing both hands on his pants, Eddie jerked a piggin off the hank. Swiftly and expertly he bound the corpse to the board it lay on.

"Okay, boss, if it does start moving it can't do anything," he said, muffled. "We can just lift board and all out of the drawer and drop it into the box. Unless you want a shroud?" Swallowing, he looked past the mortician at Bernie.

Conquering his stomach, Bernie said, "Hell no, they're not paying for any extras."

Culter nodded. He wheeled a trolley with a plain pine box on it into the cramped cold room and bent to the feet. Up, over, and down, and the corpse didn't so much as twitch. "Close the box, except the head end, and bring it out."

Culter came out of the cold room and gestured to Bernie. "We recovered the funereal briefcase with Reverend Hallowell's brief for Mr. Smithers's soul," he said. "It's designed to be cremated, for those who choose that method. Shall we throw it in the—"

"Ohm thyit!" came Eddie's food-muffled voice, accompanied by a clunk. He jumped and looked around guiltily at Bernie. His hand came out of the coffin with a bottle of Gates's barbecue sauce, his sandwich open in the other hand.

"What the hell?" Bernie said. Next to him, Judith stood staring in dismay.

"S-sorry, sir. I-I dropped the bobbycue sauce—"

Bernie hurried over to the box, the mortician right beside him. The bulging eyes of the corpse stared in two directions up through sticky red stuff, he saw. Its dumbfounded expression caused Bernie to double up and roar with sudden laughter.

"Uh—we'll clean that off—"

"Don't—don't bother," Bernie said, wiping his eyes.

He looked at the helplessly staring corpse and went off into another train-wreck of hysterical laughter.

"Well, we wanted you to be satisfied that it's your uncle-in-law, and that he was indeed cremated," Culter murmured, with a return to his professional manner. He dropped the briefcase into the box, lowered the head end of the lid, and wheeled the gurney to the crematorium's maw. A nervous Eddie took the other side—still eating, Bernie thought, choking down laughter.

"Ready?" Culter asked.

"Mmyeah." (Chomp-chomp.)

Eddie opened the door. Enthusiastic flames puffed, making Bernie step back. Culter gave the box a steady, smooth shove into the yellow inferno whose heat beat out into their faces. The door snapped shut.

Bernie sniffed and couldn't keep from laughing again. "Good barbecue."

5

Justin Waley looked away from the spreadsheet and picked up the interoffice line. "Yes?"

"It's Mr. McKay, Mr. Waley," said their elderly office girl. "On four-three."

"Thank you, Sandra," he said, and pushed a button. "Justin Waley."

"Justin," came Bernie McKay's hearty voice. "How are you?"

"Fine, Mr. McKay," said Justin. Frugally, he turned the computer's screen down. "The question is, how are you? Mr. Smithers tells me the whole family is upset."

"Oh, they've been at me all day, as if it was my fault!

He was *their* brother; I just married into the family. But thanks for your concern. Anyway. I wanted to ask you, confidentially, if you can tell me anything about the partnership audit?"

Justin lifted his eyebrows but kept his voice even. "No, Mr. McKay. Mr. Smithers is handling that himself, as the senior partner. Neither I nor Mr. Lamour are involved."

There was a moment of silence, and McKay's voice came, sharpened by concern. "Uncle Bill's doing it all by himself? Isn't that unusual?"

"Well, this is an unusual case, and I believe that he wishes to keep it especially confidential," Justin said temporizingly. "I suppose though that he will eventually ask for help from one of us."

"From you, you mean."

"That is very likely."

"Well. I just wondered . . . it seemed odd to me. It felt like a . . . well, a cover-up, if you know what I mean."

Smithersgate, Justin thought. "I believe Mr. Smithers wanted to avoid any further notoriety," he said primly. "Did you have any reason to suspect, let us say, irregularities in Mr. Albert Smithers's accounts?"

Short pause, then: "Frankly, with Uncle Albert, God only knows. We were partners, but we basically worked independently. He wasn't easy to get along with, and he wouldn't stand being questioned. He could've been doing anything."

And probably was, if gossip is any guide, Justin mused. "Obviously, as the surviving partner, you have a right to know what we find," he said. "I'll keep my eye out; confidentially, of course."

"Confidentially, of course," McKay said hastily. "Thanks for that, Justin. Not that I don't trust Uncle Bill, but . . . well, the Smithers family has its own viewpoint on things. They'd rather lose money than face."

"Yes," Justin said. Very well put, he thought. "Your concern is understandable."

"Right. Well, I'm glad you understand," McKay said. "Oh, by the way, is Gibson over there? Paul Gibson? I thought he was helping Uncle Bill, but nobody seems to have seen him around. . . ."

Gibson. That would be the third agent in Smithers and McKay, Real Estate—Justin knew him slightly and liked him about as much. "No, he hasn't been here."

"Hmm. Wonder where he could be. Well, thanks anyway."

When he had hung up, Justin poured tea and put his legs up on the dictation board. He looked out his second-floor window at the massive courthouse in the middle of Oswego's Square. After about five minutes he put his feet down and dialed a number.

"Ikle, Orson, Blanchard, Smithers, and Hadley," said a woman who was obviously not Ikle, Orson, Blanchard, Smithers, nor Hadley.

"Mr. Hadley, please; tell him it's Justin Waley."

Presently Red Bud Hadley's voice came. "Red Bud here. What can I do for you, Juss?"

"It's close enough to quitting time to think about it," said Justin. "How about meeting me at Bracher's at five thirty?"

"I'll have to call Margie, but if I don't call back, you'll find me there."

A row of Brachs's red and dark blue striped candy boxes lined the window of Bracher's Restaurant: a clever pun that had gained quick name recognition for the place. At five-thirty Justin walked past them into the restaurant, past the stuffed jackrabbit with the antelope antlers on its head, and slid into a brown leatherette booth at the back, opposite Red Bud Hadley.

When they had ordered, he said, "How do you like being junior, junior, junior partner in the second or third most successful law office in town?"

Red Bud sipped coffee, looking at him quizzically. He was almost theatrically handsome—women's heads turned when he or his brother White Bird walked by—but like his brother he was a modest, decent, and thoroughly married sort. Like Justin, he had all the unlovable virtues.

"It beats shoveling gravel, and it pays a little better than being a city cop like my brother. In other words, it's about like running a treadmill on bread and water. How do you like being junior partner of the second and last accounting firm in town?"

"Ditto. So. How would you like to be half partner in the only investment counseling firm in town?"

Red Bud stared at him a moment, his coffee cup suspended. He took a sip and set it down slowly. "Would I have to quit my day job?"

"No, and you'd better not. We'll start small, and we'll scramble. But with your legal training and my accounting background, we're well equipped at least to start. I've been reading books, and I know some of the basics."

Red Bud drew a bird on the table top with a wet finger. "You were always a hotshot in school," he said musingly. "I'll bet you do have a good leg up on investment counseling. I'll have to talk it over with Margie. But," he nodded, "it's worth thinking about."

He looked curiously at Justin. "Tell me, Juss, why this sudden desire to set up for yourself? I thought you were all set; you made full partner young, in a thriving office. . . ."

"Time to move on," Justin said. Before the Smitherses come crashing down, he didn't say.

6

"What we need is some idee of who was with 'em," Deputy Rod Parker said.

Judith Lamour looked at him brightly, with so much interest it kept surprising him. "Well, really, I mean, I've gone out with Bob Dubret, ..." She pronounced his name *Dyew-Bray*. She shook her ringletted head, smiling. "I really don't know who all his friends are, Deputy Parker."

Parker looked around the cluttered office of Culter's funeral home, trying to distract himself from the bright brown gaze that never wavered from him. Uninterrupted scrutiny from a woman, except his stepmother, was new to him. "Well," he said nervously, "you ever hear either of 'em mention friends?"

"Oh, all the time, Deputy Parker, but really . . . well, maybe they mention Jody Stetson most." Demurely she added, "I wouldn't go out with him."

Fascinated—Parker knew Hat Stetson—he said, "Why not?"

Judith tossed her head, making the brown ringlets dance. "I just wouldn't. Or Orlin Deutscher, either. Bob's different from them; he's much nicer and more polite."

"He's got sisters," Parker said. "So you like him, but not Dutchies or Stetson. And you go out with him but not them."

"Well, I never said I was in love with Bob!" She tilted her head and looked at him with a quirk of her mouth that brought out a dimple. "It's just that a girl often doesn't have much of a choice, unless she wants to go to the movies with another girl, you know?"

Her smile brought a strong, dull pain to Parker's chest; he thought he'd never met anyone so charming. "Yeah," he said faintly. He cleared his throat. "So, if, uh, Dyew-Bray was implicated, you wouldn't hesitate to tell me?"

"Well, maybe I'd *hesitate*," she said impishly. "But of course I'd tell you anything I knew! But I don't know anything."

"Uh, remember anybody else they talk about a lot?"

"Oh, Frankie Cowgill, Pfister Wainwright. Mmm. And a lot of girls," she added, primly. "Especially when they think I'm not listening." She looked at him archly. "They talk a lot, you know, but I don't think they get much."

Parker opened and closed his mouth, horrified to feel his face reddening. "Uh—right. Uh, it's the same with most men, Miss Lammers," he said.

"Lamour," she said quickly: "Luh-moor. And I know it is, Deputy Parker." She laughed, tilted her head archly. "I don't mind the way men talk. I have three brothers myself!"

To cover his confusion, Parker solemnly wrote Stetson's and the others' names in his notebook, though he didn't need to. "Thank you very much for your help, Miss, uh, Luh-moor. And if you think of anything, please let us know."

"I surely will, Deputy Parker. And don't hesitate to call me. You have my number?" She gave it to him and he carefully wrote it down as well, her name beside it. "Or drop by! Even when we're busy I can usually make few minutes to talk!"

Culter appeared in the doorway, smiled at her. "Yes,

if there's anything we can do to help, don't hesitate to call on us."

Parker thanked them bumblingly, shook hands—Judith shook as enthusiastically as she spoke—and made his escape.

Well, that was one of the reasons he'd gotten into law enforcement, Parker thought—to impress girls. Nice girl, he thought enviously. So *interested* in everything. He thought back to his schooling and came up with a word: enthusiastic. He was a little uncertain of how it was spelled, but it described her.

Quitting time. He checked out at the sheriff's office, sighed and said goodbye to Renee, the Sunshine Girl, whose stint at the radio wouldn't end for another couple of hours. Tiring as he often found his job, it was preferable to going home to Ma.

Parker thought about going by the Night Owl on the off-chance of company. But the only kind of woman there who'd be interested in him would want money, and his stepmother took enough of his pay without him throwing away the rest. Good thing Ma didn't know how much he made. He saved every penny he could, for some vague future use, when he got away from her. She'd have supper for him, but somehow even his prodigious appetite wasn't up to eating in her shrill company. He went instead to a hamburger joint, ate greasy food with relish, vaguely thought again about going on a diet.

Outside, in the graveled lot, he stood by his car, debating going to a movie. But he'd seen everything in driving distance. Just drive around a while, he thought. He had never known anyone whom he could tell of the pleasure he got in driving around St. Claude County and just looking at the hills and trees and fields and things. It was sure purty country, most folks would agree, but they never went *looking* at it. Just drove through it, on the way to the next job, or drunk, or, he thought enviously, fuck.

He debated a trip up north to Deepwell to see Eunice. Eunice might be black, might be older, might be a little dotty—but she never nagged him, or even raised her voice to him. Matter of fact, she was far and away the nicest and best-looking woman he'd ever made it with. But Ma would pester the life out of him when he got in, if he was out much after dark.

Aw, hell.

Parker drove slowly home and greeted Ma tiredly.

"So there you are," she said shrilly. She was tall and thin and cadaverous and smelled of unwash and whiskey and other nameless things. Her nose was sharp, her skin like parchment—she hadn't been out in the sun in years—and only a few teeth remained. "You didn't come home to dinner. We waited table for you for a-nour."

That was a lie, Parker knew, they hadn't waited a second. "I had a few last things to do," he mumbled. "Hadda write up my log."

"Dickie was here on time, like he mostly is, aren't you Dickie, but you, you're never on time, you're hardly ever *here*," she said.

Parker's youngest stepbrother smirked at him, reclining at ease in what had been his father's chair. By rights, now the old man was gone, it should've been his, Parker's. But Dickie was Ma's favorite, and her only son currently at home. Her boys had split as soon as they could, but came back from time to time, when they needed help. And always took his chair.

He'll soon be gone, Parker thought. He took his own more humble seat, that needed to be reupholstered, some distance from their two throne-like recliners, and stared vaguely at the shows they chose to watch, ignoring them and being ignored. Having Dick here was a strain on Parker's salary—Ma's Social Security didn't go but so far—but Parker didn't mind the expense, since it gave her someone else to think about, and pick on.

Damn them all anyway, why was he stuck with taking care of the old body? She was *their* mother. Without someone to take care of her she'd fall apart. So why was he stuck with her? When she was gone, betcher ass they'd come around quick enough and sell the place out from under him; he wouldn't even inherit to reward him for taking care of her.

Parker thought of his father. He couldn't remember the old man, who'd taken off before he was three, but Ma kept a faded picture of him on the shelf. He'd been fat like Parker, but not bad looking. Why he'd ever married a ugly ole witch like his stepmother, Parker had never figured.

Maybe he got tired of being alone; he needed someone to raise me up, and hell, maybe she was nice to 'im when he was hung over, Parker thought. Pore old bastard, it was a pore bargain. But what else could a drunk git?

Ma'd made it known, many's the time, that his father was a drunk. Parker'd made up his mind never to get drunk again, after his first time, and, now he'd put on the star, he was confirmed. A couple beers in the evening, and he'd had his. Who knew when he might come out of the daze and find he was married to such a deadly ole bag as Ma?

Dickie and Ma were sopping up whiskey, as usual, it was about all she swallowed. Needs it to keep from smelling worse, he thought. Since they slept all morning, they'd still be awake at midnight. Long before then Parker was off to bed. He couldn't wait for morning and his long day to begin.

Lying awake, which he did more than he liked, Parker thought again of Judith Lamour, and in the darkness her bright eager direct gaze pierced him again. God, he thought. What a nice girl. Dyew-Bray don't know what he's got.

7

Bernie McKay hung up and paced around the office. Damn Gibson anyway. Where the hell was he? Place was in total confusion, and Bernie needed to clear accounts for the Ikle sale—one of their most important accounts.

Bernie called the Registrar in the court house. "Smithers and McKay Real Estate. I understand that my associate, Paul Gibson, is over there checking on some deeds. Can you put him on, please?"

"I'm sorree, Mr. McKayee, but Paul hasn't been in todayee," came the lilting response.

"Thank you." Damn it.

Bernie tried to put things in order and get something done, but within twenty minutes he was tearing through the files looking for an abstract. Damn thing should've been with the rest of the damn file—who the hell took it out—he'd like to shove it up their ass—it was an inch thick, and ran back to 1894—where the hell was Gibson?

Furious, he called Smithers and Waley, but the girl there hadn't seen him; neither was he at the copy shop. Nor at the court house. He even called Gunderson's Real Estate—they frequently had dealings with each other, and Gibson might have been over on some joint matter.

"Mr. Gunderson isn't here, Mr. McKay. Would you care to call him at home?"

He wouldn't, but he did, and got Lottie Gunderson. "Oh, no, Bernie, I haven't seen Paul Gibson all day. You want to talk to Jack? He has a summer cold, and he's lying down. Oh, Bernie—" catching him just before he hung up. "Where's Angie? She was supposed to join us this afternoon."

Bernie had no damn idea where his wife was, but said so politely. Furious, he quit early and stomped off home.

The big, maple-shaded house on Coolidge soothed him a little. Bernie had worked hard for this place. His father had been a farm worker and Bernie had worn his socks three days at a time as a kid because he didn't have enough to change every day. Yet, he had married into one of the Four Families that owned and ran Oswego and much of St. Claude County.

He had sometimes wondered if that had been such a good deal.

He headed for the kitchen and the pitcher of Martinis that should be waiting. Uncle Albert's body lay at full stretch on the kitchen table.

Bernie halted, shocked—he'd *seen* them cremate the thing—

It sat up, and he realized that he was seeing the counter through it: ghost. Its liver-spotted features were whole, Uncle Albert's to the wizened life, creased in a gleeful grin he'd rarely seen when the man was alive.

"Hello, Bernie, good to see you, you thieving little bastard." The ghost sat dangling its legs for all the world like a live person, grinning at him. The faucets gleamed through it.

"Urrk," said Bernie, gripping the door frame. He felt his eyes bugging out; his breath came hard.

"Thanks for having me cremated, you little shit." Its grin widened. "That's where you let your skimmer leak. As long as I was animating my body, I was bound to it. If you'd buried me in that damn copper coffin again, I'd have been stuck there till my body rotted away—months, years maybe." He laughed unpleasantly, and slid to the floor.

"Now, Bernie, *where did you put my gold?*"

"Wha—?"

"Where's my gold, you thief, you lying cheating bastard! I want my gold! Give me my gold—"

The ghost came at him, arms outstretched, the grin now a rictus of hate, the eyes glaring wildly. Bernie staggered backward in a panic as the hands came at his throat. No poker would stop it now— He tripped over the carpet, fell at full length and banged the back of his head severely. Stars shot through his brain; tears stood in his eyes.

Move move move— Gasping and desperate, he made himself move. He was still scrambling frantically backward on the carpet when he realized that the ghost was gone and Angie was coming through the front door.

"Bernie! What are you doing?"

He was lying on the floor, his head almost on the hideous stain Uncle Albert had left on his previous visitation.

"Uh—I tripped—" In far less time than he could have put words to it, he decided not to mention the ghost. It was scandalous to be haunted— it hinted at shameful secrets—there'd been enough notoriety— the Smitherses would blame him if he was the haunted one, not their own kinsman who was the ghost—

"Well, do be more careful. What were you doing, dancing around the room like a lunatic? Never mind, I don't want to know."

He sat up groggily as she tripped youthfully by him and into the kitchen. Spitefully he hoped Uncle Albert would appear and leap at her, but he heard her singing "In die Gut Alt Sommerzeit" in the original German, an accomplishment he didn't envy her in the least. He heard the refrigerator door open and the gurgle of a martini into a glass.

She lifted it perfunctorily to him as he came in, smiling to herself. "I love the summer," she said, twirling about and making the skirt of her light sun dress swirl around her still-excellent legs. "Lottie Gunderson had a bunch of us over, and we drove out to the Sac-Osage Overlook. It's beautiful."

"A bit hot, I would have thought." Lottie Gunderson? Angie must've gotten there late.

"Oh, not so much. We didn't mind, anyway."

Bernie spent an uneasy evening, so worried about the ghost that Angie's bubbly mood was more an irritation than a relief. Gold? What stupid movies had Uncle Albert been watching? Death must have driven the man daft. Gloating over some imaginary buried treasure. His gold, my ass.

At length, watching Arsenio Hall and dreading the moment for turning out the light, Bernie jolted to attention at his wife's tone.

"You haven't heard a thing I've said," Angie said. "Pay attention! Lottie Gunderson tells me that Jack talked to Paul Gibson again yesterday. You really should make him partner soon, and let him know immediately, or you'll lose him. I mean it, Bernie," looking at him sharply. "The Gundersons know what he's worth."

"Paul Gibson," he said slowly, looking at her. He

started to tell her caustically that Paul Gibson wasn't worth the paper his birth was recorded on—he hadn't been in the office all afternoon. But he caught himself.

Where's Angie? She was supposed to join us this afternoon. He could hear Lottie Gunderson's voice clearly in his head.

Sac-Osage Overlook, hmm? "We didn't mind the heat." I'll bet you didn't, you horny old bag, he thought, and made soothing, acquiescent murmurs. Full partner? Paul Gibson? Not in *my* agency.

I'll see him dead first.

Chapter Three:

Take Me Out to the Ball Game

1

Nona Martens struggled into wakefulness, drugged and feverish from sleeping in the heat. It was late morning. She sat up dispiritedly, gathered her strength, and slid her feet out of the bed. Sitting with face in hands, she wondered vaguely why she went on, but habit eventually brought her upright. Bernie McKay had given her a second-hand air conditioner, but while he was generous with items like that, he didn't give her money. Consequently, she couldn't afford to run it much.

Why on earth I ever got mixed up with him—

She'd known it would do her no good even if no one ever found out. But McKay reminded her a little of her father—on the rare occasions when he was sober and loving. And also of her ex-husband, Kevin Martens, when *he* was sober and loving. Well, it was true what they said; you marry your father. She herself, she knew,

53

just missed being an alcoholic, and she had her fears
for Billy.

Billy—she stopped, her hand on the doorknob,
reminded—he was back with her again. In this heat,
she slept in the nude. She opened the small mobile
home's tiny closet and found her old green bathrobe.
Here where her nearest neighbor was far away and a
screen of leaves lay between her and the road, she
had gotten out of the habit of using it.

Neither the air conditioner, which she turned on
first, nor the shower, woke Billy, sleeping on the couch
in the tiny living space. The sounds and smells of
cooking breakfast did. Nona watched him rouse,
unshaven and unattractive. He was turning into another
man, she thought wistfully. Self-centered, shiftless,
insensitive—he hadn't been born so, nor had he been
that way as a child.

"What's f'breakfast?" he asked, knuckling his eyes
and sitting up.

"Bacon and eggs," she said. Good morning, she
thought. Good morning, Mom, good to see you. How
are you? Aw shit.

"Good." He got up, kicking the sheet carelessly to
the floor, and went past to the bathroom in his
undershorts. Presently he returned and hopped
clumsily into his pants, not having bothered to shave,
or even shower.

Nona debated sending him back for both operations.
She felt delicate about it, remembering her father's
wars with her brothers, remembering too how Kevin
had constantly ding-donged at Billy when he was little,
before she'd sent him packing back to the Army.

"Here you are, Billy," she said brightly, smiling.

He sat down at the counter with an uncouth grunt.
She started to pour orange juice but he stopped her.

"Aw, Mom, you *know* I only drink grapefruit juice."

"Sorry, Hon, this is all I got."

"Aw, gimme coffee."

She poured it silently, thinking, You're welcome. Should she mention his lack of manners? He was eighteen, for god's sake, and out of school. She hadn't seen him for a month, except at the Night Owl with his friends, that damned Hat Stetson and all.

Feeling guilty at not having raised him better, she sat down to her own breakfast, giving him another bright smile.

Billy responded with a sullen, hang-dog look that said: Don't talk to me. Suddenly she realized that Billy was afraid. Terribly afraid.

Oh God, she thought prayerfully. What has he done now? Hat Stetson—! It has to be. What has that damned Hat gotten him into?

2

"Today is Jane Crosby's day to come in," Angie said, buttering toast. "She's going to be cleaning your den."

Bernie McKay grunted, swallowed coffee. "Long's she doesn't touch my monster models. My Frankenstein is authentic from ancient photos; it's worth plenty." He glanced at her past his copy of the Kansas City *Star*. "The family made any decisions about the agency?"

Uncle Albert's will would be read today, but the family already knew what was in it. He'd left all his possessions to his brothers and sisters, share and share alike. That didn't include the real estate agency; by the terms of the partnership agreement, the surviving partner inherited everything. But the family had part interest in many of the assets, and had done a good deal of investment with Uncle Albert. Bernie wasn't worried. None of them knew real estate, so they couldn't move in on him even if they could agree to do it.

"Oh, Bernie, you know they haven't. Why, the will hasn't even been read yet. Maybe he surprised us."

"Yeah, maybe he left his share of the family assets to Paul Gibson."

Out of the corner of his eye Bernie saw Angie's swift sharp glance, but he was folding his paper, face rigidly placid. He pretended to study the business section, watching her peripherally. Angie dabbed a bit of apple jelly on one corner of her buttered toast and bit it off, crunched it thoughtfully, with a glance at him.

"Why do you say that?" she asked with so noncommittal an air that if he hadn't known, Bernie might have thought her innocent. But he'd caught that swift sharp glance.

"Say what?" he asked absently, still looking at his paper.

"That Uncle Albert might have left his share of the family's assets to Paul Gibson. I thought he didn't like him."

"Uncle Albert didn't like anyone. Nah, if he wanted to surprise us, he'd have to leave it to the church or Save Our Children or something like that." He glanced at her. "Why, did you ding-dong at him about making Gibson a partner like you do me? Stupid, if you did. Uncle Albert was stubborn, too. Surest way to make him not do it."

Angie smiled and shook her head. "No, I never dreamed of mentioning it to him. The family had to twist his arm to get him to let you in, when we were married. Without you, he would soon have been broke, and we all knew it, even him. But he was too stubborn to admit it."

"True. Nobody liked or trusted him. Gibson's a lot like him. He's good-lookin' now, but he'll be an ugly old man like your uncle, and about as mean." Bernie shook his head, folding his paper. "These self-centered types always turn mean and stingy at the end."

"Well, maybe. Even so, he's young enough yet to learn better. However, it's your agency now; don't mind me. He'll make partner soon enough with Gunderson." Angie pushed her plate back. "Look, I've got to run; the church committee meets at nine."

"Right, dear, see you this evening," Bernie said absently, and studied his paper till the door closed behind her. When he heard the starter of her car, he looked out the window, smiling tightly.

Little jumpy this morning, are we, Angie?

Best to call Uncle Bill before he gets to the office, Bernie thought, and got up. When the older man came on the phone, Bernie said, "Uncle Bill, how are you? Looks like it's gonna be another scorcher."

"Bernie, uh, good to hear you, how are you? Maybe it'll rain and cool things down; radio's callin' for a chance of thunderstorms."

"Yeah, I hope, things're gettin' too dry. Listen, how are you comin' on the audit? You know they'll read the will today, and since the family's gonna want to rush it through probate. . . ."

"Uh, yeah, they are. And we'll have to have a list of the partnership assets, of course. Uh, but these things take time. I'm workin' on it myself. . . ."

"Right, I know you are. Gibson tells me it's comin' kinda slow, though. . . ."

"Yeah, these things take time."

"You havin' any problems? I mean, Uncle Albert was a secretive old bird, he never told me half the stuff he was workin' on. Some of his transactions—"

"Oh, no, no problems, nothing like that, it's just a big agency and we need documentation of everything, these things take time. . . ."

When he had hung up Bernie lit his after-breakfast cigar, the only one he allowed himself anymore. No question about it, he thought. Uncle Albert's books are rotten. Either he was stiffing me big time, or he was losing money big time. I hope he didn't run me too much in debt, damn his black soul. Well, Waley's straight and honest, he'll tell me if he learns anything. Gibson won't, that's for damn sure.

3

Deputy Rod Parker pulled up at the building that doubled as jail and sheriff's department. Evelyn Anderson came hurrying out, his blue eyes sparkling.

"Good, you're back; come with me."

They jumped into the sheriff's cruiser. Anderson peeled out.

"What is it?" Parker asked, trying to suppress his excitement.

"Smigly kids. You know old man Hennessey? Lives south of Jackson City on Highway H?"

"No." But the Smiglies—

"He complained couple times the past month about stuff bein' stole from his yard. Small stuff. We figured it was the Smigly kids, remember?"

Parker remembered the complaint about the Smiglies. These kids were yelled at a lot by their parents, but had never been hit. They had all—five or six of them—grown up completely contemptuous of authority of any kind, and sneered at punishment, which they believed to be a myth. The oldest boy had already done time in jail.

"Couple of 'em come into Hennessey's yard this morning, boy and girl. About nine and ten, maybe, small for their ages. The boy was carryin' a pitchfork, prob'ly Hennessey's. The old man went to the back door—he's about sixty-five, seventy—to ask 'em what they was doin' there. Boy jammed the fork into his chest, 'n' they ran like hell. The old woman called us, and we sent out the ambulance. I was just up to the hospital, talkin' to her."

"She identify 'em?"

"Not well, but the Smiglies live just back of them through the woods, and the description's close enough. She was shook up pretty bad."

"Well, no wonder."

"Oh, that too, but mostly by the ambulance ride. Pinky White drove it."

Parker grunted. "We pickin' up the kids?"

"Right. I got a warrant for 'em from juvenile court. We'll turn 'em over to Miz Harker; they need a firm hand."

The sheriff settled down to driving. Parker said, "I had a little talk with Poochie Doo-brett. Dyew-Bray. Wouldn't talk."

"Didn't expect him to. How'd he act?"

"Guilty. Kep' flinchin' an' wouldn't meet my eye."

"Well, Deputy Nordstrom finally found Orlin Deutscher and asked him about those keys to the graveyard shed. He claims he give 'em back to Judith Lamour—you know her, girl who works for Culter the mortician."

"Yeah, I talked to her m'self, yestiddee. Figured she'd

know who Dutchies and Poochie was runnin' with.
What did she say?"

"She said Deutscher was lyin'. Doesn't like him much.
Every set of keys was accounted for, the pastor's, the
handyman's, Culter's, and the two sets of spares. But
Judith Lamour says she never put that set back in the
box, where we found it. What d'you make of it?"

Parker mulled it over. "The Lamour girl don't
remember Dutchies giving them back to her. She also
don't remember puttin' them back in the box. She
might fergit one of those things, not likely both. Hmm.
Could Dutchies have snuck the key back into the box?"

"Must have. Culter thought so. Deutscher showed
up to see if there was any work for him the following
morning."

"Prints is not gonna be much help. They could've
left their prints on the tractors or shovels durin' the
day. Hmm. Unless we can find one that matches one
'a' their friends."

"Yeah."

At length they pulled up into the littered yard of
the Smigly place. It was covered with car bodies far
gone in rust, with old refrigerators, a defunct buzz
saw, a pile of corrugated sheet metal that had been
or might some day be a shed, pieces of nondescript
farm equipment meant to be pulled by horses, and
piles and piles of just plain junk. Jake Smigly had spent
years hauling it all in.

Parker followed the sheriff's deceptively lackadaisical
progress to the equally littered porch of the tiny
decrepit house.

"Come in," came Jake Smigly's voice sullenly.

The inside of the house was a continuation of the
yard. A tiny front room had a wood-burning heater
in its center, a flour-sack cover over it. Decrepit

furniture left only footpaths around the stove, and every horizontal surface was covered with household items and just plain junk. The TV was broken; must've been, for it was off.

The family huddled in its lair and stared at them. Eyes glittering.

Two skinny, dirty kids with tangled hair glared from near their mother Clothilde, a weary, graying woman, as thin and sharp as they. Two older kids glowered sullenly from other corners. Jake Smigly, a smallish, gray-unshaven man older than his years, warmed himself by habit at the cold stove. His large untidy mustache twitched nervously.

Smigly had some kind of disability pension, did odd jobs, sold wood off his twenty acres, and scrounged by. ADC supported the kids. Smigly was a paranoid. Last year's tornado, which had touched down on a distant corner of his property and done him no real damage, was a problem for him. He had never been able to figure how his imaginary enemies could have arranged it, and the concept of a universe that did not revolve hostilely around himself shook him.

Evelyn took off his hat, revealing his pale forehead above the tanned lower part of his face, but wasted no time. "Got a warrant here for the arrest of Randy and Cordelia Smigly. Assault with a deadly weapon."

The smaller kids screeched: "We never done it!" "We was here all morning!" "We never been *near* ole man Hennessey's!"

The older ones chimed in: "Yeah, they was here all mornin'!" "You go away, you old nasty nigger sheriff!" "Yeah, you fuck off an' leave us alone!"

"Jake?" Evelyn's quiet voice cut like a knife through the clack.

"Well, Sheriff, I don't know who's been tellin' you

these lies, I mean, I got lots of enemies who'd love to see my kids in jail, you know how they railroaded Jake Junior—"

"Yeah, ole man Hennessey's lyin'!"

"He just hates us!"

Evelyn looked at them. "If you done nothin' and been here all morning, how do you know who was stabbed?"

Silence; they glanced at each other. Parker had never seen such feral eyes since the time he'd had to shoot the mad dog.

"The old woman got a good look, and what's more, Hennessey will live to testify."

Stubborn silence.

"Right, I'm takin' you in." And Evelyn Anderson uncoiled with the speed of a serpent; had both of the kids before they could blink.

Parker had seen the sheriff in action before and was ready; he stepped forward to help. At that moment Clothilde Smigly landed on him, shrieking, moving with speed even more surprising than that of the sheriff.

"You let my kids alone! They didn't do nothin,' you bastards, you let 'em alone—"

Parker recoiled and flung up a meaty arm. Fortunately the woman was small and half starved; she rebounded, came at him again. This time he used both arms, one eye nervously on Smigly. Mouth open, Jake made no move to help, and after a moment Parker realized he could concentrate on the woman.

She was a handful, but fought without any training. She clawed and struck futilely overhand with her fists, and his hat distracted her for fatal seconds. Finally he got her wrist, forced it down, and in a moment had her twisted around and bent over, though he almost uprooted the woodstove when he bumped into it.

He looked around, panting. Jake Smigly was opening and closing his mouth, getting ready to be indignant when he got his wits back. The older kids, early teens he guessed, and also small for their ages, were on their feet ready to throw the items they'd picked up. Evelyn was just snapping cuffs on the girl, his foot on the manacled and writhing boy. He'd had as bad a scuffle as Parker.

Parker shoved their mother into the kids, breaking up their formation, and crouched facing the three, discounting Jake. Parker might not be tall and slim and good looking, but there was a solid strength about him that even half-grown fools could recognize. The kids hesitated and uncocked their arms.

Clothilde struggled back to her feet, screeching. Behind him, Evelyn hustled the screaming kids out onto the porch. Parker picked up his hat and backed away, but Clothilde had no further ambition for combat; she'd bumped her head, by the red mark. The Smiglies contented themselves by following them to the car, screaming at every step. They didn't throw anything till the car was in motion.

Randy and Cordelia never ceased to shriek in the back seat. Parker leaned back between seats and manacled them to the floor, though there were no door handles in the back. The girl spat in his face, and he slapped her chops with a cannon-crack sound. Wiping his face, he found the scratches Clothilde had left, not having noticed them before. Panting and sweating and more than a little shaken, he looked at the even and seemingly untroubled features of Evelyn Anderson.

The sheriff surprised him by leaning over and saying, under the screaming, "Hell of a thing. 'Druther deal with werewolves."

Parker shivered. He had a superstitious fear of

werewolves. He glanced back at the feral children. "How do you know we ain't?"

Anderson had no answer to that. They drove in tense silence to the town.

Once there, things seemed a little more rational. "Where'll we keep 'em?" Parker asked, holding the squirming children. The bars on the cells were too far apart.

Anderson looked around. "There," he grunted, "until I get hold of Miz Harker." He indicated the supply closet. "Here—I'll unlock it." He worked the sturdy lock on the door. "This ought to hold them."

Parker shoved the kids inside, and Anderson closed and locked the door. Later—when he saw the lock hanging, partially unscrewed, the inside of the door broken open with the edge of a metal ruler and the kids gone—Parker remembered they had gone in suspiciously easy.

4

Bernie McKay had a sheet of paper ready to hide quickly under the other papers on his desk. On it, to the best of his memory, he was tallying up the times Paul Gibson had been out of the office long enough to have gotten it on with Angie. And then there were Sundays—Bernie went to church only when bullied into it—and often she went out on Saturdays. She wouldn't have put up with quickies; even so, the total was startling. Even discounting half of them for sheer jealousy, it was still startling.

Just when did she start in on me to make him partner—aaah!

Uncle Albert's ghost opened the door and walked

in, just as the living man had so often done. Bernie stared with bulging eyes, noting that the actual door had not opened. Uncle Albert's fleshless Scrooge face was as dour in death as in life, louring down sidelong from beetled brows in the old fashion.

"Hi, Bernie, you little shit," said Uncle Albert.

Bernie stopped himself from asking the automatic, *Who let you in*? "Wha— What are you—"

He became aware that his mouth was open and shut it with a clop. His erstwhile partner put his immaterial hands on the desk and thrust his liver-spotted features into Bernie's. Bernie recoiled, goose-pimples on his back.

"Where's my gold, you lying thieving little asshole?" The dead old man glared, eyes like chips of gray steel. "Where's my gold? You white trash, you bum, you *thief*! I'll—"

The door opened behind the ghost and Paul Gibson stepped in. "Mr. McKay? Mr. Smithers called from his office. He gave me a list of deeds he wants researched. I expect to be at the courthouse most of the morning."

Bernie had a little trouble hearing this because of the screeching of the ghost, which Gibson did not seem to see or hear. Bernie nodded jerkily, trying not to see or hear it himself.

Apparently Gibson only noticed Bernie's distraught air after making his little speech.

"You all right, Mr. McKay?"

"I'll hound you, Bernie, I'll be with you day and night till you give me back my gold!" The ghost shook its finger in his face.

But Bernie heard the hint of hope in Gibson's tone. He pretended to be a bit woozy, looking through the gesticulating ghost at Gibson's image.

"I'm fine. Just need more coffee, I guess." He hoped he wasn't yelling over the ghost that Gibson couldn't hear. "I don't sleep well in this kind of weather, even with the air conditioning."

"Yes, I expect it'll break and we'll get a storm soon. Anyway, I'll be out for a while—maybe till after lunch."

"Okay." Bernie stopped himself from saying anything that would reveal his suspicions.

With a smug smile, the other turned and left. Bernie's rage was so great he found the ghost, a moment ago so frightening, now a mere distraction. He waved it off, irritably saying, "Yes, yes, yes," and picked up the phone.

He caught himself halfway through dialing his own number. Absolutely the stupidest thing he could do, trying to check up on Angie. "Oh, shut up," he said to the ghost. It was pounding loudly on his desk.

"Don't you tell me to shut up, you mangy little fuckhead—"

He tuned it out, thinking furiously. The Gibsons were a family of plumbers, carpenters, and odd job handymen from way back. Paul had spent two years at Central Missouri State U in Warrensburg, and a couple of years in community colleges in Kansas City. Angie'd possibly met him at the church; she was on some damn kind of committee that oversaw the renovation. Or even at the house, some day when Bernie was at work and she'd called a plumber or whatever.

This could have been going on for years.

He turned fiercely on the blathering ghost. "Gold? Gold?" He tried to keep his voice down; others could hear *him* talking to *it*. "You never had any gold. You're dreaming, you ghastly old creep. You're crazy. You're dead! Go back to hell."

"Oh yes I had gold, don't tell me I didn't have gold, you know I did, you stole it, you—"

"Knock it off! You never had gold. What on earth would you buy gold for? Where would you keep it? How did you pay for—"

Bernie checked, staring at the ghost. Uncle Albert, halted in full cry, clamped his immaterial jaw and turned partly away, glancing sidelong at Bernie, sullen, stubborn. A look he'd seen a thousand times in arguments.

Uncle Bill Smithers was, after all, examining the books—with a great deal of nervousness.

"Why, you swindling old *bastard*," Bernie said softly, almost whispering. "You used partnership funds to buy your damn gold—and then forgot where you hid it! You stupid fucking old—"

The ghost was already on its way to the door, glancing back sullenly one last time. Before Bernie could get around the desk, it opened—but did not open—the door, and was gone.

Bernie glimpsed something white in the mirror. It was his own face, pale with rage. "*Bastard*," he whispered.

5

Justin Waley stood up, feeling his lean cheeks crease in a broad grin. "Red Bud, Margie! Sit down. Good to see you, Margie, and you're even prettier than ever. Too good for this mug. How's Tyler?"

Margie Hadley was a young woman with dark brown hair, currently in an ear-length wave. Justin had always found her more attractive than many better-looking women, because of the warmth of her personality.

"Oh, Ty's wonderful, Juss, and looks just like Red Bud did when he was six. We looked at old pictures and they're just alike. Gonna be a real heartbreaker! He's already reading and writing, of course."

"Starts school this fall," Red Bud said. He seated her on the red leatherette of the booth.

"Already," Justin said. He sat down across from them. The Night Owl's normal roar was mute; the lunch-hour crowd was always sparse. Nona Martens wouldn't be in till evening. "It seems like just last year he was born," he added.

When the waitress had come and they had ordered their burgers, Red Bud said, "Tell him about I Know," looking fondly at his wife.

Justin raised an eyebrow. "You never did tell me how you came to name that cat."

The young couple laughed. "Oh, that's on account of our dumb neighbors," Margie said. "One of them had this dog, and couldn't think of a name for it, and so they would say, 'You know, the hound.' To this day the hound's name is You Know. So one of the other neighbors thought that was funny, and they named one of their dogs I Don't Know. So we named our cat I Know."

Justin laughed. "A good name for him. What about him?"

"I was up in the attic yesterday," Margie said eagerly, "and I Know was looking at a big box up against the wall, and up at me, like he wanted me to pull it out. I figured there was a mouse behind it, so I said, 'Oh, I Know, you wouldn't be able to catch it,' but I went ahead and pulled the box out and I Know jumped behind it. A mouse ran out, and I said, 'I told you so!' But I Know didn't come running after her, so I looked over the box, and there he was with his paws in a nest.

There were two half-grown mice in his mouth. He twisted around and killed them both and laid them down, then he lifted his right paw and killed the two under it, and then the two under his left paw. He sat there with six dead mice in front of him and looked up at me, as much as if to say, 'You told me what?' "

Justin laughed with them. "Reminds me of our old family cat. —But if we get started talking pets, we'll never get done."

"Yes, what did you decide?" Red Bud said eagerly.

"Well, you know I never thought Oswego was big enough to support an investment counseling service. We'll have to open an office in Clinchfield. There are good offices fairly cheap, but that's a bit of a drive. And if we keep our jobs, we'll have to have someone in the office on the days we're not there."

"I could be your office girl five days a week," Margie said eagerly. "I can leave Ty with Shirley; he loves his aunt and cousins, and when school starts it's even easier."

"That'll be a big help," Justin said. "Thanks! We've also got to decide whether we should incorporate or set up a partnership. You're the lawyer; what do you think?"

Red Bud shook his head. "I'm still looking into it. I'll have to get back to you on that. Oh, and those books on investment and money management; I need to start studying up."

"They're in the car," Justin said. "Though as I told you, the people around here like to invest in land. I've had a few conversations with Bernie McKay— not so many since his partner died—and it can be fairly lucrative, especially around Clinchfield."

"Could we work with McKay?" Red Bud asked.

Justin smiled frostily. "We won't. I think he's honest,

but he knows his business too well. He'd get all the profit."

"So we need to be studying the real estate market to the north," Red Bud mused.

Margie looked brightly around. "Ah, here comes our food. Thanks, Betty! It's like old times, isn't it, dear? Don't you think so, Juss?"

Justin smiled wistfully and thanked Betty.

6

The rough sound of an ill-kept engine aroused Nona Martens from her desultory housekeeping. Billy continued to stare sullenly at the TV.

"It's that Hat Stetson," she said, exasperated.

Hat jumped jauntily out of his old pickup and slammed the door. Surveying him through the machine-lace curtains, Nona felt a sinking sensation. Of all the people she didn't want knowing where she lived, Hat Stetson topped the list. He strode over the more or less flat stones of the walk with the exaggerated swagger that three generations of "macho men" had learned from John Wayne. *Just what I need,* she thought.

She opened the door when he stepped onto the tiny plank deck.

"Nona, my favorite sweetheart!" He swept off his cheap white cowboy had and turned on all the freckle-faced country boy charm he had. It wasn't much. "Good to see you! Hey, put on your glad rags. I'm takin' you and Billy to Clinchfield."

"Sorry, Hat, I can't go."

"What? I didn't hear you say that. I *won't* hear you say it!" Seriously, he added, "I'm buyin' and it'd do you good to get out."

Nona worked in a night spot; she got out more than she wanted to.

"Sorry, Hat, not interested. Besides, I have things to do." She became conscious that she was letting cool air out, but she wasn't going to let Stetson in.

"Hey, really, Nona, why don't you come?" Plaintively but still country boy charming. "I really like you, you know. You're the only reason I go to the Night Owl. What's the matter; don't you like men?"

Nona looked at him and fought down her stomach's answer to the question. "I do like men, quite a lot. But I have my own definition of 'man' and it includes 'job.' Get it?"

A sullen expression crossed his face, but he was persistent. "Hey, is that any way to treat your best son's friend?"

She turned to Billy. "You want to go with him, Billy?"

Billy never looked away from the TV. "Naw. I got to mow the lawn." He had never mowed her lawn.

"Aw, come on, Billy, don't you give *me* that high hat!" Stetson cried. "It ain't my fault we didn't make out. It's more yours!"

Billy rose and came slowly to the door. He looked at Stetson. "Nothing's ever your fault," he said with quiet bitterness, and closed the door firmly, simultaneously locking it.

The knob immediately rattled as Stetson tried to open the door, saying, "Hey, listen—"

Nona fully expected him to kick the door. She and Billy stood close together, holding their breaths, he still gripping the knob. Then she heard Stetson say, "Aw shit." A hollow wooden tramp on the deck, the clap as his boots hit the flagstones, the stomp of his steps, and the slam of the pickup's door.

Billy relaxed and so did she, as the pickup's engine

ground, then caught with a roar. Stetson peeled out
in a circle, tearing up as much of the weedy lawn as
he could, and rattled off down the long drive.

Nona wanted to hug Billy, but knew he'd resent it.

He scowled at her. "You'd be better off not getting
involved with Stetson," he said. "He's a bad 'un." He
went back to the TV.

Nona followed, to look at him with wild surmise.

He looked up, an irritated expression in his blue-
gray eyes. "I'll mow the lawn soon's this show's over."

7

Hat Stetson roared and rattled down the county
highway, seething. He didn't know which he hated more
at that moment, Nona or Billy. I'll have her ass yet,
he thought. Get a job! Sounded just like his damn
mother. A job! In St. Claude County? Who was she
trying to kid? Alls she had was that lousy waitress job
in the damn Night Owl; hell of a job.

God, she looked good in those old tight jeans. Hat
wandered off into a fantasy, with a naked Nona at his
knees.

He was still fantasizing when he went down the long,
long hill into Monegaw Springs, a town built on a slope.
There was a small, Baptist church; Abner Mazarofsky's
unpainted store; and across the street from it, a
building that had been a store owned by Abner's father
till the older man retired. A dozen houses drowsed
under the spiky oaks. A crude handlettered sign—
CAUTION HOG CROSSING—gave warning of
Abner Mazarofsky's livestock. Monegaw Springs;
population, a hundred people and about three times
as many dogs.

Parking next to Abner's store, Hat slouched in and bought a beer with change. Have to hit the old lady up for a loan, he thought. "Seen Orlin Deutscher?" he asked Abner.

Receiving a negative, he slouched back out onto the concrete porch. It was no higher than a curb at one end; four feet high at the other. Hat jumped off the high end, landing with more of a jolt than he had expected.

"Hey, you— Snyder!"

The boy across the street, with a baseball bat over his shoulder, was about fourteen. He'd shot up, or was wearing his brother's pants, for his lean shanks stuck out below the pant legs for a palm's breadth. As he was the color of a good gunstock, he had to be a Snyder— there was only the one black family in the small town.

The Snyder turned to face him expressionlessly. A big old hound that Hat recognized as Knuckles sat down and panted with polite interest in Hat's direction. A much smaller dog, a purebred Heinz named Winnie-the-Pooch, laid his ears back warningly. His mutt face registered suspicion.

"Yeah?"

"Seen Orlin Deutscher?"

After a moment's deliberation, the Snyder said, "He ain't in the store?"

"No."

"Checked the church shed?"

"No."

A freckle-faced boy appeared out of a vacant lot, one of the few nearly level places in town, even here near the bottom of the slope. He glanced at and ignored Hat. "Hey, Gus! Come on, game's startin'!"

"I gotta go. If he ain't there, try his Mom."

❖   ❖   ❖

Poochie Dubret and Orlin Deutscher were sitting on Deutscher's mother's porch, cracking pecans, drinking cider, and throwing walnuts at a Siamese cat. Hat jumped out of his pickup and ambled in a friendly manner toward them. After one sidelong glance, they ignored him.

Hat realized that they weren't throwing at the cat, but past it. The cat went after each skipping walnut as if it were a mouse.

"Hey, that cat's wild," said Hat. "Does he bring 'em back?"

They didn't answer. Somewhat daunted, he picked up a walnut and threw it past the cat. The cat killed the walnut and looked hopefully around for more. Poochie threw.

"How you been makin' out?" Hat asked.

Deutscher grunted.

Poochie looked at him, at Hat, and pursed his lips. "Broke, as usual."

They all looked at the frantically sprinting cat. Hat felt a certain constraint, as well as exasperation.

"Well, hell, is that my fault?" he said defensively. He knew he shouldn't get mad, but damn it—

"It was a damn fool idee in the first place," said Deutscher stonily.

"Yeah," said Poochie.

"We tole you the ole man was movin'."

"Yeah."

"You wouldn' listen."

"Yeah."

"You always got to be the big shot, the one who's runnin' things—"

"Oh, fuck that shit! Who was it run away and left me to fight the damn thing off? 'We'll just bash it on the head,' you said. Sheeyit! If you would only have stood with me, we could 'a' taken care of it. Hell, ole

McKay, that ole man, took care of it single-handed when he was half asleep."

"So what?" said Deutscher. "The whole idea was stupid. It would 'a' never worked. Somebody would 'a' reckonnized the pieces of copper, sure."

"Yeah. That damn depitty Parker's been all over my ass," Poochie said, pushing out his lips angrily.

"Yeah. Depitty Nordstrom's been sniffin' around me," Deutscher said. "What's more, ol' Culter's gonna fire us, bet on it. He's pretty sure I snuck them keys back into the box; he ain't fuckin' stupid like you, Hat. You forgit other people got brains too."

"Yeah, that damn depitty Parker—"

"Well, shit, I never promised you a rose garden. I don't see where the fuck you get off, bein' mad at me when it was you that let me down—"

By the time he left, Hat was in a rage, and his fantasies alternated between gruesome deaths for Deutscher and Poochie, and them crawling to him for a share of the astonishing wealth he would realize in some hazy fashion. The copper coffin swam in and out of his visions, gleaming like gold. If only— Too late now, it was gone, but if only—!

A pair of grubby little kids ran out almost in front of him, near the top of Monegaw's long hill, and he stomped his brakes savagely.

"Out of the damn way, little assholes!" Hat yelled out the window.

"Fuck you, shithead!" the little girl cried shrilly, and gave him the finger.

"Why, you—"

But before he could put the old pickup into motion after them, they had scrambled up the weedy bank. They ducked under the barbed wire and vanished in the sultry forest.

Even the goddam kids got no respect for me, Hat thought bitterly.

8

The battered old bat struck the ball with a crisp, clean *crack*, and Winnie-the-Pooh danced his forepaws up and down on the sideline, yelping delightedly to the children's yells and running. He had no idea of the score, but he enjoyed the game as much as anybody who played it. Beside him, Knuckles was clearly uninterested, even in the part just after the *crack* that so delighted Winnie-the-Pooh's doggy heart. The big hound instead watched the baby who sat pawing at the dirt and cooing in the shade.

The baby smelled interestingly of milk and baby food, and even more interestingly of urine. It was the last that told the dogs that the baby was human, very very young, female, well-fed, and bursting with good health. Every now and then Knuckles's head, bigger than the baby's, would swing over and he would take a few luxurious sniffs. She would babble at him and reach up to grab at his nose or lips, and Knuckles would grin and submit.

Only in the quiet intervals of the game did Winnie-the-Pooh go wagging over to the baby and lick her face, causing her to squirm ecstatically and laugh. The light was fading to twilight sooner than normal, and at intervals in the game the children pointed up toward the sky, calling out. The storm Winnie-the-Pooh had been smelling all day had finally taken visible shape as a bank of high, massed clouds in the northwest.

Winnie-the-Pooh smelled a warm, musky animal smell. He looked around, growling.

Two children came out of the woods.

Knuckles greeted them with restrained but dignified courtesy. The ball players paid them no attention, for the newcomers were smaller than they. Winnie-the-Pooch regarded them with deep suspicion. They smelled wrong.

Normal children might smell dirty, but there was always an underlying clean animal odor about them, and reminiscences of soap. These children had no soapy undertone, and in fact, they smelled far more like Knuckles—who had never in his life had a bath—than like normal children. Not that they were hog-filthy. Winnie-the-Pooch did not know how to express the concept of infrequent and sketchy washing, but his nose told him the tale.

One of the girls in the game looked over and called out to the new children that the baby's name was "Linnie." Her tone was brisk and not unfriendly; she was obviously addressing strangers. But Winnie-the-Pooch's suspicions were not allayed.

There came again the crack of the bat and the disappointed yells that told Winnie-the-Pooch that this hit didn't count.

Then the baby screamed.

It was a long, loud, shrill scream of pain and terror. The two new kids were all over the baby, down on hands and knees, the baby flat on her back, screaming. Knuckles was springing back in an attitude of total astonishment. The hot savage smell of blood was in the air. Winnie-the-Pooch was already in furious motion as he took in these details, and a moment later, with feral pleasure, he felt living flesh between his teeth-- the boy's animal-odored leg.

The boy screamed in pain and rage and kicked, struck back at him. Winnie-the-Pooch tasted blood and wasted

a moment in another savage bite, then shifted over
to the oblivious girl, lunging forward to get her in the
buttock. She screamed also and jerked away from the
baby, her face smeared with blood. The boy struck at
him and Winnie-the-Pooch leaped for his face with a
bark that was more like a shriek of rage. The boy went
over backward, screaming and striking out wildly.
Winnie-the-Pooch got home a couple of juicy ones,
but felt a furious blow on his back.

He rolled and scrambled away, turning to the girl
again, but the fight was over. The ball players were
yelling and running toward them, some waving bats.
The bad kids scrambled up and ran off into the woods.

Furious, Winnie-the-Pooch followed and heard with
fierce pleasure the deep-chested baying of Knuckles,
coming strong after him. The huge hound was a mighty
hunter of great nasal prowess, and though a little past
his prime, still formidable. The bad kids ran fast, leaving
a broad spoor of old unwash and fresh blood.

With a great bell-mouthed baying, the hound
followed. Knuckles would have pursued them all night.
But Winnie-the-Pooch abruptly realized that there was
nobody following them. He hesitated, looked back,
and barked the big hound into submission. Knuckles
stood panting in the middle of a spoor as broad and
easily "seen" as a paved road, not understanding
Winnie-the-Pooch's concern.

The big hound's blunt old teeth and amiable heart
unfitted him for close-in combat. Winnie-the-Pooch
wanted backup. He stood panting, listening. Distant
yells, but no sound of anyone following. He barked
at Knuckles and started back, but the hound was
stubborn. It took a long time to persuade him, but
finally they came despondently back into the open areas
of the people place.

Knuckles was plainly disgusted with him, and Winnie-the-Pooch couldn't blame him. They sniffed the spot where the baby had been attacked, and followed the trail to a nearby house. There was a great deal of excitement about it, people coming and going, and they heard the baby crying inside, but not in terror, only in pain. The children were not permitted inside, but congregated without, talking in shrill excited voices.

He and Knuckles came in for a good deal of attention and fierce petting. Every passerby was invited to examine the blood on Winnie-the-Pooch's face where his tongue didn't reach. He and Knuckles whined anxiously and several times tried to lead people into the woods, but no one would follow.

Finally a strange man came over to the children and talked to them for a long time. He smelled of leather and khaki and guns, and sweat and a hint of beer over an underlying pleasant odor of clean man-smell and soap. He spoke patiently to the kids, forcing them to talk one at a time, and made scritching sounds on a flat thing in his hand. Presently he also came over and examined Winnie-the-Pooch's muzzle, and petted him and Knuckles.

It was he who finally urged them into the woods, making it plain that he would follow. But it was too late.

The rain had come at last.

Chapter Four:

Lady Sings the Blues

1

Justin Waley held a sword, point up, in his right hand, bare left foot advanced, left hand at his side. He held the sword steady though it weighed five pounds and by its long hilt was clearly meant for two hands. The CD player made mechanical noises as it prepared to play the cuts he had programmed. Through the open door of what he called his barn, Justin could see the sun setting behind the wall of trees beyond the back yard.

From the CD's speakers came a female chorus singing the opening words of "Amazing Grace." Simultaneously Justin let the point of the sword fall backward from the vertical, the long hilt tilting up before. Smoothly he reached up with his left hand to grip the hilt just above the steel ball that was its pommel.

Then Homer William Randolph the Third swept into

"Amazing Grace" on the saxophone, long cool mellow sounds. A brilliant artist playing at the very peak of his career, with a control that few artists of any sort ever hope to achieve.

Justin brought his five-foot-long claymore up, over, and down, slowly, slowly, stepping forward with his bare right foot. Trying to match the saxophone's cool graceful control with a control as complete and as graceful. Slowly, slowly—handsomely, as sailors say—sweeping the great sword in a precise arc.

At the end of that sweep he turned his wrists over and brought the sword back, slowly caught a theoretical enemy's blade on his own on the backhand, stepped back—handsomely, handsomely!—disengaged, and counterattacked. All the while keeping time to the flow of the music.

The CD finished "Amazing Grace" and played a faster, jazzy cut from Jean-Michele Jarre's "Magnetic Fields." Justin stepped up the pace to match. The next cut was Vangelos, and a faster pace yet.

Once he had warmed up, the CD switched over to Homer William "Boots" Randolph's "Yakety Sax," back in his younger and wilder days. Again Justin's tempo picked up, and the speed of his great sword. His bare feet skipped and thumped across the hardwood floor of the renovated barn, the gleaming blade a flashing blur. Sweat started out on him, his breath came fast. At five pounds the claymore was almost twice as heavy as most swords—its blade alone three and a half feet long—but he handled it deftly, after a year of practice.

Justin Waley was doing battle.

He hacked and slashed imaginary foes with vim and vigor, till the sweat ran and his breath came short. His was a sedentary occupation, and he tended to spend his evenings reading. He'd found riding an exercise bike boring, not to mention that it did nothing for his upper body. So he'd paid nearly four hundred dollars for a replica of the great two-handed Scottish claymore.

When the CD player went back down through Vangelos and Jarre to Homer William Randolph the Third again, this time playing "Me and Bobby McGee," Justin was panting, aching faintly. He made his tired muscles respond, waving the sword slowly, slowly through the cooling-off exercises. Finished, he pushed his thinning hair back from his damp brow. He'd done himself a lot of good—and hadn't been bored.

Next: precision. He lit candles and whipped the great sword at them as fast as he could swing it. The first one he knocked flying, but he steadied himself, and despite his exhaustion, neatly tipped out the flame of the next without touching it. Of the next four, he only hit one, putting the others out neatly, after several tries. Two out of three, after a year of practice. Not bad, he thought. Even when tired, he usually put the big blade where he wanted it.

Grinning, he racked the claymore—no scabbard came with it—beside the rattan practice swords in the recessed nook where once there had been a feed box. Swinging the panel to, he locked it, turned off the CD player and threw a piece of canvas over it for a dust cover.

Justin looked around, his breath still coming fast. He'd spent a good bit to renovate the small barn, insulating and paneling the interior and replacing the splintery old floor with one he could have held a dance on. Overhead, the mow still held hay, an artistic touch.

Justin padded across the hardwood floor and looked out at the encircling forest. The long summer twilight was gone, fireflies punctuating the dusk, and the air felt a little cool. Locking the door securely, he trotted barefoot back to the old farmhouse.

Kicking out of his sweaty pants, he took a shower. Afterward he wandered out into the living room wielding a towel vigorously. The light glowed on his answering machine. Justin damned it faintly, but his sense of duty got the better of him. Flinging the towel down, he played it back.

There was only the one message.

"Justin? This is Bernie McKay, calling about, uh, about seven o'clock. Uh, I wonder how far you've gotten . . . I mean, I wonder if you've noticed any . . . uh, any, uh gold purchases . . . you know what I mean. I wonder if, uh, he, uh, he bought any, uh, any gold. Could've bought any uh, gold. Any time in the past, uh, eight or ten years. Uh."

Gold?

Justin frowned. If Albert had wanted it kept secret, he would have dealt in cash, of course. Better call McKay back now.

Presently McKay's voice came over the line.

"Mr. McKay? Justin Waley here, about your message. Want my thoughts now, or shall I call you with a more complete report at work tomorrow?"

"Now will be fine. Angie's out with her friends," said McKay. "Any record of Uncle Albert buying gold?" Eagerly.

Justin nodded thoughtfully. "I take it that you think he might have done so secretly. In that case he would have bought in cash. Nor have we found certificates in any of his safe-deposit boxes. Unless he hid them in his house—"

"I don't mean certificates. I mean gold—coins or bullion or whatever."

Justin's eyebrows went up. "Well," he said, and rehearsed the obvious to give himself time to think: "The simplest way to buy gold is through mutual funds that own bullion or gold mining stocks, or both—"

"I know, I've got seven percent of my own retirement in a gold fund."

"Yes. Other ways of buying gold are through futures contracts with commodities brokers, or bank gold certificates, representing bullion stored in vaults. But if Mr. Smithers actually took possession, he must have gone to a dealer. They sell new gold coins, usually in one-ounce sizes, for a few percent over the value of the gold. Krugerrands are a popular choice; they're also available in half and I believe quarter-ounce sizes."

"He'd have had to go to Kansas City, then," McKay said musingly.

"I expect so. If he bought gold."

"He did, all right," McKay said grimly. "Well, thanks. And if you turn up anything like checks to gold dealers, let me know."

"You think he may have used partnership funds for these purchases?"

"God knows. With Uncle Albert, God alone knows," McKay said bitterly.

Justin hung up, shook his head.

In the past several days William Smithers had gotten more and more haggard as he went over the books of Smithers and McKay. Obviously, there was something more rotten there than Albert Smithers's corpse.

William Smithers would of course try to cover up the defalcations, Justin mused. As McKay had once said, the Smithers family would rather lose money than face.

But of course, any attempt to cover up was stupid. Justin had already had hints. Their assistant, Darrel

Lamour, clearly knew something, by the way he watched William Smithers. McKay obviously guessed— and he wasn't one to take being cheated. There'd be hell to pay if the Smitherses tried it.

Justin went to get dressed. Wonder how McKay knows the stolen money was invested specifically in gold, he thought. Maybe Albert's corpse had let drop a few words before he ceased it with that poker. Wonder where the gold is.

McKay played his cards close to his chest.

2

"This'll hafta do ya, Jody honey," his mother said. "I cain't spare no more till my nex' check comes."

Jody "Hat" Stetson gave her his charming grin by reflex, pocketing the "loan" while concealing his disappointment at its size. "Yeah, well, thanks again, Mom. I'll pay ya back someday, I promise you."

Her claw-like hand squeezed his forearm; a grin wrinkled her thin features. "Yeah, well, Jody honey, you know I just want you to be happy. You go have yourself a good time while you're young, all them girls all the time followin' you around."

Hat patted her scrawny cheek, concealing his wince. "Hey, thanks for those good words, beautiful."

"Too bad you quit that nice job at the cheese plant—"

The phone interrupted, to Hat's relief; he'd been fired. He slipped out onto the splintery porch, not letting the screen door bang. Here he waited just long enough to be sure the phone wasn't for him before sloping off toward the battered, empty rabbit hutches at the back edge of the narrow lot.

Hat inhaled the hot summer air with effort, and looked around glumly. His mother was currently living in a slovenly little house along one of the winding streets that connected Oswego to Highway 13, in a semi-rural setting. A wooded hill rose precipitously behind the house, constricting it against the road; to either side, similarly low-rent houses were occupied by a shrill collection of neighbors and their dogs and a few chickens, despite city ordinances. Trees, and what could be called shrubbery or just plain brush, gave the scene its only relief. The asphalt exuded the odor of tar; the day was hot and blindingly bright. Cicadas buzzed deafeningly.

Hat kicked vindictively at a rickety hutch's hind leg. "All them girls all the time followin' you around." He kicked the hutch again, harder. That was ten years ago, Ma, he wanted to say. All those girls were married now, and none had ever been married to him. That had seemed like a good idea at the time; now he wondered. They were married off mostly to dumb bricks who had never been as cool, as smooth, as good-looking, as he had been. He'd gone off to the Army rather than fall into that trap, marriage and a shit-level job. *He'd* had travel and adventure and seen the world, and been footloose and fancy-free all this time.

But now those dumb bricks were getting it every night. And he—?

Hat winced at the memory of the last time he got it: with a wistful older woman nearly as wrinkled as his mother, with flat pendulous breasts and a flabby ass. The last time he made it with a girl just out of high school, was that waitress with the eager snaggly grin. She was practically a moron, and had embarrassed him by making over him so loudly in public every time she saw him afterward that nobody could doubt he'd screwed her.

He didn't get it nearly as often as a cool with-it dude ought to, and with young good-looking women, practically never. He dreamed vaguely of finding some dissatisfied housewife like from the Four Families who'd go for him like crazy, that he'd fuck like a jackhammer. But all the housewives he met—none from the Four Families—were repressively faithful.

Or just uninterested in him.

Well, anyway, he thought hurriedly, there was Shirley McGinnis. She'd come around soon, couldn't help it, he'd been laying on the old charm, showing her a good time and not pushing her. Play it cool, hard to get, let her know he was available. He'd give her a call tonight when she got off work. Maybe tonight—who could say?

A twinge of frustrated desire went through him. It better be *soon*, he thought resentfully. He really needed it—but not badly enough to screw another dog just yet. He thought of his last tryst, and winced.

Wonder what the guys're doing, he thought wistfully. Hangin' around, I guess. Whatever, they didn't want him doing it with them. When he'd called Orlin Deutscher, the bastard had refused to come to the phone, and the last time he'd seen Dubret, Poochie had made an excuse about having to fix his mother's washing machine and left him standing on the damn porch. Hat seethed for a bit at the memory, then sighed.

It was hell, having no one to hang out with. He kicked the hutch again, and his sigh was almost a groan. There is nothing so boring as hanging around on a flat hot summer day in Missouri, all by yourself. A quail called, "Bob White? Bob . . . White?" wistfully.

Meantime, out there, things were happening. Movie stars were screwing in airconditioned bedrooms and all.

He thought yearningly of Nona Martens. Too bad the guys 're pissed off at me, he thought. I could really go for Nona, but that damn Billy's been talkin' to her about me. Little bastard, like to twist his neck. God, what a great ass she's got. Wisht she always wore them tight skirts like when she's waitressing. But she's good in jeans, too.

I really go for that type. She's been around, not some kid or some dumb old lady that's never been anywhere but church. Too bad she sounds so much like Mom. "Get a job." Huh! I seen what happens to guys that git jobs. They just shrivel up and die. I wasn't made for that.

There has got to be a better way. Win the lottery or dig up a treasure; something. Anything!

Anyway, he'd see Shirley tonight, he made up his mind to that. And by God I'll put it to her: Does she want it or not? Not going to be taken for a ride much longer, he thought sullenly. Not unless I get to ride, too.

"Jody!" his mother shrieked. "Oh, Jody! Phone! It's Mr. Wainwright!"

Hat stepped reluctantly toward the house. Wainwright owned a little convenience store at Gobbler's Knob. Hat owed him considerable and Wainwright had taken to pushing him about it, especially since Hat had turned down the other's offer of a job. With all his drinking buddies, Wainwright had thought Hat a good bet for a clerk; wanted all his buddies to hang around the store. But Hat wasn't born to slave behind a counter and be polite to everyone.

"He's got a job f'you!" She was delighted for him and wanted the whole community to know.

Shit, Hat thought.

3

"You ready to go?" Paul Gibson smiled his smug handsome smile.

Bernie McKay stretched his lips back at him, trying to conceal his own smugness. "Not really," he said. "But I'm as ready as I'll ever be. Foolishness, traipsing off and letting the business go for three days. Especially with the audit and all."

Gibson smiled sympathetically. "Yeah, well, I'll do my best to keep an eye on things."

I'll bet you will, Bernie thought, closing his desk drawer and getting up. He'd spent a couple of days laying the groundwork for his supposed absence. Everybody knew he was off to Kansas City to talk to investors about the river resort deal. In reality he was going no farther than Clinchfield, where he'd rent a car and return by night—with his camera.

"You sure you're up for this?" Gibson said, well-simulated worry in his tone, as he helped Bernie on with his coat. "You don't look right."

Bernie hadn't slept much for several nights, between the noisy ghost of Uncle Albert and his rage at Gibson and Angie.

"I'll be all right," he said, taking pains not to stumble going down the steps.

The ghost. It had stopped being frightening, now that he knew its secret. Bernie's only fear was that it would cease to be invisible and inaudible to Angie. If she heard about the gold—

Just this morning, Justin Waley had called and told him that his preliminary study suggested that Uncle Albert had gotten into the agency for nearly two hundred thousand dollars. Bernie could guess at a total somewhere around a quarter of a million dollars, stolen and hidden.

If the ghost was to be believed, hidden in the form of gold. Over fifty avoirdupois pounds of it, at current prices.

His gold, since he now owned the agency. But if he could find it, he need not pay taxes on it—

Gibson closed the maroon Cadillac's door and said, "Oh, don't forget to stop off and look at those strip pits near Appleville. I told you—I think there's a gold mine in it."

"Too big for us," Bernie grunted, fastening his seat belt. But he had agreed to at least look. Gibson was no fool.

Bernie started up the big Cad and purred across town to Coolidge, stepped into the house, gave Angie a muted goodbye—apparently it never occurred to her to kiss him—and picked up his bag, already packed.

She'd sing a different tune soon! A few pictures would bring her into line. He'd have her back in his bed, or know the reason why!

The threat of divorce would bring her around. Slinging the bag into the car, he thought savagely, She'll crawl to me on hands and knees and give me head till the bulls come home. I could cut her off completely, if she won't. Pick up some *real* blonde half her age. Yes, by God, and I'll fire Gibson, see if I don't!

And then there was the gold. If he could just bait the ghost into letting the wrong word drop. Even though the ghost couldn't remember on one level, on another it knew where the gold was. One little word, and Bernie would have it all. . . .

Thus daydreaming, he sent the big car hurtling north on highway 13. As highway A came up, he hesitated, and turned left onto it. Appleville and the strip pits were out of his way, going to Clinchfield, but he would have gone past them on the way to Kansas City. Might as well check them out.

After half an hour the ridges above the pits reared up to the left of the highway. He slowed, watched for the turn-off, and waited till a farmer's tractor howled by in road gear.

Bernie frowned a little as he drove in; there was only the stub of a graveled road for a couple of car lengths from the highway. After that there was merely a dirt track, kept open by fishermen. The ground was firm, however, despite the rain of a couple of days ago.

The strip pits were an old coal mine. Dirt and shale dug out of deep pits now full of murky water had been piled up in high shark-back ridges. A field of giant furrows. The ridges had been planted with trees thick as bristles on a brush.

Fifty years and more ago.

Now they were a considerable forest. Nobody had bothered logging them; they were quick-growing softwoods and hardly worth cutting even for firewood.

Gibson had a scheme to bulldoze the tops of the still-sharp ridges, saving the biggest and best of the trees, and turning the area into a retirement complex or some such development. It looked like a damn expensive proposition to Bernie. Those slopes were steeper than most house roofs. To make it work would mean sacrificing most of the trees, and the pits, too, would have to be filled or something. The mosquitoes—

"Gibson!"

At least it was Gibson's blue Honda, parked by one of the deepest of the murky pits. Squinting, Bernie got out and peered at it. Gibson came out of the dense forest growth.

"Mr. McKay! I didn't think you'd stop, so I came over myself to take a few pictures. What do you think?"

Bernie crossed to him, frowning around importantly. The other's enthusiasm made him doubt his own instincts, and he tried to think of some way to make any investment here pay.

"Well," he said. "I don't know."

"It'd be a big investment, of course," Gibson said. "But look over there, where those trees—"

Bernie followed the pointing finger and saw a couple of old soft maples, far gone in age and decay but beautiful, reflected in the tarn at their feet. Then he glimpse shadowy motion and felt a terrible blow on the side of his head, was conscious of Gibson's grunt. Darkness came and went. In the same instant, it seemed, he was looking with astonishment at his hands in front of his face, the stubby fingers plowing through the dirt and dead leaves.

Then came another jolting blow, and starry darkness returned. He tumbled down into it, jolted again, and the stars vanished. His last emotion was astonishment that Paul Gibson—*Paul Gibson!*—would do it to him. . . .

4

Deputy Rod Parker was scratching himself when the Sunshine Girl looked into the sheriff's office. Embarrassed, he stood up.

"Yes?"

"We got a report from a rural mail carrier," Renee said. "Thinks he saw two kids duck into the woods not far from the Smigly place. Evelyn says you're the only one available; wants you to check it out."

"On my way," Parker said. He grabbed his hat. "See you."

Gunning his engine, Parker reflected that the last thing he wanted was a return match—single-handed—with the Smiglies. But he'd gotten bored sitting around—and he felt honored that Evelyn would trust him on such a tough case.

He'd never doubted that Clothilde and Jake were helping, or trying to help, their fugitive kids, but what could the sheriff's department do? They'd have needed an army to watch the woods around and on the little twenty-acre Smigly place.

Out of sight of the junk-littered place, he eased to a stop, as nearly off the narrow gravel road as he could get. He closed the door quietly and walked in the weeds on the shoulder, ducking under occasional untrimmed limbs, rather than in the noisy gravel.

The rusty old Smigly van was in the yard, but no other sign of life about the place. After watching it for a bit, Parker crossed the yard. The Smigly dogs were too tired to notice, apparently; they made not a sound.

From the house came a muted chain-saw sound. He stepped quietly up on the creaky porch, crossed it carefully. Nobody in the littered living room. He stepped off the porch and swished through the weeds to the kitchen window. No sign of Clothilde, but Jake was there.

The man was sitting rocked back in a kitchen chair with his bare feet up on another, wearing bib overalls.

There was nothing between Jake and the Lord but
them, as far down as the unbuttoned sides revealed.
His head bobbed and his gray-shot four-day beard
opened and closed to his snores.

The only other living thing in the kitchen was one
of the family cats. Parker thought he'd never seen a
more miserable creature, so starved that its fur stood
out in all directions, rough and lacking all sheen. It
was up on the table, looking warily at Jake. The table
was covered with dirty dishes and things like salt and
pepper shakers and vinegar cruets and mustard jars,
a jelly glass full of spoons, etc., which obviously were
never put away. In addition, there were things like
bread and mayonnaise and an open jar of peanut butter.
Jake had obviously just had lunch.

The cat jammed its paw down into the peanut butter,
pulled it out, and licked it clean, nervously watching
the bobbing, snoring Jake. To Parker's amusement and
pity, it repeated this performance three times before
a more extravagant snore and movement on Jake's part
sent it ducking to the floor. He left as the cat cautiously
hopped on a chair, on its way back up.

Where was Clothilde?

Parker looked around. The dogs slept heavily in the
shade; probably so starved they had no energy. Even
the chickens clucked about listlessly. That appeared
to be the sum of the Smigly livestock.

There was a narrow trail leading off across the weedy
back yard to the nearby forest. Maybe the kids were
hiding out in some shed out back?

Parker followed the trail carefully, observing that it
had been used recently, enough to have kicked all the
dead leaves out of it. One step off it would make a
crashing of dead leaves and twigs audible for a quarter
mile on so quiet a day. He followed it carefully.

The trail turned sharply around a heavily leafed oak sucker and Parker was in full view before he realized. But Clothilde Smigly had her back to him. He stepped back behind the bush and watched.

She'd built a fire on a knee-high rock, he thought at first. Then he realized that she was burning an incense stick, like they sold in the Rexall Drug store. Burning incense in front of a crude, unpainted clay idol the size of a cat. Home-made, he guessed. Frog, dog, hog, he couldn't tell what it was supposed to represent. Nor could he make out her mumbled chant. He wasn't sure it was English; he doubted it was any real language.

There'd been an article in the *Reader's Digest*, Parker remembered. Much of this "Alternative Worship" had lost all meaning, if it had ever had any. Some could simply have been impressive nonsense to start with.

Froggy Would A-Courting Go, he thought. High muhnee cantivo. Staddle laddle laddle bob-a-laddle bob-a-linktum, rinktum, boddley mitchie cam-bull.

"Alternative worship" had been considered witchcraft a century ago. Now they invoked the Bill of Rights, and laws against it had been struck down. Nobody'd been lynched for "witchcraft" in Missouri for a hundred years.

The thing on the low flat rock shimmered, heat waves rising off it as off a paved road, though it was in the shade. Parker shivered, staring at the wavering thing. The air all around it was distorted and quivering. This wavering area grew bigger and more distinct as Clothilde mumbled and waved her hands about, sprinkling a black liquid thick as blood on the rock altar. All the idol's attention was fastened hungrily on her.

Shivering, Parker backed away.

One thing he was sure of: this was no "alternative worship," no variant approach to worshipping God. This was the real thing: paganism, witchcraft, whatever. He'd heard a preacher prove in a sermon when he was a kid that paganism and witchcraft were the same thing, devil worship. True alternative worships, like what Jews and Catholics and Ay-rabs and those Chinamen who drink the beer do, were all ways of worshipping one God who had a different face for each worshipper.

He ought to stop her. Parker shivered again at the thought. No telling what that thing would do—or what it could do. At the very least he could set himself up for seven years of bad luck, nightmares, things like that. A curse.

And it would be his word against hers. She could claim that hunk of clay was her idea of God.

Parker tiptoed back down the path between the spiky oak trees, breathing quietly and taking great care not to step into the leaves. That little shrine was within range of a yell from the house. Back in the weedy, littered yard, the sunshine seemed dimmer than when he'd gone into the woods, but Jake's snores came as before, and the hens clucked, and the dogs slept in the shade.

Dog, frog, or hog?

Parker took great care not to awaken the dogs, stepped quietly along till he was out of the yard, and eased into his car. For a long moment he hesitated, fearing that the sound of the starter would be a bugle call of alarm on the still, somnolent air. But when he did start it up, no devils roused up, and no dogs. He backed quietly away till he could turn around, not wanting to drive by the place.

With a chill beneath his sweat, he drove back to the

office. Have to report this to Evelyn verbally, he thought. No way I'm gonna write this down.

5

Justin Waley stood as she entered his office. "Mrs. McKay," he said politely. "This is a pleasure."

"It's a pleasure to be here, Mr. Waley," Angie McKay said, and to his surprise she sounded as if she really were pleased to be in his functional, rather untidy little office.

Justin was no authority on women's clothing, but he observed vaguely that Mrs. McKay was as well-dressed as if she were going to church. But not the same as if she were going to church. Then she sat down and leaned a little forward, and the corner of her blouse fell away from her neck, as it was styled to do. The amount of skin it revealed was not great, but the style suggested that much more might be revealed if the proposition was stated properly. She crossed her legs, with a glimpse of silk-clad thighs.

Justin turned slowly and shut down his computer, thinking quickly. This, he reminded himself, was Angie *Smithers* McKay.

"How can I help you?" he asked pleasantly.

She leaned forward earnestly and put her hand on the corner of his battered desk. "It's about my husband," she said. "I'm worried about him. I'm afraid his business isn't doing as well as he thought. He's been acting very strange lately—like there are things he doesn't want to talk about with me. You see," she said confidingly, "he's always had this thing about being a poor boy, and showing that he was worthy to marry into the Smithers family. Well, it's nonsense, but it's how he feels. And well, you know my Uncle Albert didn't have a good reputation. I'm just worried that Bernie's— my husband's—business is failing and he is afraid to tell me. Uncle Bill, your partner, won't talk to me either. So I came to *you*," she added confidingly.

She was very good, Justin thought. Her tone was that of the worried, appealing wife; her pose made other promises. Her hand might as well have been on his knee.

"Well, as you know," he said slowly, "your Uncle William is handling the audit. He has not confided in me, which is understandable. The Smithers family has large interests and those might be damaged by a premature revelation, if there's anything to reveal. So I really can't tell you much."

"Oh, please, Mr. Waley—May I call you Justin?— please, Justin, you know I'm more than a Smithers family member." She hitched herself closer and leaned more toward him, increasing the visual promise. "I'm Bernie's *wife*. By the terms of the partnership agreement, the surviving partner inherits the whole business. I'm more than just an interested Smithers family member. I have a right to know if my husband is worried about going bankrupt, don't I?"

Justin nodded slowly as if considering. His heart was racing, almost audibly. Just how far would she go to get what she wanted? Clearly she wanted more than mere information about her husband's business. She wanted an ally. That, she might pay high for.

Alarmed by the thought, Justin said, "Well, obviously you do have more than ordinary interest. I can't give you final figures, but it's becoming evident that Albert Smithers borrowed against partnership properties purchased by him—the men worked independently, of course. We have not been able to find where those monies went. Such loans were normally used to leverage purchases of still more land. So it seems that Smithers and McKay has a sizeable debt that your husband was not aware of."

"And that might worry him, very much, mightn't it . . . Justin?"

"Not knowing your husband that well, I couldn't say."

"Call me Angie—please. Still, it might account for him going off to Kansas City on a business deal, in the middle of the audit," she said, apparently to herself. She frowned, puzzled, and looked at him. "I never understood that. But if he's worried, and figures he has to move quickly to recoup his losses . . . do you think, Justin?"

"Very possibly . . . Angie."

She looked at the struggling airconditioner and swiftly touched the top button of her blouse, without altering anything he could see. She took a long breath, and Justin found himself startled at the size of her bosom— the stylish blouse underplayed it. Justin swallowed, to avoid clearing his throat nervously.

Angie sighed. "There have been so many rumors about the audit that I became alarmed myself," she said. "You can understand. I'm afraid this isn't good for my husband's business." She shook her head and stood up.

"Well, thank you, Justin, for all your help." She bent and took his hand before he could stand up, and for a moment Justin didn't dare try to stand. The top button made the difference; the blouse fell open as she bent, revealing a modest amount of lightly tanned cleavage and one sweet freckle. Her attitude made the sight more alluring than any amount of nudity could have.

"If you learn anything, please call and tell me," she said wistfully. "And may I come and see you again?

Please, Justin? I really don't have anyone to tell my worries to, until Bernie is willing to talk to me again. May I?"

"Of course," he said, managing not to sound strangled. Justin stood up, glad he'd had so much practice, as a much-teased nerd of a kid, at keeping his face straight.

She clung to his hand for a moment more, looking appealingly up at him. "And please don't tell my poor husband I've been here," she added. "I don't want him to worry about me knowing."

"Of course," Justin mechanically repeated. He watched her hips switch till the door closed behind one last, bright glance.

Justin took a breath and let it out, relieved. Surely the temperature had jumped ten degrees in here.

He sat down slowly, embarrassed by the memory of the way he'd looked during the interview. Like a total nerd, as usual. He wasn't sure he was glad or sorry she meant to stay in touch. Maybe next time he could act less like a nerd; or maybe he'd overreach, make a pass or something and get frozen.

The whole town knew Angie McKay liked good-looking young men—a category into which Justin had never put himself. Darrel Lamour, their assistant, had once repeated a catty remark that everyone knew Angie got into church committees and school and town event committees in order to meet young men. They squired her to public events when Bernie was busy or out of town. How far she went with them had long been a matter for speculation.

Justin suspected she'd go much farther with an ally in the business. Was he glad or sorry that he'd been such an unresponsive, terrified nerd? He had a fleeting, wistful vision of an affair with Angie. It might be very good. Even if her only interest in him was purely commercial.

Then his shyness rose up and embarrassed him at the thought. Blindly Justin turned on his computer and sat looking at the screen. Out of his welter of emotions one surfaced: a fearful eagerness at her promise to see more of him.

He slowly passed the palm of his hand back over his balding head, and sighed again.

6

Jody "Hat" Stetson pulled into the Amoco station on Highway 13 and grandly up to the *Full Service* pump. Pfister Wainwright waved drunkenly out the passenger window at Bob "Poochie" Dubret as he slouched over to them, and lifted a bottle of whiskey.

"Hey, man, come with us!" Hat said pacifically. It'd been several days since he'd seen any of his friends; he'd been lonely. Deutscher was bull-headed, but Poochie was usually more pliable.

"Cain't. I just started this job t'day," Poochie said enviously. He pushed out his lips. "Where'd you git the bottle, Fester? Rip it off your ole man?"

Hat grinned. "Never mind. Come on, we're goin' out to visit Joe Bumgardner."

Poochie looked nervously over his shoulder, pooching his lips. "Cain't, I said. I got to keep this job for at least two weeks. Haveta git my ole car fixed. I shouldn't even be talkin' to you 'less I'm fillin' you up."

"Fuck the job, git in the truck," Fester said, waving the bottle.

Hat saw that Fester was too drunk to persuade anyone to do anything. And Poochie meant it about the job. "Hell. Well, we'll catch you on the flip-flop."

Poochie waved as he peeled out, and Hat felt a little better about the trouble. Poochie'll come around, he told himself.

"Fuck him, we don't need him," said Fester, reaching down for a beer from the 12-pack.

"Just don't drink it all before we git to Joe's."

Joe was renting a rusty old trailer house back in the woods five-six miles from a thriving small town called Laura. The trailer hadn't been lived in for a dozen years before he had rented it. In front of it was a rickety sort of deck, once roofed with an awning, that did duty as a porch. It was shaded now only by a persimmon tree that had grown up since the trailer was last occupied. Joe was sitting aimlessly in this shade, talking to himself and giggling, when they pulled in over the dried ruts that were the drive.

"Howdy, howdy!" Joe cried, starting up and coming eagerly toward them. "Oh, it's you, Stetson," he said, as Hat got out of the car. "And young Wainwright! Good to see you boys."

" 'Member that fifth I owe you?" Hat asked, waving the bottle. He saw the sudden thirst in Joe's eyes.

"Cain't say as I do, but I won't dispute the word," said Joe. He took the bottle and immediately unscrewed the cap.

"My dad sent me along to see how you're doin', Joe," said Fester, struggling through the weeds around the car, lugging the twelve-pack.

Joe blew out his breath. "I needed that, Stetson. I ain't hardly had a drink since you boys gimme them beers in the cave that day, 'member?" He made a gesture toward the shade on the porch. "Take the cheer, Feaster. Stetson, you can sit on the block; I'll be okay leanin' agin' the wall here."

"So how you doin', Joe?" Fester asked. "We ain't seen you in weeks."

Joe soberly took another drink. "Oh, well, fact is, I made up my mind to save my money. Figured I'd save it up this month, after I paid my debts, and put it in the bank. I ain't gittin' any younger, and I cain't always work. My back gits to hurtin' me and them docs in the VA Hospital in Kansas City don't do me much good any more. So I figure to save money ever' now and then. So I ain't been by."

The Wainwrights owned a country convenience store, Gobbler's Knob, one of Joe's favorite places of resort.

"Good idea," Hat said easily, taking a drink when the bottle came his way.

They alternated whiskey with beer and listened to Joe ramble. From where he sat Hat could see into the rusted-out trailer. Joe had kicked the junk to one end and contrived a dry sty in the other, with a tangle of moldy quilts on a warehouse pallet, more a nest than a bed. A crazy old kerosene stove and a blackened skillet were the only articles for cookery. There was electricity, but no running water, only a well out back and an outhouse down the hill.

With a thrill of quiet horror, Hat thought, This is old age. Living like a pig, with no woman, no friends, no family, no one who cares. Someday they'd find Joe dead in some place like this. Till then his only pleasures were drink and talking to himself. He didn't even have drinking buddies: he and Wainwright weren't even that.

The talkative Joe had told everybody of his resolution to save money: Hat and Fester were here to break it. The elder Wainwright had provided the whiskey and offered to cancel Hat's debt for the favor.

Judas, Hat thought. But what can I do? I owe the old man too much to back out. And when Joe was

sufficiently lubricated, Hat kindly persuaded him into
the car.

Back at Gobbler's Knob, the afternoon got drunker
and drunker, at Joe's expense. Memory faded in and
out, but Hat's mood remained dark. He'd seen the
future, and it was bad.

"You know whose fault it is?" at one point he
remembered saying to Fester. "Shirley McGinnis's,
that's who!" He'd spent much of the week pursuing
her, to no avail.

"Yeah?"

"Yeah. She keeps pushin' me away. Not now, Hat.
If it's not now, when is it, huh? That's what I want to
know! When is it ever gonna be Now? Huh?"

"She's been leadin' you on," Fester said wisely, and
hiccupped.

"Yeah! Well, it's over now. Know what I'm fuckin'
gonna do about it? I'm gonna take her out soon's she
gits off work. And I'm fuckin' gonna have it out with
her. Now or never, I'll say. Now or never. Or it's fuckin'
all off!"

Memory came and went unstably from then on, but
much time must have passed, for it went from being
blazing sunlight to being warm night when Hat found
himself in the McGinnis yard, hearing Mrs. McGinnis
yell at him and Shirley's fat kid sister laugh. The scene
was eerily lit by drunkenness and the mercury-vapor
lights, a feverish blue-green frost over everything. All
the faces were like corpses in that light.

Hat later remembered his defiance in flashes when
Shirley refused to come with him. He remembered
half a dozen father McGinnises and several brothers
leaping on him, while his feet were rooted nightmarishly
to the ground and his arms too heavy to lift.

At one point he was bent over beside his car on a

dark gravel road, his guts wracked, mouth full of vomit and mind full of self-loathing. *Poor ole Joe Bumgardner, I really screwed him over, I oughta be hung.* Then without perceptible interval he was driving through the night, pounding the steering wheel in rage and trying to find his way back to the McGinnis place to have it out with them. He vaguely remembered changing his mind; the image of Nona Martens came to him, wearing tight jeans and an apron. It was tied up with an image of a copper coffin and more rage.

If they hadn't let me down, I would 'a got the coffin, and could of took her out on my share, the cowardly bastards. . . .

Then he was bumping across a field toward the line of trees that marked the river. Sometime before this he must have emptied his bottle, for the haze lifted slowly at this point and did not return. The anger had burned out, replaced by the wrenching melancholy of a black lady singing the blues. He stopped under the trees with his lights on the turbid water and wandered sickly down onto the bank, utterly wretched. He felt that he had been abandoned and betrayed by all women and would never know happiness, not ever, he'd die an old man with gray unshaven whiskers in a rusted-out bus, like an animal in a hole.

It was too much effort to scramble down to the water for a drink, supposing the Osage River was fit to drink. He sat down on the bank, clutching his stomach. For a while he just sat, then a memory came to him, stereoscopically clear: old man Wainwright tucking a paper into his pocket and saying, "Here's your bill for this afternoon."

So he hadn't wiped out his debt, only made it worse. Weakly Hat scrabbled in his pocket for the bill, but when he found it, the headlights were too dim for him to read it. He dug out his lighter and held the flame as steady as he could, squinting. He still couldn't quite make it out, but he got that it was enormous, stupendous, more than he could pay. More than he could pay in a year, in a lifetime, a crushing destroying debt.

He was sick. He was terribly sick. He fell over, hoping he would puke, but he didn't. Instead came tears. Hat huddled in the dirt, gasping and sobbing over the waste of his life, the bill crumpled in one hand and the lighter clenched in the other.

Weeping, he wondered: was it twenty pieces of silver, or thirty?

Chapter Five:

Didn't He Ramble

1

Deputy Rod Parker looked up nervously from his menu, feeling clumsy—even clumsier when Judith Lamour smiled brightly at him.

"Better have cold sandwiches," she said. "There won't be time, otherwise. Lunchtime is the busy time."

"Uh—right," he said, looking at her rather than at the menu.

Judith was the brightest thing in Bracher's dim-lit restaurant. She was so bright she sparkled, he thought. Bright brown eyes, short bright brown hair in curls all over her head, uptilted nose, light freckles over light tan, bright light-yellow dress over neat little figure. But it wasn't any of that. It was her attitude: she *sparkled*.

"I'll just have the ham sandwich," she said to the harried waitress, laying the menu aside and looking eagerly at him.

Hurriedly Parker lifted his menu, looked blindly at it. "Uh—yeah, that sounds like a good idee," he said. "And I'll go for a side of fries. Gotta keep my weight up." He instantly regretted the last.

Judith laughed. "You know, you could have the dinner salad for about the same price; it's just as filling, and a lot better for you."

"Yeah? Well, I'll give it a try," he said to the waitress. When she had gone, Judith leaned eagerly toward him. "Have you learned anything more?"

"Not learned exactly, no," he said, and sipped his coffee to give himself a moment. He had to shift from thinking about her to thinking about the digging up of old man Smithers. "You been seein' Poochie—Bob Doo-bray," pronouncing it carefully. "Have you maybe picked up a hint of who he was runnin' with about then?"

"Oh, I haven't seen Bob since then," she said, tossing her head and making the ringlets dance. "I already gave you all I know. You wrote it down!"

"Yeah," Parker said, flipping open his notebook. "Thing is, Poochie—Doo-bray—was one of Hat Stetson's gang of friends. Seems like the gang broke up. Word we been gittin' is that they ain't talkin' to each other no more. Could they of argied over what happened that night?"

"Could be. But anything would do. They're always having spats, like little girls."

He laughed. "Yeah. You haven't thought of anything more?"

"Not since Mr. Culter thought about the keys. I just know that nasty Orlin Deutscher snuck them back into the box, but—"

"Yeah." Parker sipped his coffee again. At least she wasn't still seeing Poochie. Parker wondered who she was seeing now. He sighed.

The waitress arrived with their sandwiches. "That was quick," said Judith enthusiastically.

Parker bit into his. "You heard about this rumor that's goin' around that ole Smithers stole gold from his partner 'n' hid it away, Miss Luh-moor?"

She looked conspiratorially around, and leaned forward. "My brother works for the accountants. He says it's definite! A quarter million!"

Parker nodded. "We ain't been told nothin' officially, but word's leaked out. I was wonderin' if maybe someone dug up the grave lookin' for the gold."

"But who would do that?" she asked. "If nobody knew about the gold."

"Anybody that took a wild notion the gold was there," he said, swallowing. "Meaning it had to be somebody on the inside, not Stetson and Dutchies and Doo-bray."

Judith looked at him over the rim of her cup, her eyes startled. "Oh, no, Mr. Parker. Don't you know why those boys dug up the casket? You should have asked Mr. Culter! They wanted the copper. I suppose it would be worth hundreds of dollars, cut up for salvage."

"God damn it," Parker said in a suffocated tone. He almost hit himself on the head. "I feel so damn stupid! Sheriff Anderson and me figured it was just some dumb joke or something. We never thought of the copper. Damn." He took a bite of his pickle.

Judith was laughing. "Oh, you poor guys! And we never mentioned it 'cause it was so obvious! I thought you knew all this time!"

Crushed, Parker said, "Well, I'm sorry to've dragged you away from your work for such a bullshit idee." He winced. "S-sorry, Miss Luh-moor," he mumbled. "I usually hang out with men, and so I talk kind of rough."

She looked at him, head tilted roguishly, eyes sparkling. "Good thing you never heard women talking among themselves! You'd be shocked."

"I'm sorry you told me that, Miss Luh-moor," he said. "I always thought women were special and neat and nice."

She shook her head in smiling mock regret. "Now I've disillusioned you! Call me Judith. And you're Mr. What Parker?"

"Huh? Oh, my first name? Rod."

And to his chagrin he felt his ears and face reddening. For a moment, so great was his embarrassment at being embarrassed, he thought the tears would come to his eyes.

"If I say one word about your name, you'll never forgive me," she said. "You'd never speak to me again!" She slid out of the booth. "Goodbye, Mister Rod Parker," with an impish twinkle. "Thank you for lunch. See you soon!"

Unwillingly, he maneuvered his bulk out of the booth. "G-goodbye, J-judith." He shook her proffered hand, watched her bounce away, sprightly.

It was over. Somehow or other, he stumbled to the cashier's, and out.

2

Jody "Hat" Stetson said, "Thanks for the beer, Poochie. That job o' yours any good?"

"It's a helluva job," Poochie said, pushing his lips out sullenly. He exhaled tobacco smoke dispiritedly.

"Least it pays money," Pfister "Fester" Wainwright said.

Frankie Cowgill grunted in greedy agreement. His

freckled face looked almost as red as his hair in the colored light.

They were sitting on the porch of the white-painted little store, Gobbler's Knob. Hat sipped beer and observed the red-painted sunset sky.

"Hell, I only been on it four days," Poochie said, pooching his lips. "Ain't seen a penny. And ole lady Flynn works me like a mule, the bitch."

Hat sympathized absently. It felt good to be sitting around with the gang again, even if Fester and Cowgill and Poochie weren't much. Hat had done his best to get on all their good sides, but Deutscher was still adamant. Even Poochie was still pretty sulky.

Pity about Billy Martens, too, Hat thought, on account of Nona. The boy wouldn't even talk to him.

"Got time for another round?" Fester Wainwright asked, nodding toward the now-pale drained dregs of sunset.

"Guess not," Hat said reluctantly. "That reminds me. 'Member that buck I owed you for buyin' gas?" He pulled out a crumpled bill and handed it to Fester.

Fester looked at it in bemusement, looked at Frankie Cowgill. "Well, Cowgirl. This'll knock my bill for that transmission fluid you bought me down to three fifty," he said, handing the dollar to Cowgill.

Frankie grunted, looked at the worn bill. He looked at Poochie Dubret, shrugged. "What d'I owe you for oil, the time I changed it? Down to nine bucks? Eight now."

Poochie looked at the bill, shrugged in turn and handed it blank-faced back to Hat. "Does this square us?"

Hat took back the bill, laughing. "Aw right, the buck stops here," he said. "I ain't startin' it back around."

They finished their beers, a little edgily. The sun

had set. The only light in the sky was from clouds and the saw-edged horizon.

Hat said, "Guess it's late enough."

The others jumped up eagerly; he himself walked more slowly toward Fester's decrepit, once-white Ford. Behind the wheel, Fester dug out. In the car and safe from being overheard, Frankie addressed Poochie.

"Tell us again what the Lammers girl told you," he said eagerly.

"Lamour," Poochie said, pursing his lips irritably. "Like Dorothy Lamour. Her older brother works for Smithers and Waley—the accountants. They're goin' over ole Albert Smithers' books. Smithers family is tryin' to hush it up, but they figure he got away with millions. Anyway, a million. And word is that he put it into gold and hid it, and nobody don't know where."

"It's stolen from his pardner?" Fester asked, steering around a pothole in the blacktop.

"Yeah—McKay, that's his pardner," Poochie said, sounding important. "In Kan' City on some deal. Anyway, the ole man didn't git out much in the last two or three months he was alive. But one place he went to was the old Smithers place in Laurie City."

"The old Smithers house is way out on the outskirts, half in the woods—it's an ole farmhouse," Hat said. "I fixed the eaves oncet. Nobody lives there now."

"It's a cinch the gold's there," said Fester eagerly. "The Smithers been tearin' up ole Albert's house in Ozzy-go. If they'd'a found it, word would 'a' gotten out."

"Yeah," said Hat. Privately he wondered; he remembered an expedition after Albert's coffin. That had been a cinch too. "Anyways, it's worth a look, and if we don't find gold, we might find—somethin' worth while."

Fester flicked on the one working headlight, the right

one, and they turned off the blacktop onto a rutted gravel road, to approach Laura City from the back side. The light faded as they drove, until the trees along the road were vaguely seen masses. Presently they topped a long hill and started down.

"Lookit that!" Frankie cried, surging forward till his head was between Hat and Fester.

Hat looked and heard a strangled sound emerge from his lips, along with one from Fester's. Poochie sucked in his breath behind Fester. A yellow-and-black tiger-striped locomotive was charging up the left lane toward them.

They glared at it in almost superstitious horror. We're all cold sober, Hat thought indignantly.

As their car descended the hill, its one weak light flickering yellowly over the apparition, Hat saw that the locomotive's own light was not working—that was just reflection from theirs. And it was moving more slowly than he'd at first thought. Fester slowed, and for some seconds they all stared at the locomotive as they approached it.

Hat realized that the road at the foot of the hill trended toward the right, so the locomotive was not in the left lane, it was on the shoulder. And it was not actually moving, just sitting there.

"Oh!" said Frankie, on a note of intense relief.

"Yeah!" said Fester a moment later, also relieved. Poochie grunted.

Then before Hat's eyes the locomotive shriveled, collapsed, shrank down into a road-grader a third its locomotive size; darkness, flickering light, and liberal imagination having done the rest. Hat caught himself before saying anything, lest they realize he was the last to see it.

"What'd you guys see?" he asked.

"Locomotive."

"Yeah. Freight engine, with tiger-stripes."

"That's what I seen. Funny thing, wasn't it?"

Presently the old Smithers farm house loomed beside the road. Beyond it was a small sign, dimly seen in their light: City/LAURA CITY/Limits. As they pulled into the recently-graveled drive, the light glanced off another sign: FOR SALE/Smithers & McKay. Fester jerked the car to a stop and for a moment they regarded the house.

There was an old-fashioned yardlight, greenish-blue. It revealed the recently cut lawn—more weeds than grass. The old farmhouse had been built in the most utilitarian style of the early century, a wooden frame boxed with vertical boards, battened with more boards nailed over the cracks. Unpainted, it had weathered to a dull light gray except here and there where newer battens had replaced older ones. The windows had at some time been ripped out and replaced with larger, more modern ones. A pair of brick chimneys tottered atop all, the irregularities of their bricks visible in the dim light.

"Looks okay," said Poochie.

Instantly jealous of his position, Hat said, "Yeah, let's git goin'."

Entry through the kitchen door was not difficult, though a little noisy. There followed three hours of frustration as their flashlight batteries grew weaker and weaker. They ransacked every likely place inside—looking for places where the woodwork had been disturbed, and in natural hidey-holes like that under the staircase or inside the flues. Frankie had the idea that the gold might have been dropped down inside the walls, and went around banging on them. Hat thought that ridiculous.

"How'd he git it out when he wanted it?" he asked, and went out to check the shed.

Fester Wainwright had given up on the house and was crawling around the yard, looking for places where the soil might have been disturbed anytime in the past two months. The shed, Hat found, was full of empty mason jars. It was a mere adjunct to the cellar, which was a crudely-laid stone house, its floor below ground level. This stone house had been buried in dirt, now heavily sodded with grass. It was empty—Hat didn't bother with his flashlight, he turned on the overhead, closing the door—empty and refurbished. The walls and floor had been painted with white water-proofing paint, from which spicules of light glanced. The paint showed no breaks.

"Shee-yit," said Hat to the others when they gathered back at the car, all irritated and exhausted. "Bastard must've hid it somewheres else."

"Maybe in his house. Maybe the fuckin' Smitherses found it and ain't lettin' on," grumbled Fester.

"Didn't git a fuckin' thing," growled Poochie.

The house was totally empty.

"Shee-yit," Hat said again. "I did hope there'd be somethin' in the house." He felt that his star had descended, but didn't know what to say or do to save the situation.

"I need a drink," Fester said sourly. "Anybody got'ny money? I got a couple bucks."

They pooled their money and drove to one of Laura City's convenience stores, where they bought beer. They took it back to the Smithers house, where they drank and glowered and cursed Albert Smithers. When the beer was gone they had a little trouble finding another open place, and had to go down onto Highway Thirteen—it was well after midnight. Again they returned, by some nameless compulsion, to the Smithers house.

Finally, with the drink and their money gone, they wearily decided to call it a night. Frankie Cowgill, as marginally the least drunk of the four, elected to drive. Fester they just shoved without comment into the back seat. Poochie sat on him.

When he cranked up the engine, Frankie grunted, squinting at the dash. "Damn thing's outta gas."

Hat leaned over and peered blearily at the dial. Damn if the hand wasn't on "Empty." "You got'ny money lef'?"

"Nope. You?"

"Me neither," said Poochie blearily.

"Fester! Hey, Fester! You got'ny money?"

They shook Wainwright until he responded with a soggy negative.

"Shit farr and save matches," said Hat, hating Albert Smithers more than ever. "We got to take all four of us home, and that's a long way round. What're we gonna do?"

From the back seat, Fester muttered, "Cipher. Can. Trunk."

Hat looked at Frankie; Frankie looked back. Poochie stared at them.

"Guess that's all we can do," said Hat.

"Yeah."

They got out and opened the trunk, finding not only the promised can, but a promising length of rubber tubing. It smelled of gasoline, suggesting that Fester had solved similar problems in a similar manner in the past.

Wainwright pushed the back door open and stumbled out to join them. Poochie suggested that they all go together. Quickly taking charge, Hat made the idea his own. "Less noticeable," he said, meaning that a group of four going down the road would seem more natural than a lone individual. Moreover, they could conceal the can more readily. It was a dubious proposition at best, but Hat made it sound sensible. Frankie Cowgill, no lover of walking as exercise, demurred at first, but Hat argued him around. Poochie grunted.

They set out down the back roads of Laura City, Fester wavering along behind. Presently they found a van parked on a side street, if a graveled road is a street. Fester tried to take over, as an old hand, but was too drunk. Hat, something of an old hand himself, masterfully took command, brushing Poochie aside.

"Here's how we did it in the Army," he said, sliding the tube down into the gas tank. From the feel, he had to go around a corner. Then he applied his lips to the end of the tube and sucked mightily.

Instantly his mouth filled with gasoline, and reflex made him swallow. He coughed and choked, head full of the indescribable burning flavor of gasoline, emitting fumes from every pore and gasoliny tears from his eyes.

"Haw-haw, way to go, Hat!" Poochie said. "You reelly got it flowin' good!" He hastily picked up the spouting tube and tucked it into the five-gallon can.

"Fuckin' goddamn hell," Hat gasped weakly. His vocal cords felt burned, worse than by whiskey. "Bastard must be full." He belched curses and gasoline fumes.

"Haw-haw! You cipher gas like a expert," Frankie said.

"Aw, fuck you and shut up, Cowgirl." Hoarsely.

When the siphon had run for some time, a barking dog panicked them and Poochie jerked the tube out and ran off with the can. Hat ran, lost the others, and finally staggered back to the car. Frankie looked around white-faced from where he was pouring the gas into the car.

"Where's the others?" Hat asked.

"Poochie's layin' down in the back seat. Where's Fester?"

"Dunno. I—"

Crunch of footsteps on gravel and a hoarse muttering and drunken laughter heralded Fester, who was waving the van's gas cap like a scalp.

"Oops," said Frankie, at the gas spout. "Damn thing's spittin' back at me. Hey, Hat, the damn tank's full. I ain't put in more'n two gallon."

"Damn gauge must be busted," Hat said, still tasting gasoline. "We had plenny gas. Hey, Fester, you bastard, your gas gauge work?"

"Shee-yit, you guys, come on, git in, we gotta go," Poochie said, grabbing the keys out of Frankie's fumbling hands He slid in behind the wheel.

Hat was too miserable with his belly-full of gas to resist Poochie's taking charge. "You fuckin' tell 'em, Poochie," he muttered, and got sullenly into the passenger side.

The disgruntled silence wasn't broken for ten minutes.

"Long about here's where we seen the locomotive," said Fester, leaning blearily over the seat back.

"No ih-tain't, it wuz furder down," said Poochie.

"Aw, shee-yit, Poochie, you don't know your hand in fronta your face," Hat said, out of pure spite. "You always gotta be right."

"Shit yourself, man, if it wuz here, the road grader'd still be here, right?"

"So someone come and moved it," Hat said.

"Yeah," said Fester, bobbing his head between them.

"Aw shit, only one way to find out." Poochie pulled over to the side of the road, killed the engine and turned off the headlight.

Hat opened his door and looked down, not into a ditch, but onto gravel. He looked up. "Shee-yit, man, you jus' pulled over into the lef' lane and stopped. Should'a pulled over to the right, onto the shoulder, asshole."

"You're the asshole. Who cares? Nobody's gonna come by at this time—"

A faint engine grumble and grind of tires on gravel burst into a roar as lights bloomed at the top of the hill before them. A car topped it at high speed and instantly hit its brakes. Paralyzed, Hat watched it come in a cloud of dust and scream of tires. It drifted on the gravel till it was traveling right fender first.

Its right headlight caught them square between the eyes and caved in their radiator. Hat's head rebounded from the windshield and stars shot through his vision; Fester was hanging gurgling over the seatback. Frankie Cowgill squealed in the back seat.

In front of them, in a haze of dust and steam, the other car reversed and jerked back out of their front end, put its wheels over, and did a U turn. It gunned its engine and in a moment was back over the top of the hill, gone. Faint engine and gravel grumble. Silence.

"—time of night," Poochie finished his sentence.

"Shee-yit," said Frankie, dumbfounded.

Hat belched gasoline and spat out the window, shaken.

3

"Stop, stop!" Nona Martens cried, one hand on her brow where she had bounced off the windshield despite the safety harness. Her shoulder and chest felt like one great bruise.

"I cain't stop!" Billy cried back over the roar of his engine. The old car rocketed down the gravel road, leaving a rooster tail of dust.

"But those men—"

"They were parked on the wrong side of the road with their lights off."

"But—"

The car tipped over forward and went down and down and down an incredibly steep hill on an incredibly bad road, jouncing over ledges of rock. At the bottom it rumbled across an ancient plank-floored bridge two car lengths long, then climbed and climbed and climbed an equally steep and rough road on the other side.

Nona looked uncertainly over at her intent son. Driving through here—wherever *here* was—took all of his concentration, obviously. Equally obviously, he didn't want to talk.

Of course, she thought. He had too many points on his license—and probably didn't have insurance on his car. If there was any question at all about his driving, he'd lose his license. No wonder he rarely drove, preferring to ride with his friends. But her car was in the shop, and he'd agreed to drop her off and pick her up—sullenly, she had thought at first; reluctantly, she now realized.

They topped the rise and jounced along for a bit, then climbed some more and abruptly surfaced on blacktop. Billy gunned it. He got them nearly home before giving up. His gauge had been in the red for a long time, and when the idiot light finally came on, he snarled and pulled over, shutting down.

For a moment they sat, staring into the leaf-lined darkness along the gravel road, about a mile from the mobile home.

"Engine too hot?" she ventured.

"Radiator busted."

"It'll cool?"

"In five, six hours, maybe."

It was plain he meant to sit there till it did. Nona sighed and unhooked her harness, picked up her purse from where it had fallen to the floor. She rubbed her shoulder.

"Right. I'll walk from here. Maybe I could call someone—?"

"Who? I don't have any friends who'd come, 'specially at this hour." Bitterly.

"Yeah," she said. With a sigh she got out, closed the door gently, and edged along the clay-banked ditch to the front of the car. The right fender was stove in, but she could see no other details in the dim light. Sighing again, she started for home.

It was a twenty-minute walk in solitude. Call someone?

Tow charges would literally be more than the car was worth. And they just needed someone to haul it home, that was all. Back home in Ohio, no problem; one of her brothers would turn out grumbling, as she had turned out for them when they were young together. But she had no relatives here, and no friends she felt she could impose on to this extent.

Yet, there was that boy of hers, sitting grimly and somehow heroically in his ruined car. Ruined helping her.

4

Justin Waley smiled at Nona Martens as she poured coffee for him, but she didn't seem to notice.

"That be all?" she asked, not smiling.

Justin opened his mouth to ask what was wrong, but instead said, "Can I have extra creamer?"

"Sure, be right back."

It was earlier than he liked to eat, but this early there was no crowd in the Night Owl, though the evening shift of waitresses had come in. As a result the service was usually good. When the promised creamer did not materialize, Justin went looking for Nona. She was in the doorway to the kitchen, having stopped to answer the questioning of one of the other waitresses.

"Yes, I picked it up today," she was saying. "Just needed to have the carburetor adjusted, thank God. But Billy put his car in the ditch last night, taking me home, so he's on foot till we can replace it."

"You going to junk it out?"

"Yeah, it was a junker when we bought it and he 'n' his friends fixed it up. His old friends, from high school, that was. Oh, I'm sorry," seeing Justin. "I was on my way, but I got distracted. I'm sorry." Nona flurried off and came back with a handful of sealed creamer cups.

"Thank you," he said. "Don't worry about it," as she visibly started to apologize all over again. "I hope your son can soon replace his car," he added, feeling clumsy.

"Thanks," she said, and made a wry face. "I wish he could get a job. He'll have to buy an old junker and fix it up, and they're cheap, but fixing it up—" she shook her head hopelessly, her reddened hair flirting around her face.

"Ain't no jobs in St. Claude county," said the other waitress grimly.

Nona said, "Yeah," glumly, and hurried off to another of her tables.

Poor Nona. Poor Billy, Justin thought, methodically eating his sandwich. But he couldn't think of any way to help. Nor could he join easily into the commiserating talk, with his self-conscious shyness. He ate silently and glumly, as usual, till he was finished, and only spoke to her once more, when she stopped briefly by, to accept a last cup of coffee from her.

She was nowhere in sight when he got up to leave.

Another evening wasted, he thought wistfully. Not that the whole evening was wasted. But he'd spent most of the day just waiting for the moment when he could see her again. And as usual, she hadn't seen him.

5

"Bernard McKay's missing," said the sheriff, hanging up the phone.

Deputy Rod Parker pushed his hat back, standing in front of the fan. He wished they'd get the air fixed in here. "Been gone long?"

"That was White Bird Hadley. Accordin' to him, McKay went off to Kansas City four days ago on a deal. Should've been back last night. Mrs. McKay called up to the hotel and found he hadn't been there. So he's been missin' four days." Evelyn Anderson flipped a page in his notebook.

"This was the first she knew he hadn't been at the hotel?" Parker asked quickly.

Evelyn shot him a shrewd glance. "Yeah. And White Bird says McKay's assistant, guy name of Gibson, was there at her house when he went around to interview them. Not exactly holdin' her hand, but—" He grinned. "Hadley's kind of ironical."

Parker grinned back, but he had trouble thinking of a woman of the upper class playing footsie. In fact, he was always rather shocked when one got pregnant. It was so undignified.

"Gibson?" he said, coming alert. "I know a family of Gibsons." A shifty lot; dishonest, but rarely lawbreakers. The sly kind who twisted everything to their own advantage. He'd a damn sight druther deal with Smiglies—

The sheriff was nodding. "Paul Gibson. The same family you're thinking of, I guess."

"Don't know him." Parker shook his head.

"It don't look good to me," Evelyn said frankly. He pushed at the sweaty, graying hair at his temple. "Partner dead, but walking, suggesting something wrong. There've been rumors that the partnership accounts are cooked. And now the surviving partner turns up missing—*and* his assistant is hanging around his wife." He shook his head. "Formula for murder." He looked sharply at Parker. "Don't mention that."

Parker grunted in acquiescence. "I suppose Hadley's already put out an APB on the car?"

"Right. Big red-brown Cadillac. Hadley's called the hotel and confirmed McKay wasn't there. Neither the wife nor the office has received phone calls or any other messages from him since he left for Kansas City." He tapped his fingers thoughtfully on his notebook. "Any other ideas?" he added, looking up hopefully.

"No," said Parker, then checked. "Uh—this deal McKay was on. Anybody talked to those people in Kansas City? The ones he was goin' to see?"

"Good thought!" Anderson reached for the phone.

"I'll pass it on to Hadley; he can talk to Gibson, find out who they are." He shook his head grimly. "I don't like it. I reelly don't like it. Well. Your time up? See you tuhmorra."

"Yeah, I guess it is. Guess I'll swing by the Night Owl."

The Night Owl wasn't his favorite place—he felt out of it, among all those happy young couples—but Parker had no desire to go home to his stepmother. Her son Dick was making noises about leaving again, and that would leave only Parker to care for the old bat. She'd fall apart without someone to care for her, but by God it was hard. Even worse when she felt deserted and turned weepy and demanding. Jesus, when he was little Ma even used to kiss him.

Parker shuddered at the memory.

6

Awareness.

Hatred.

After a long time of awareness and hatred, came: Movement.

He moved. He was aware of himself, and he hated, and he moved.

He fumbled. He hated and was aware, and fumbled and pulled himself upward and along. He pulled himself along something: Smooth. Metal, he identified, and Glass.

. . . The Cadillac.

Pausing, his hands on the Smoothness, he perceived an Image inside himself: a car, The Cadillac, standing alone in a blaze of golden light. It was of a rich color: Maroon. A car. Not just a car: The Maroon Cadillac.

It meant much to him. To be near it almost soothed the hatred, and he could have gone back into . . . sleep, into the Darkness.

But Purpose came now, Purpose driven by the Hatred.

He pushed and pulled and fumbled away from The Maroon Cadillac, upward, over a rough soft substance. And then Light was born around him, and he thrust upward and upward, fumbling and sometimes slipping back, but ever upward, into the Light.

And then the world parted from him and fell away from him and poured from him, and he thrust and pulled himself farther up the soft muddy bank, into the Light, above the cascading world he'd been in. Water, came the thought from far away.

With Light came Vision: the higher world above the water was Green. He pulled himself out on it and more water poured from him, and he looked about. Trees, and a Black Pool, and impossibly steep Hills covered with old softwoods. The Light was very very bright. He looked back at the Pool and realized that The Cadillac was there, down there. He hesitated over a feeling of loss, and almost went back to it.

Back into the Strip Pit.

And with that Bernie McKay realized who he was, and what his Purpose was: Revenge.

Angie, he thought. And Gibson, but mainly Angie. Swaying, he turned from the dark pool from which he'd been born, and looked across the world. From here to Oswego was not over thirty minutes in a car.

It was going to take him a couple of days, Bernie realized. For one thing, he wasn't moving very well. For another, he mustn't be seen; if he was, his revenge would go glimmering. For some minutes he assessed the situation. His route here, Highway A, lay through prairie. He decided to go south three or four miles, into the wooded country down Highway H. Turn east about Jackson City—the partnership owned a lot of land around the tiny town, and he knew the area well— then keep to the woods all the way east to Oswego.

Twenty-five or thirty miles, if he didn't wander around in the woods too much.

The first stage, through the strip pits, was no problem. He skirted the ends of the ridges and the pools, and the trees screened him from the highway. After that came open fields with only minimal protection. But he ventured, staying well out, away from the road, but keeping near the edges of the fields. Don't stomp through the crops; that they'll notice. From a distance, he told himself, he must look fairly normal.

It was slow going. Patience, he told himself. I've got lots of time. Dear Angie will wait for me, won't you, dear? I know you will. . . .

At long intervals he circled three houses, dreading dogs more than people, and was hopeful of soon coming into forested regions. Then came the birds.

The blue jays found him first, shrieking and yelling and swooping about. Some called him "Thief!" and others disagreed, calling him "Jay!" Their quarrel brought the crows.

At first Bernie's fear was that the swarming yelling confusion would attract attention to him. Even here in the wilds of rural Missouri, he was rarely out of distant view of a house. Then a crow landed on the shoulder of his blue suit and aimed a peck at his eye with its big blunt beak. He jerked away and it missed, striking him over the cheekbone. He felt no pain, merely a jolt. Horrified, he watched it gulp the pale shred of flesh it had torn free.

He brushed it off, crying "Get away!"

His voice came out with a great hoarse sawing sound, not unlike the voices of the crows. Other crows swooped at his face. He felt blows to the back of his neck. Desperately he stumbled into a staggering run, the birds swooping and screaming and cawing about him, the crows going for his eyes, or any area of exposed skin. Stark fear of blindness went through him.

"Get away, get away, damned crows, damned birds, damned . . . damned—" He alone could have understood his words, he knew.

Head down, hands above it, he stumbled across the field while the birds attacked. Alfred Hitchcock would've loved this, he thought wildly.

At least he didn't get tired. Running, he thought of stopping, hiding in a fence row. But no, they'd just continue to shriek around him, and the commotion would likely draw a farmer with a gun, thinking they'd found a hawk.

The fence rows got denser with trees, more hills appeared, and here and there were standing clumps of trees. Houses thinned, and finally the fields were no longer ringed by tree-lined fence rows, but were visibly hacked out of the encircling forest. Bernie crossed blacktop a couple of times, plowed through thin outlying forest, and crossed gravel roads. Finally he found the narrow, poorly maintained, and nameless track he wanted, running east from Jackson City.

It saw about a car an hour on a busy day, he supposed, but he stayed alert to plunge into the woods and hide. It would mean ducking under barbed wire, but because of the hills he'd hear them long before they saw him.

The damned mob of crows and blue jays thinned out here; poor country for them.

Bernie's hate hadn't thinned, nor his purpose. Revenge, revenge, revenge, it beat more steadily than his heart had when he was alive. He wondered if Angie and Gibson were married yet. I'll be with you on your wedding night, Angie dear, he thought, and a nasty slobbery sound came out of him as he chuckled inwardly.

Furiously he swatted at a crow. Off to the south, he'd been hearing gunshots but had paid them no mind. Presumably some foolish hunter braving what must be the heat of the late afternoon. Now, distracted by the double-damned crows, he almost walked over a small hill into view. The gleam of metal through leaves warned him, then voices and the clunk of a car door.

"Birds! What are they carrying on about, huh?" A woman's voice.

"Likely they've found something." Male voice, so audibly Missourian as to make the woman's non-Missouri origin obvious.

Hurriedly Bernie stumbled through the small ditch here and struggled under the fence, tragically hanging up on a barb for long moments. With a tearing sound he got loose and scrambled on all fours into the dense brush of the gnarled oak forest, leaves rustling under him, twigs and small limbs crunching.

The shooting and stomping to the south drowned his own noises: *kaBLAMM. Crash crash crash crash kaBLAMM. Crash crash crash crash kaBLAMM.* Forty-five, he thought, or maybe a forty-four magnum. Handgun. Being fired at everything interesting, by some city yahoo. He burrowed under a dense clump of trees and brush. At least he was hidden from the damn birds.

He heard a crunch of feet on the road's brown river gravel.

"Phew!" said the woman's voice.

"Well, whatever they've found, it's long dead," said the man. "When's your husband coming back?"

"Soon. Aren't the sounds getting louder?"

"Guess so. What's he huntin'?"

"Well, whatever, you know? I mean, I know it's out of season, but wouldn't it be great if we could take a deer back to California, huh?"

Crash crash crash crash kaBLAMM. Crash crash crash crash kaBLAMM, drowned the man's reply, as they walked back toward the car.

Yeah, Bernie thought dryly. It sure would be great. It'd be more than great; it'd be a miracle. Every deer this side of the Osage must be in hiding.

Muted voices, a car door closing, a car engine starting, and a car drove off. Tensely Bernie lay hidden while the Californian hunter came *crash crash crash crash*ing up to the road. At least there was no earth-shattering *kaBoom*. He hadn't shot his wife. A murmur of distant exultant voices, another car door slammed, and another car started up and drove toward him. Bernie got just a glimpse through the leaves of the shiny red machine, and it was gone.

So had the crows. Maybe I'd better stick to the woods, he thought, though I'll be as noisy as the Californian, except for the gun. He struggled on for a ways, surrounded by a great cloud of flies, frequently falling down. His clumsy dead legs didn't do so well on this rough terrain. At one point he fell, and in picking himself up, he saw in the sunset light that a chunk of flesh had been torn from his left knee, from which the pants leg had also been torn. He hadn't felt a thing.

This was going to take even longer than he'd thought. He heaved himself to his feet, his hatred beating strong in him, and staggered on. Almost immediately he fell, crawled for a space, then stood. Protecting his eyes with his outstretched hands, he struggled on. In the fading light he saw that shreds of dead flesh hung from his hands. The back of his neck must be shredded too.

Don't worry, Angie, I'm coming, he thought. He chuckled in his nasty way. I'd be there even sooner, but parts of me keep falling off.

Chapter Six:

There'll Be A Hot Time in the Old Town Tonight

1

Justin Waley entered the McKay home warily, smiled politely and responded to Angie McKay's eager greeting. She took his hand and drew him in, the moment the door closed enough to block the view from the street.

"Oh, Justin, I'm so glad you came," she said, with just a touch of breathlessness.

Justin wouldn't have been greatly surprised if she had greeted him in a negligee, though he would have been greatly embarrassed. In fact she was quite modestly dressed in loose blouse and slacks. Her tone almost suggested the negligee, however, and he was embarrassed anyway, but puppyishly pleased that he had come.

Nervously he looked around. Wealth in small

Midwestern towns expresses itself as middle class, written larger. Kitsch and bombast: a huge reproduction of a nineteenth-century impressionist picnic full of satin dresses, a gigantic up-to-the minute audio system, a huge TV on a walnut stand, a small tasteful wooden bookshelf. About half the items on the shelf were books, handsome gold-stamped imitation leather classics nobody had ever read. The furniture was the essential giveaway: overstuffed, immensely comfortable, but so pristine and virginal, it seemed no one had ever sat on the sofas or chairs or put a coffee cup on the coffee table.

With a skillful maneuver, Angie seated him on one of the sofas. "Just a moment, let me get you some lemonade," she said, and hurried out of the room. Justin observed that her slacks were much tighter than he had thought.

In a moment she returned with a tray. On it was a large glass pitcher full of lemonade made with real lemons, an ice bucket, a couple of glasses. "Such a hot day," she chattered, "a cold drink is the thing. Here you are!"

She gave it to him on a saucer with a coaster on it. Justin thanked her and took a sip: it was excellent, and so pure he suspected that it was mixed with distilled drinking water, and the ice frozen from the same.

She sat close to him and looked at him anxiously. "I'm so glad you came," she said. "I'm at my wits' end and I don't know who to turn to. Bernie is still gone, I don't know why or where."

Justin heard real worry in her tone. Not, he thought, that she cared so much for Bernie. "Yes," he said, encouragingly.

"Daddy McKay—Bernie's father—such a dear old man—he's talked to me. He's worried too. And Paul

Gibson." She paused, looking at him, swallowing. "Do you know Paul Gibson?"

"Slightly," Justin said dryly.

She leaned forward and he saw that her eyes were large and very blue. She was only ten years older than he, he knew.

"Well, I used to think that Paul was all right. I-I'd been pushing Bernie to make him a full partner, after Uncle Albert died, because it's too much work for just Bernie. P-Paul knew that—anyway, since Bernie d-disappeared, Paul has been acting very strange."

She paused and again she swallowed. Their thighs were touching and Justin felt her tremor.

"Strange in what way?" he asked, suspecting the answer.

She surprised him: "Acting like a full partner. Making decisions and coming to me to agree, only I'm not a real estate agent, I don't know if what he's doing is right or not. He shouldn't be closing deals; Bernie will be back soon and . . ." Her voice trailed off.

Justin's scalp crawled as if his scant remaining hair was trying to stand up. So Gibson was acting as if Bernie wasn't coming back! "And he hopes to marry the boss's widow," he added aloud.

Angie nodded, frightened. "It's nothing I can put my finger on," she said. "Even if he d-doesn't hope to marry me, he's acting like I have no choice, I have to make him partner. I'll sell the agency to the Gundersons before I do that!" she said, her eyes twin bolts of blue lightning.

Justin nodded in silent sympathy.

She softened and put her hand on his arm. "But I don't want to sell. The agency was my uncle's and my husband's—it *still is* my husband's!" Angrily. "But I need someone I can trust, someone who knows business. I mean, all my Smithers cousins are hopeless, I can't trust Paul, Bernie has no relatives who know anything. You're Uncle Bill's partner, he trusts you," she said wistfully. "Can I trust you too?"

She was warm all against one side of him, and Justin realized that he couldn't retreat without spilling lemonade all over himself. Tall narrow glass on a silly little saucer—unstable. He looked into her large, anxious blue eyes and tried not to sound strangled.

"I certainly will not cheat you," he said. "Though how good my advice would be on real estate—"

"Oh, I'm so glad! I just need someone to turn to—" She bent her shining head next to his, squeezed his arm, leaning against him. "Oh, I'm sorry—don't worry—here, I'll get it—"

She snatched the tottering tumbler from him and quickly mopped his lap with the cloth from the tray. "Don't worry, it won't stain—lemon juice—"

Back in his office half an hour later and staring at his computer screen, Justin was still shaken by the interview. But he was not sorry he had promised to help her however he could. On the other hand, the rational side of his mind thought grimly, Bernie couldn't come home too soon for his, Justin's, safety. That was a dangerous woman.

Uneasily he wondered if she knew where her husband was.

2

"God damn it to hell!" Jody "Hat" Stetson shouted, slamming the wrench down in the dirt and glaring at the broken bolt in his pickup. The nut had rusted to the bolt, which had twisted right off when he put his strength on it. "I've got the Midas touch in reverse. Everything I touch turns to shit!"

"That's good," Frankie Cowgill told Pfister Wainwright. They slouched in the shade of the tree while he sweated. Overhead a damn squirrel chittered angrily.

"Gimme a goddam hammer!"

Fester Wainwright brought him one and looked at the bolt. He shook his head sympathetically, his blond ponytail swinging. "I think I got one that'll match that," he said pacifically. "Hey, Cowgirl, fetch me that coffee can full of bolts. Not that one—the blue one—right."

Angrily Hat pounded the bolt in, crawled under, and teased it out from behind. "Here's the rest of it," he said sullenly, tossing it to them, and went to get a Coke.

They had drinks in an ice chest and one of the jackasses had left the lid off; half the ice had gone to water. Hat splashed the icy water over his face and, lifting his white cowboy hat, over his hair. Sighing, he replaced his hat and the ice chest lid, and popped his drink tab.

"—had this big ole mole on 'er face," Frankie Cowgill was saying, touching his freckled face. "Her mother told 'er never to mess with it, when she was a girl, on account it would turn to cancer. Anyways, she knocked it off when she was a young woman—banged into the edge of a window. She was so scairt it would turn to cancer she took and glued it back on with Elmer's. It growed back, and it's still there, after thirty years. I seen it myself."

"That's amazing," Fester said. "Shit, I ain't got one of these after all. Listen, though, my brother's old Buick's out back. He's off in the Army, and he won't care. We'll knock one of 'em out of it. C'mon, Cowgirl. Be right back, Hat."

Hat sat in the shade of the Wainwright home farm, wiping sweat, batting at flies, gulping Coke, and brooding on the perversity of fate. God damn all God damn cars anyway. Should 'a' gone to Springfield and got that job at the airport. Too late now. Too damn late. Story of his entire damn life.

"God damn it t'hell!" he roared in pain, jerking. An unripe hickory nut had bounced bruisingly off his shoulder. "Fuckin' God damn squirrel!" He glared up at the angrily chittering squirrel. "Blow your fuckin' head off!"

It objected to people under its tree. Fester'd warned him it was a good shot with a nut.

Presently the others came back, carrying a bolt. Fester was saying, "But you cain't git bobbycue in California, alls they got's some damn chain that's like bland, you know? So when we got to Albuquerque I said I wanted bobbycue, and we went out to like the best place in town, and it was awful. It was like they took bad bobbycue sauce and watered it down about half."

"Yeah, I know what you mean," Frankie said. "It's the same in Texas. My cousin Bradley says they cook the meat okay, slow and right through. But they don't know shit from shinola about bobbycue sauce. They got good salsa, though."

"Just the same on the East Coast, I guess," Fester said. "Here's your bolt, Hat," tossing it to him.

"Thanks," he grunted. Setting down his Coke, he crawled under his pickup.

"My Mom was tellin' about her cousins from Noo Jersey bein' surprised by bobbycue. They didn't know it was supposed to be hot!" Laughter.

"Guess they was expectin' ketchup!"

Hat called, "Gimme the plarrs and that piece of arrn

warr." Someone handed him pliers and wire and he secured the bolt temporarily. He crawled out and sat down in the shade to paw through the can of nuts.

Frankie Cowgill was wearing a thin, vestlike jacket despite the heat. Fester abruptly jerked it down off his shoulders, binding his arms. While Cowgill was momentarily incapacitated, Fester struck him a light blow in the stomach. It was a joke they did a lot in Spring, when everybody wore coats or jackets, usually open.

Cowgill wasn't expecting it now. "Ha, funny," he gasped.

Fester dodged a nut and that restored Cowgill to good humor. Laughing, they took to throwing rocks at the angry squirrel.

Hat went on pawing through the nuts, and later banging away on his pickup, brooding sullenly, their conversation an unheard background. His hands were all over grease and raw sores and old scabs. Gold, he thought. Walking corpse. Midas touch. Shit.

Damned old Smithers. Bastard prob'ly took his gold with him. Be just like him. Absently Hat worked his wrench, not seeing the nut and bolt. How could he have taken it with him? Well, think about it.

He did so, and slowly an idea came to him. Maybe, he thought. It just might be! Because the grave they'd buried him in was open for a week. Smithers had been took sick, so bad they'd dug the grave. Then he'd sat up and cussed everybody out, and the grave was covered over with slats and canvas till he needed it. What if Smithers had been faking—and paid it a visit that week before he died?

Hat started to speak to the others, larking in the shade, and checked himself. These two bums were all that was left of the old gang. Deutscher refused to speak to him, and had turned sullen. Poochie Dubret jeered at him every time they met. Young Martens— he was no loss, though. Except for his mother, Nona.

A million dollars—gold—it was all just words. It was the fun of the search that had drawn him, when they broke into the old Smithers house, Hat realized. He hadn't known what a million dollars meant.

Now he knew. It meant never never never having to dig into a damn car's greasy guts again. It meant living like on TV: a great house, a hot fast car—bought new, not used—and everybody looking up to him. It meant girls all over. Real girls, not dogs like Shirley McGinnis, but girls like on TV, with big tits and great asses.

Maybe even Nona Martens.

Fester and Cowgirl were laughing about the wreck, when that drunk slammed into Fester's car. Hat saw them for the first time, and saw them plain. Losers. A couple of no-good losers. Share it with them?

Hat turned his face away and silently finished fixing his pickup.

3

Deputy Rod Parker leaned sideways to pick up the phone, his feet up on the wastebasket. "Sheriff's department."

"Is that the sheriff? I gotta talk to the sheriff! He's dead! Sheriff?"

His boots hit the floor. "Depitty Parker. Sheriff ain't here. What is it?"

"I gotta talk to the sheriff!"

"I'm his depitty! Can I help you?"

"Yeah, yeah, you gotta git the sheriff on down to

Monny-go Cave right away! Them Smigly brats killed my dog!"

It sounded like a nigger kid, and Parker frowned. But it couldn't be the kind of half-assed joke the Department sometimes got; he could hear the shock in the kid's voice. "Okay, I'm on my way."

He hung up and stuck his head in the next office. "Hey, Renee, call the sheriff. Tell him I'm checkin' out a report of the Smiglies in Monny-go Cave."

Renee nodded and started to speak, but her radio spoke first. "Hello, Sunshine Girl?"

"Sunshine Girl here," she said.

"I'm on Thirteen about three miles north of Oswego and there's this red Corvette speedin' and cuttin' in and out, southbound. Pass the word on, okay?"

"I hear you. Sunshine Girl out." She immediately punched up the State Highway Patrol, nodding and gesturing to the dial to indicate that she'd call Sheriff Anderson in a moment. Satisfied, Parker ran.

He made time on Highway B to the turnoff for Monegaw, which was also blacktopped. A mile or two from the tiny town, he turned off into a dirt track through a wooded pasture. He had to park at the top of the hill, where he glimpsed the brown Osage River vaguely through the trees, far below. No other cars were here, and he frowned, paused to call the Sunshine Girl on his car radio, then patched the walky in to it.

A black boy sat on a rock, watching him.

Parker got out into the sweltering heat and contemplated the walk down the hill. The climb back would be even worse. Already he was panting. This had better not be a joke, he thought, and walked deliberately toward the kid.

The kid acted scared all right, but relieved also. It began to look more and more like the real thing.

"Sheriff?" the kid squeaked, disappointed.

"Depitty Parker," Parker said. "Sheriff's busy. You wanna show me where you saw the Smiglies?"

"Yes sir," said the kid, swallowing.

Parker looked sharply at him. The kid was scared, upset, sick, but game. Parker nodded in approval, feeling excitement. Maybe this time they'd get the little bastards. "C'mon, boy," he said.

"Don't you call me 'boy,' " the kid squeaked, hurrying after him down the hill.

Parker was too excited to feel the exertion. "You ain't a girl, are you?"

"No, but I'm not a boy. I'm fourteen!"

"You're boy size an' boy age, what should I call you?"

"Call me 'man'!" he said. "You know, like 'my man.' Okay?"

"Callin' you a man don't make you one," Parker said automatically.

"Oh yeah? I screwed more women this month than you did, *Depitty!*"

Parker grinned, concealing his wince. " 'Spect me to b'leeve that?"

"It's true! Hell, I screwed more *white women* 'n' you did!"

"Yeah? Well, I screwed more nigger wimmin than you did. Quiet."

They'd reached the slope above the mouth of the cave. Parker narrowed his eyes at the sight of a piece of thin old rope hanging from a tree limb. The dirt here was partly covered with old leaves, partly with weeds here and there, and where the light reached, clumps of tough grass. But in many places the dirt was bare. It was fairly dry, except down in the gulch where the spring inside the cave wet the ground. There were only scuff marks in the dirt, not real tracks. Old beer cans. The other end of what looked like the same rope, made into a hangman's noose.

"It was like this when you first came down here?"

"Yeah, man."

"Where'd you first see the Smiglies?"

The kid pointed down into the muddy-bottomed gulch. "My dog smelled 'em and started after them, but they hit 'im with rocks, I heard 'em while I was comin' down the hill, and I heard 'im holler when they hit 'im, and I seen them. They run inside when they heard me runnin' down the hill. I seen them look up at me. They looked like apes all in raggedy clothes." The kid gulped. "My dog was dead, and his head was all bloody, and his tongue was hangin' out in the mud." He sounded as if he were about to cry.

"Right," said Parker. "The Smiglies ran back into the cave when they heard you?"

"Yeah, man, I seen 'em go."

"But where's your dog?"

The kid approached close enough to see that the bottom of the gulch was bare except for tracks. "They must 'a' dragged 'im off!"

"Yeah." Those were drag marks all right. Parker unlimbered the camera. Something heavy had been dragged into the cave, and small footprints in worn-out sneakers were all over the muddy bottom. Parker got pix, and pulled his big five-cell flash out of its loop. "Let's go."

The body lay in the Bat Cave, the first wide spot inside. Parker hadn't been here in years. In high school it'd been a favorite haunt. Judging by the beer cans, it still was, for high school kids. Prob'ly Brad Schiereck and the Watsons and Lesslies, that bunch. He moved the flashlight's spot over the interior, seeing nothing else.

Monegaw Cave was not beautiful. There were no stalactites or stalagmites, no gleaming crystals, no interesting rock formations. There was only the gray-brown limestone and the sticky red clay. Beyond Bat Cave, Parker remembered, a twenty-foot vertical crack in the hill dipped down through a wet-weather pool, then climbed, and finally dead-ended. Up above, there were low rooms branching off in two directions. It would take an hour or two to go through the cave.

He brought the light back to the pitiful body. A big old hound, its head battered bloody, slumped on the mud amid the beer cans. A rude attempt had been made to peel the loose hide back and get at the meat of the hindleg. Parker bent over to look, and jumped.

"My God! It's Knuckles!"

"You know him?"

"Hell, yes, boy, he's older'n you are. A grand dog." Parker had occasionally been invited on coon hunts, and twice had hunted behind Knuckles. His eyes stung and he slapped his gun hilt savagely. "Damned Smiglies!"

"Yeah," said the kid tearfully, and for a moment they stood shoulder to shoulder, mourning.

Parker handed him the light. "Hold it on him." He took several pictures.

"Guess we ought to git him outta here," he said. "Smiglies is holed up by—"

Look out look out look out!

Parker looked up and jumped back. Shadowy motion in the vertical crack beyond—and the flash blazed by reflex in his hands, pinning it against the farther darkness. Ugly, wet, shiny, big night eyes, teeth, claws—firing the camera as if it were a weapon, he shot it again.

Look out look out—

Scrambling backward, he dropped the camera on its strap and tugged at his .45. The thing was on him instantly, in the dark—the flashlight, behind him, wobbled wildly as the kid kept screaming. Its claws tore at him.

He fended it off with his left arm: "*Shit, shit, shit—*" —and fell over backwards into mud and beer cans.

The kid brought his light back to it, over Parker. He looked up at a thing like a man in a shiny black rubber wetsuit, only *it was no suit*. There was a strong, choking, musky lizard smell. It bent to claw at him, and Parker fired the big Colt twice—he had finally overcome his panic enough to release the safety.

Deefen us all, he thought, as the concussions pounded his ears. It fell back, but he was too paralyzed to move. He stared helplessly at it for an eternal moment, his ears ringing. Then it spun about, as he belatedly raised his gun again, and dived back into the inner cave.

From a deafened distance as he struggled to his feet he heard the kid crying, "You hit it! Git it, git it, git it!"

He ran forward with the light. Panicky, Parker ran after him, peered into the crack. Dimly he heard a splashing as it went through the pool. It wasn't hit hard, he thought.

"Aw right!" the kid cried. "C'mon, man, we got 'im!"

Parker hauled the kid back by his belt loop. "You wanna run into an ambush?" he said. "C'mon, out. We gotta call for backup."

Seemingly, that decided the kid. Parker hesitated and peered into the darkness of the cave. Awe and wonder had begun to seep through the shock and fear. What was it? Something that should have been left alone. Had the Smiglies stirred it up? Maybe

Clothilde's prayers to that idol had been answered, gruesomely. . . . Unless this thing had killed Randy and Cordelia Smigly.

"Whatever it is, it's meaner than my Ma," he muttered, and the kid, hushed, said, "Yeah."

. . . Outside, the light was so bright it was impossible to believe in anything so dark as the interior of the cave, let alone the Thing. Blood was dripping from his arm, and the scratches stung sharply, like giant paper cuts. Hell of a time to start sweating, he thought. What the *hell* was it?

He called the Sunshine Girl through the car radio patch and tersely reported the situation, hoping the sheriff would believe it. His hands were shaking a little; he didn't believe it himself.

"Stand by and I'll call the sheriff," Renee said.

He sat down on a rock facing the cave mouth, gun handy, and looked at the kid, who had copied him. Gutsy little bastard.

"What's your name, kid?"

"Don't call me kid, man! I tole you—"

"Yeah? Just how many white wimmin *did* you fuck in the last month?"

The kid looked at him defiantly, then looked down. "One."

"Yeah?" Parker could tell it was the truth. "What she charge?"

"I don't haf ta pay for it!" cried the kid, stung. "Do I look like I got money, anyway?"

"Aw right, aw right. She good lookin'?"

"Well, she's not so much. Older than me, older'n you." Reluctantly he added, "Gives me cookies."

With sudden defiance, he looked at Parker. "What about you, how many black women you fucked this month?"

After a moment, Parker confessed, "One."

"Don't tell me it's my mom!"

"No, she ain't from around here."

"What *she* charge?"

"Nothin'," Parker said gently. "Do I look like *I* can pay? Older than me, too," he added. "And—sometimes she bakes cookies. Yours bake her own cookies?"

"Hell yes she does!"

Parker started to laugh, and after a moment the kid joined in. Parker got laughing so hard he almost fell off his rock.

"What's your name, man?" he asked.

4

When you're dead, you draw flies, Bernie McKay thought, returning to consciousness after a period of blankness. Flies of all colors and sizes swarmed about his head. He was, he thought, south of Laura City and maybe five or six miles from Oswego. He could remember his decision to wait until dark before pressing on, in this populous region. He had holed up here in deep brush under a spiky blackjack, and he remembered putting his head down on his forearms out of ancient habit.

Then, blankness, till now.

What time is it? he thought. What day is it?

He brought his watch up to his dimmed eyes and peered at it, but apparently it had stopped underwater. Then his fading vision focused on his hand: it was covered with industrious ants tearing it apart. With a croak of dismay he pushed himself up onto his knees and beat his hands together.

They must be all over my head, too, he thought,

but hesitated to try brushing them off. Might rip my face off.

He knelt, shuddering with fear of blindness. Hate beat in him, and the yearning for revenge. Blind, he would be destroyed, doomed to agonizing frustration.

After a moment, he scrabbled up a handful of dead leaves, shook them to dislodge any ants, and brushed them over his face. They crumbled, but he thought they helped. Next he tried it with a twig loaded with green leaves. That should get rid of most of them, he thought. Now, just walk away from them.

With clumsy effort, he got to his dead feet and blundered noisily out of the brush into a more open space. Swaying, he turned about, looking at the sky beyond the trees and hills. If that was west, it was late afternoon, coming on for sunset. No, not as late as he thought: that was a black wall of cloud eating up the western sky. The sun had set behind *that*. No point in waiting longer—soon he'd be covered by the storm. Besides, he was too impatient to wait.

Trailing his cloud of flies, Bernie pushed on to the east.

Hours passed. His route stumbled widely through woods and pastures, avoiding farmhouses, hurrying across roads. Field and forest diminished as he went east, and houses became more plentiful. But the light waned fast as the storm came on, and he was able to follow the back roads.

An hour or more after he started, the storm broke with a savage glare of lightning and burst of thunder. The trees bent to the blast and showed the pale undersides of their leaves. Blue-black darkness came on under the raging clouds, periodically relieved by blue-white light so intense it paralyzed the raindrops in the air. Thunder was almost continuous, and at first Bernie staggered with the vehemence of the wind. Welcoming the darkness that hid him and the rain that covered his scent, he stumbled on through the early night to the river.

There were only two ways across the Osage: The long bare concrete bridge on Highway Thirteen, and the old railroad trestle. Bernie tripped, almost fell down the bank. Rain sheeted white on the river below, thunder drowned the river noises.

His fading vision worked imperfectly in the darkness and the raging rain. A searing flash of lightning didn't help. He saw nobody, but over there was the railroad trestle. Oswego lay, lights dimmed by rain, on the other side. In his present clumsy state, it would be no simple task to scramble over the trestle. If he fell, could he swim? Thunder answered no.

Barking dogs ended his hesitation. With a despairing rush, Bernie hurried out onto the tracks. He quickly realized that he could not walk the slippery ties. Lightning revealed him pitilessly, rain-heavy wind lashed at him. Going onto hands and knees on the rough, creosoted wood, he scrambled carefully but rapidly across. At least it didn't hurt; he had no sensation in his hands and knees.

At the other end he stood up and tottered. In the rain-dimmed glow of a streetlight he grimly surveyed his hands and knees. Bones showed in both places; his pants were abraded, and the knees no longer worked as they should. But he could still walk—even run, slowly and clumsily, as he found by experiment. And this body didn't have to hold together much longer.

He was only a few blocks from his house.

Making a nasty rasping sound in lieu of the chuckle he felt well up inside him, Bernie plunged into the back streets and alleys of Oswego. Rain, wind, and lightning guarded and guided him to his own back door.

The house was dark.

Bernie made his nasty rasping sound again, and looked under the proper flowerpot: there was the key to the back door. Gripping it clumsily with both damaged hands in the light of the back porch, he inserted it carefully into the lock. With a little struggle, he twisted it, and entered.

Catch her in bed, he thought, a jolly joke. Maybe with Gibson!

Eagerly he bumbled his way upstairs to their bedroom, dripping nasty water over the stair carpet, pawed open the door, and turned on the light with a triumphant rake of his crumbling hand over the wall.

The bitch wasn't home.

Damn her! he thought, suddenly raging. He lunged forward and tore the covers off the bed. Damn the fucking bitch! He kicked over her nightstand. Where the hell is she? *Crash* went the picture on her side of the bed, a litho of some damn modern art he'd always hated. Out whooping it up with that damned Gibson— He flung her closet door open and raked all her clothes off their hangers. Evil-smelling rainwater dripped and puddled all over the room.

Eventually he calmed. Wait for her, he thought. She'll be back sometime tonight. Downstairs. He turned off the light and fumbled his way back down the stairs, thinking black thoughts.

In the front room, in a blaze of lightning pouring in through the broad window, Uncle Albert stood up from the easy chair and grinned at him nastily. The lightning went and the ghost's suddenly shadowed smile was revealed only by the watery streetlight. The crash of thunder didn't drown its words.

"Well, boy, good to see you again. I'm really *glad* to see you—you're looking so good!" Uncle Albert cackled shrilly. "Well, it didn't do you a bit of good to steal my gold, did it now? Angie's got it, and she'll split it with that Gibson boy. They'll have them a time—"

"You son of a bitch!" Bernie lunged toward the ghost, blundered into the TV stand, knocking it and himself over.

"That's it, Bernie, go to it!" The ghost cackled again, haloed with lightning, thunder an ironic accompaniment.

Scrambling up, Bernie stumbled after it, knocking over the floor lamp, bouncing off the easy chair, caroming off a wall, and bringing down with a smash the big Impressionist reproduction Angie had stuck up there. He paused, peered with dim vision at the mocking figure of the ghost.

"Stand still, damn you—"

Uncle Albert slipped easily into the kitchen, gave him the finger. Raging, Bernie plunged after it, floundered around in the kitchen, goaded into mindless fury. How long this lasted, he couldn't say; the kitchen was a wreck when he finally fell to the floor, helpless despite his best efforts to rise. Lightning flashed weakly, thunder distantly answered; the storm was moving on.

Rest, he thought, though he felt nothing, not pain or exhaustion or breathlessness. But then, he wasn't breathing, he never inhaled except when he tried to speak or laugh. Hate alone drove him.

Even so: rest. Uncle Albert wasn't worth it, maddening though the bastard was. Angie was his target, Angie and Gibson. Ignore the old bastard, he thought. Play dead, be the fox.

Hard to do when the rage and hate within him demanded utterance.

But he did it. He lay there in the darkened room,

lit only by light shining through the windows, waiting, waiting . . . until at last he heard footsteps on the front porch, the clack and sudden rush of rain and wind as the door was thrown open.

"That's enough, Paul, I don't want to hear another word," came Angie's impatient tone. "I——" She screamed. "My God, what happened here? What's that stink? *Oh my God!*"

Get up, *get up*. Bernie willed his dead body to move, but there was no response. Up, up! No response. Uncle Albert's shrill cackle maddened him, he managed barely to move his head, to see the old man's ghost rocking with laughter and slapping its thigh.

"Now's your chance, Bernie boy, here's your revenge! You've got 'em both! Get up and choke the bastards! Hyeh-hyeh-hyeh-hyeh!"

Bernie couldn't move. In fact, every sensation was fading, vision, hearing. For the second time, his spirit was slipping out of his body. His failing body, so used up and rotten that not even his hatred could move it more. Uncle Albert, he thought, as darkness settled over him. Uncle Albert——! Deliberately kept me moving till I collapsed——I'll get him! I'll *kill* him——

Then he had a vague, dreamy vision of the wrecked room, looking down from near the ceiling on his slovenly decaying corpse in its ruined business suit, sprawled in a puddle on the tiled floor. Angie appeared in the kitchen doorway and shrieked, distantly to his ears. She fell back into the arms of Paul Gibson, who looked as shocked and surprised as she, and much more fearful.

I'll get you yet, Bernie thought, hatred holding off the compelling tug of the afterlife. I'll get you all—— I'll *haunt* you——I'll——

5

Mount Pisgah Baptist Church was a stark white box with a mildly peaked roof; there was a once-gold cross nailed on the gable end above the entrance. It was faded now to pale yellow. Such details came dimly through the storm, despite the yardlight and lightning. Jody "Hat" Stetson frowned. There was a light on in the building.

But he was already halfway turned into the driveway. He drove warily on in, parked the pickup behind the unadorned building, frowned at its clapboard sides. There were no curtains, of course, but the windows were too high to see into from his seated position. Apparently his engine hadn't been heard, or the crunch of tires on gravel, over the rain.

He got out and ducked quickly through the rain to the building. In the narrow dry strip under the eave, he listened beneath one of the windows. A male voice muttered something, and giggled. It answered itself, giggling, and interrupted itself.

"So I said to him, ha-ha, I said to him, You . . ." Mumble mumble, ending in a giggle. Footsteps and more mutterings.

Flattened against the wall, Hat sighed in relief. Joe Bumgardner. Then he frowned. Joe had a nervous disability that made him an insomniac. He'd be waking up all during the night, and he usually got up when he woke up—Hat had heard him recite his complaints often enough.

He thought for a bit, then nodded.

The little porch was a mere platform with a small shingle roof. Hat strode up its four steps, knocked at the church door, and grinned at the old man when that surprised individual answered.

"Hi, Joe! Thought that was you I heard." He held up the bottle. "Can I come in?"

"Why, it's young Stetson! Sure you can come in, anytime, boy! Glad to see you." But he was looking at the bottle.

Hat stepped in and glanced quickly around, shaking the rain off his hair. Beyond the varnished brown pews, he saw an air mattress in the pulpit end of the building and a pile of bed clothing on it. "So what're you doin' here, Joe?"

"Couldn't pay m'rent," said Joe, leading him along the aisle to the sleeping area. The barnlike box of a building was ovenlike with the day's accumulated heat, despite the rain, but he had opened windows on opposite sides and was getting some cross ventilation. "Babtiss let me sleep here fer a few days, till I git my nex' check."

"Mighty nice of 'em," Hat said. "Here, lemme pour you a little of this."

"You're a real friend, Stetson, a real friend," said Joe sadly. He sat dispiritedly on a pew. "Times I don't know what's gonna come of me. Thank God I got a few friends. Them Babtiss is good people, and Mr. Krespo that let me sleep here, he's a good man. And that Miz Withers that give me fried chicken t'eat. And now you. It wuz reelly nice of you t'think of ole Joe." Shakily he lit a cigarette.

"D'I ever tell you about the time I eat the fried chicken at ole Arree Allen's? I wuz a-he'pin' him out around his place one day, and his wife Maude, this's when Maude was still alive, Maude, she fixed up a big plate o' fried chicken fer us. I was purty hungry, and so I et a lot of it. I kep' on a-eatin' fried chicken, and you know ole Arree is just a little runt of a ole guy, he could only eat a little bit. He watched me eat, a-grinnin' at me, and he said"—falsetto voice—" 'You su-ure mus' like chicken!' " Joe went off into one of his giggling laughs.

"Pore ole Arree," Joe said. "You know his ole mule Jack died same summer Maude did. He got down low after that, and he said, 'It's a turrible thing when a man's wife and his bes' friend both die.' Ain't it the truth."

As he became drunk Joe became more and more maudlin. Hat waited patiently. Joe had a mighty capacity, but it went to his head quickly. Unfortunately, he hadn't passed out by the time they'd reached the bottom of the bottle, though Hat gave him most of the whiskey.

"I can't b'leeve we run out so soon," Hat said, mentally reckoning his resources. "You sit tight while I go and git us some more."

Joe sat, tight, while Hat made the run, and was still tight when he returned. But he was wide awake. He got half through the next bottle before he began to snore between words and giggles.

It was late enough now to be safe. Hat put the bottle near Joe's hand and stepped outside. The rain was steady but light, the lightning and thunder away to the east.

Mount Pisgah Baptist Cemetery exhaled sweet green wetness in the summer night. It was profoundly quiet out here; Oswego's lights came faintly from over the hill. No cars and nobody in sight. Hat crossed the road, vaulted over the gate with his shovel, and quickly lost himself behind the tombstones.

There was the Smithers plot. He shivered faintly at the memory of the corpse leaping from its coffin. He wasn't exactly ashamed even now of having fled. But old Smithers was gone, cremated in fact. Hat walked cautiously under the trees to the site of the grave.

Shit. They'd covered it over. He kicked the half-sunken mound despondently, stuck the shovel into it. Have to get the tractor out, dig up the grave again. No doubt in his mind, old man Smithers'd slunk out here after he had recovered from his fake "illness," and buried his gold in his own grave. Prob'ly not very deep, Hat reflected. He was a sick old man, after all.

Damn him. He was going to have to sift the damn mud for it. In the dark.

Hat hesitated. He wasn't scared of ghosts, but— Well, it was going to be a damn tough job, in the dark and rain and all, especially watching out all the time lest somebody was to come by. And what if, after all his pains, there wasn't any gold there?

He slunk about the cemetery for some little time, dithering and despising himself. All right, all right, he finally said to himself. So I'll go for it.

He prowled down to the equipment shed, ready to duck at the first sign of anyone, and examined the lock. He was gloomily unsurprised to see that it had been changed. No mere hasp and cheap padlock now, there was a heavy lock in a sturdy steel plate. Just my luck, he thought.

He needed a crowbar. What he had was a tire iron. Cautiously he crossed the road in the pittering rain, ducked behind the church with heart pounding as a pickup roared by, and heard Joe's snoring on the same note. He got his iron and quickly recrossed the road, stood listening intently, wiping his dripping hair out of his eyes. Silent as a bunch of graves.

He decided that the hinges were best. They were of the long sort found on a barn door, and were on the outside. He drove the iron's thin end into the rotten wood and pried, and the nails gave with a rusty screech that nearly stopped his heart.

Hat looked around, listened. No one appeared, and no ghosts. Taking a deep breath, he went at it again, and soon had the hinges off. Again he listened, heard nothing. Inside was the tractor. He pushed it out, and with much gasping and cursing, shoved it back into the cemetery, away from the ears along the road. He couldn't get it far, just to the foot of the first slope, but better than along the road. He hotwired the tractor and listened critically as it cranked over.

About the time he got it positioned to start work, it sputtered and died. A brief examination showed him that the fucking thing was empty! The bastards had drained it.

Cursing with more feeling than imagination, he sloped across the road a second time and siphoned some gas out of his pickup, and presently had the tractor running again. Except for the rain and darkness—he dared not use the tractor's lights—digging the empty grave out was simple. When he felt, and heard in the engine, greater resistance, he knew he was at the bottom of the grave.

He killed the engine, and with its silence a host of fears rushed upon him. He sat in the seat, looking cautiously around. That row of ragged bushes along the back fence—did they harbor a watcher? That shadow under the tree—was it someone standing there? That tall pale blotch half behind the tree—a tombstone, or a ghost?

Hat got down and prowled nervously around, but heard and saw nothing alarming. He returned to the empty grave, so briefly occupied, and looked at the oblong hole, a shadow in the shade, with awe. It seemed a mouth that would reach to a hell-haunted domain, ready at any moment to belch forth skull-faced liches with reaching, bony fingers, grinning at him. He remembered sharply the sickly rotten chemical odor the *thing* had breathed out. Hat shivered and fought for self control.

He pawed over the surface of the mound of dirt he'd turned up. The rain was very light now, but enough to turn the dirt into clay-mud. There were small tough clods of clay, small rocks, bits of wood. But not the distinctive regular feel of coins. He'd have to get down inside with the shovel.

A hoarse cry electrified him. Hat dropped the shovel, crouched, staring. It came from the front of the graveyard. No, from the road. From the church, he finally realized. Must be old Joe. Action was a relief after his fears; he ran for the front of the cemetery, crouched behind the line of shrubs and rank weeds that grew along the once-decorative loop-topped wire.

Old Joe was pissing in the church yard, weaving on his feet and still occasionally calling out drunkenly: "Hey, Stetson! Where you at? Ste-et-*son*?"

Even so drunk he could barely stand, Joe didn't call him "Hat." Hat was pleased by that. Good ole Joe, he thought. Now, he didn't regret a penny he'd spent on whiskey for the old bastard.

When the other had managed to light a cigarette and stumbled back into the church, Hat returned to the grave, much less fearful than he had been. Jumping matter-of-factly down into the puddle in the grave—then pausing to look quickly about—Hat shoved the shovel into the loose soil. He worked quickly but methodically, listening for the clink of metal, stooping to play the flashlight over the dirt, or feeling for coins.

Nothing.

He went through all the loose dirt, then drove the shovel into the harder, undisturbed subsoil, looking for soft spots. He also checked out the sides of the grave.

Nothing.

Shit! Son of a bitch must not of hid it here, he thought despairingly. His frustrated rage overcame his caution.

"Smithers, you bastard!" he shouted toward the treetops. "Where the hell is it? Where'd you put it? Show yourself! I'll choke the answer out of you, you—"

Aw, shit.

Tiredly he crawled out and stood contemplating the hole, the mound, the tractor. Better cover this shit up again, he supposed wearily.

Light caught his eye, a flicker. At first he thought it was a car along the road, but there was no sound of tires or engine. Glad to postpone the disheartened part of his labor, he walked over the rise of ground in the middle of the cemetery and stood petrified for a moment.

Red light flickered in the windows of the church.

Hat took off running, vaulted the gate without pausing, and crossed the road. Panting, he stumbled up the steps of the stark porch and opened the door. Hell leaped out at him.

He recoiled, said breathlessly, "Joe!" and looked under the flames.

No sign of Joe, unless he was lying down, behind a pew. Flames were all over that end of the building. Briefly Hat thought of going in, but the flames were running laughing toward the open door. Pews, cast off from more prosperous churches and fifty or more years dry, roared as their varnish caught.

"*Joe!*"

No sign of him. He must've got out. Anyway, nobody could get in there and make it back out, Hat thought.

Another tornado of flame reached for the door and

he jumped back, slamming it. For a moment the fire seemed quieted. There were no windows in this end. Then he saw the firelight from the sides.

Running around behind, where his pickup was parked, he saw the flames leaping high from the windows Joe had opened for cross ventilation, and knew he had been right: he could never have gone in and come out, even if Joe was able to walk. And maybe Joe had gotten out, he thought.

"JOE!"

The flames leaped for the roof. Urgency gripped Hat; that would soon be seen, as late as it was, rain or no. There'd be people here, questions asked— "*JOE!*"

No answer.

He jumped into the pickup and almost died of panic while it ground, cranked reluctantly, sputtered, died, and had to be recranked. Racing the engine, he took one last look around the church yard, bright as day. No sign of the unlucky old man. Hat peeled out, throwing gravel.

Behind him, the flames laughed hotly.

Chapter Seven:

Mack the Knife

1

Justin Waley gagged at the smell.

"Yeah," said Walter Lyons, the coroner and medical examiner. His dry, wrinkled, brown face split in a grin. "It ain't much like 'Quincy,' is it now?"

The odor of formaldehyde did not begin to cover the stench. Justin stepped back from the table with its sheet-wrapped, utterly relaxed occupant, sat down on a chair near the wall of the mortuary's workroom.

Rick Culter smiled at him sympathetically. "You never get used to it. But they're not usually this bad. The old bum they found burnt up in the Baptist church, now, smells downright pleasant. By comparison, anyway."

Justin grunted at that, looking with fascination at the sheeted form on the table. It looked bloated, but that might be his imagination. "How long was McKay in the water?"

"We figure three days, and he must've spent the fourth walking in the sun," Lyons said. "Two walking corpses—not just moving or talking, but *walking*—in one year. Not bad for a small county like this."

"Why do they walk?" Justin asked, fascinated.

"Well, McKay is more like the usual walker than Smithers—murder victim," Lyons said. "Evidence is that he was struck on the head at least twice. Concussion, fracture, unconsciousness, but not death. That came from drowning."

"Thanks, I don't want to see," Justin said involuntarily as Lyons made a gesture as if to pull the sheet off the head.

"Amen to that," Culter said.

"Okay," said Lyons, grinning. "Anyway, no question it was murder. When I heard about the disappearance, I figured McKay'd found that million in gold, and had taken off. But apparently not."

The coroner looked sharply at Justin. "Just what are you doing here, again?"

"Damned if I know," Justin said sourly. "Actually, I suppose I'm representing the Smitherses, or something. My partner, William Smithers, sent me down here. I think the family wants to know the results of the autopsy."

"Well, you got'em," Lyons said. "It won't make the Smitherses happy, though. Murder. This could tear the Four Families to pieces."

It had already nearly destroyed Smithers and Waley, Accountants, Justin thought. William Smithers was a wreck of what he'd been, before Albert Smithers sat up at his funeral. In fact, the whole Smithers family was in a state of shock. William had sounded like a broken man, begging Justin to come down here and find out what had happened to Bernie. Angie McKay had called him twice from the hospital, where she was recuperating from her discovery of Bernie's corpse in their kitchen. She was just lucky he wasn't still moving when she walked in—and she'd been out with Gibson!

Already there was loose talk that she was implicated in her husband's death. Remembering how she had appealed to him, Justin didn't believe it. So just who *was* the murderer? I'd be looking hard at Paul Gibson, if I was Sheriff Anderson, he thought. As for me— good thing we got going on Waley and Hadley, Financial Planning.

"Doesn't leave much of Smithers and McKay, Real Estate, does it?" Culter asked, paralleling Justin's thought. "Only one assistant left. What's his name?"

Culter's assistant spoke up through a mouthful of food. Justin had already been unnerved by the sight of the young man eating in that appalling odor. "Name's Gibson. Paul Gibson. A smooth one. A little older than me. Old Oswego family."

"Yes, I know him slightly," Justin said. "The heirs of course haven't had time to make any decisions, but I assume they'll break up the firm and distribute the assets."

"Too bad about Gibson," Culter said. "I heard talk he would have made partner within a year. As it is, I guess he's out in the cold."

"Who are the heirs?" Lyons asked. "Mizzez McKay, of course. McKay's relatives?"

"Don't know; the will won't be read till tomorrow, I suppose," said Justin. "McKay have relatives?"

"Yes," said Culter. "Sheriff's office notified his father. He had to come in and identify McKay, before Walt here could start."

"Yeah," said Lyons. "Tough old bird, old McKay. Must

be eighty if he's a day. He just leaned over, took a long hard look, and said, 'That's my boy. Who kilt'im?' "

"Is it true that he's renounced all claim to the missing gold?" Culter asked.

Justin hadn't heard any of this. "Renounced it, did he?"

"Yeah," said Lyons, with a leathery grin. "If he followed through, anyways. He was going to see old Johnny Meiklejohn and draw up a what d'you call it, a legal document formally renouncing any claim to Bernie's half of the missing gold, on behalf of the whole McKay family."

"Tough old bird, indeed," Justin said, musingly. He wondered what Angie would think of that. With a sharp pang, he hoped she *was* innocent—of everything.

"We'd better get this into the freezer. Wheel it over, Eddie," Culter said. "I hope the family doesn't want an open casket. I doubt there was much to work on before you peeled the skull, Walt."

"Not much," Lyons admitted, grinning, rather skull-like himself.

"Murder," Justin said reflectively as he watched Culter and Eddie maneuver the crumbling corpse into the deep freeze. The smell didn't diminish noticeably. "Maybe I should touch base with the sheriff. He in his office?"

"Out chasing the Smigly brats again, according to the Sunshine Girl," Lyons said, gathering up his wicked-looking implements.

"The whole town knows about the hidden gold," Justin said. "Is that why he was killed? Wonder where it is."

"Smithers took it with him," Eddie said, around another mouthful. He and Culter stripped off their rubber aprons. "That old bastard leave it behind? Ha!"

Justin grinned wryly. Culter and Lyons laughed.

"By God, somebody already thinks so," Culter said. "They dug up his grave last night."

"Is that so?" Justin asked sharply.

"Yeah," said Lyons. "Apparently it was being dug up while the church was burning. Judging by rainfall and all that. Probably the fire scared 'em off."

"Unless they burned the church to kill off the witness?"

"Naaah," said Lyons. "Old Joe, this old bum the Baptists let stay in the church, was a drunk and a smoker. No sign of foul play—I was up half last night, checking. Coupla bottles found by what was left of the corpse. He couldn't've witnessed anything."

2

"Monster," said the sheriff, musingly, looking at blurry photographs.

Deputy Rod Parker squirmed a little, trying not to let it show. The other deputies were silent, but glanced at him, some oddly, some smiling. Early though it was, the sheriff's office was hot, perhaps because of the crowd, or Parker's embarrassment.

Good thing I got them damn pix to back me up, he thought.

Evelyn Anderson rubbed a hand through his thinning, nondescript brown hair and crossed over to the gun rack. He didn't even glance at the full-automatic rifles. Instead he unlocked a row of short-barreled shotguns. He shook his head. "Sixteen gauges might be safer in a cave, but these 're what we got. Buckshot. Double-ought. Should settle it." He opened a drawer and pulled out boxes of ammunition.

" 'Course, we're short-handed as usual," he added.

Parker kept his face blank.

"I want to leave someone here, and someone on patrol." Sheriff Anderson looked at Parker. "Parker comes with me, of course."

Parker's heart leaped and he missed the next exchange. He'd seen the monster, but they didn't need him to point out the place; they all knew what he knew. Anderson didn't have to choose him, but he had. Parker had to wipe his mouth to keep from grinning like a goof.

Nordstrom was stepping forward to pick up one of the shotguns, so Parker guessed he'd also been chosen. Figured. He lived down Monny-go way, and was in on the Smigly business from the beginning.

Parker had to keep wiping off his grin, all the way to the hayfield on the bluff above Monegaw Cave.

"What's this kid doing here?" the sheriff asked, getting out.

Parker, easing his bulk out of the car, looked quickly. A black boy he recognized was arising from the rock he'd been sitting on. A cheerfully ugly mongrel dog wagged beside him, tongue hanging out.

"Victor Emmanuel Snyder, sir," he said. "Gus. He's the one called in the report about the Smiglies yesterday."

Deputy Nordstrom pulled his shotgun from the car. "Bug off, Snyder," he said. "We don't want no kibitzers."

The kid registered disappointment.

"Ah, hey, Evelyn," Parker said. "Why can't he wait outside? He can keep in touch with Renee on my walky."

Sheriff Anderson shook his head, a faint smile on his face. "You was a boy yourself, Parker. You know he won't stay outside."

"Yeah, and he won't go very far, was we to chase him off. Come back with friends, is more likely," Parker said.

"Hey!" Gus said. His voice cracked and he took a breath.

"Winnie-the-Pooch was with Knuckles when the damn Smiglies bit Linnie Pasley! He knows what they smell like, and he hates 'em! Take him along with you."

Anderson started to speak, stopped, and exchanged a glance with his deputies. He pushed his hat back, clearly thinking it over. "Have to carry him up and jump over with him, to get him into the upper cave," he said.

"But after that he could travel on his own," said Parker slowly, visualizing the cave. It had been years since he'd been back in it, and he was frankly dreading the ordeal now. He had a nightmare of getting *stuck*. "He can go places we can't, in fact," he added.

Even Nordstrom seemed impressed by that reasoning; he nodded. "He's right about the dog; I reckonnize him. Got a good nose on him, I think; and for sure he got in several bites on the Smiglies."

"The dog goes with us," Anderson decided. "Them Smiglies are little bastards. You seen 'em, Parker, you know what I mean."

"Yeah." There were many small blind holes in the cave.

"You got to stay outside, Gus," Anderson said, his slight drawl more pronounced. "You got to promise me that. You hear shots, you notify the Sunshine Girl, and gen'ly keep her posted. Okay?"

Gus nodded, eyes shining, gulping with excitement. "I kep' my promise last night an' never told no one about the monster me and Depitty Parker seen! Me and Winnie-the-Pooch won't neither one of us let you down now!"

"Let's go, then."

Winnie-the-Pooch ran eagerly ahead of them down the hill, and when they caught up with him at the gulch below Monegaw Cave, he was scratching around on the grave Parker and Gus had dug for Knuckles. He looked up at them eagerly, then froze, looked down in dismay. Apparently he'd caught a whiff of who was buried there, for he suddenly howled, nose to the sky, in a whiny, cracked, mongrel voice.

Parker looked at the sheriff, and saw Evelyn looking regretfully back; Gus looked imploringly at them both. Nordstrom, big tall broad Nordstrom, who Parker would have said had about as much sensitivity as a slab of Norwegian salt herring, jumped down and took the little dog's head between his big hands, muttering rough soothing words.

Released, the little dog shook his head hard, looked at them, gave one last brief cracked howl, and looked up at the cave, back at them.

"Yes, yes, go on," Nordstrom said, his ugly big-nosed face tense.

The gallant little dog charged up the gulch and into the cave, barking only once.

"Hey!" Parker slid down into the gulch, handed his walky over to Gus, and said, "Push this to talk, and let go to listen. It's already on the right channel. Got it?"

"We'll hold the dog," Anderson said, running after Winnie-the-Pooch.

Hurriedly Parker called the Sunshine Girl, confirmed arrangements with her, and signed off, showing Gus how. Gus gave him a thumb up, grinning.

"I'll find me a rock and sit tight," he said. "See you."

Parker hurried after the others. He found them in

Bat Cave, Winnie-the-Pooch circling around and
growling, his hair prickling.

"He smells something, that's for sure," Nordstrom
said.

Evelyn Anderson shone his flashlight on the tracks
farther back in. "Barefoot—and lookitthat. Claw marks
in front of the toes!" He shook his head. "I'm glad
you had a tetanus booster last night, Parker."

Parker looked, and gulped, remembering the Thing.
He saw Nordstrom tense and grip his shotgun.
Nordstrom preferred his own cartridges—hand-loaded
triple-ought buck—six huge pellets to the cartridge.
Good idee, Parker thought.

The sheriff led the way cautiously back into the cave,
his shotgun at the ready, turning sideways in the narrow
passage back of Bat Cave. Presently the passage
widened, then ended, and their boots splashed ankle-
deep. The whole cave was wet and dripping after last
night's storm. Their lights circled, circled, grouped
finally on the wall to their left. Winnie-the-Pooch
reared up, sniffing at it.

The left-hand wall leaned away from them and was
mostly clay. Claw marks scrabbled up it. The right-
hand wall was solid rock and near vertical.

"Right," said Evelyn. He slung his shotgun, put his
flashlight in his belt loop, picked up the dog, and
scrambled up. At the top he crouched under the low
roof and searched the cave to their right with his light.
"No sign of it."

Parker was ready, though he dreaded the ordeal.
He scrambled up, his heart pounding, and stood
crouching next to the sheriff under the sloping roof.
It was like an attic here, but they had maybe ten feet
of slippery wet clay footing, sloping down to the bank
Nordstrom was now scrambling up.

"Bring the dog, Parker," said Anderson. The sheriff hung his flashlight again and gripped the shotgun in one hand. As soon as Nordstrom made it to the top, he ran toward the slash, and leaped, landing cleanly on the other side—which was two feet higher than this one.

Parker gulped and grabbed Winnie-the-Pooch before the little dog jumped. Taking a breath and bracing himself, he made the same desperate leap. The crack wasn't all that wide, eight or ten feet. Still, the jump was across a twenty-foot fall in darkness.

Panting on the other side, he set the dog down, unhooked his flashlight and looked around as Nordstrom jumped. The ceiling was quite high over here, a gray-domed tent that leaked in drops here and there. Winnie-the-Pooch immediately cast around, then made for one of the two low tunnels that led off.

"It's the main branch," Nordstrom said, duck-walking after under the low overhead, his shotgun ready. "The other tunnel just goes a short way and dead-ends."

Parker ducked and sloped his shotgun as he followed. Glad I'm last, he thought; hope everybody's on safety. He banged his head, heard Nordstrom curse in a whisper. Bosses of rock the size of a man's head stuck down out of the low ceiling. He heard Nordstrom's shotgun grate against rock.

The tunnel opened and he stood up, trying to catch his breath. He couldn't. Grimly Parker steadied his breathing, realizing that it was claustrophobia, not exertion, that clamped iron bands around his chest.

"Should've put the dog on a leash," said Anderson, flashing his light around.

"He's gone on?" Parker asked, alarmed.

He hurried in the dimness toward the passage the sheriff indicated with his light. This was waist high but more than ten feet wide, the ceiling sloping down at the sides, a passage cut by running water. Parker went to hands and knees on rough, unyielding stone splotched with wet clay, and started to crawl in. He banged his head, and felt the dissolving limestone smear off on his hat. Flattening himself, he pushed on, calling, "Winnie! Winnie-the-Pooh! Winnie—"

"Goddam!" yelled Nordstrom, and instantly there came the roar of a shotgun.

Deafened, frightened, Parker scrambled around to shoot his beam of light back. He glimpsed one man at the entrance to the passage, spinning about and falling back; even as he watched, that shotgun roared, pointed at the roof. Beyond, the other man was already down.

There was just the glimpse of something shiny and black, flashing past them. Then it was gone. The farther man fired after it.

The man at the passage scrambled up, yelling in Anderson's voice, distant from deafness: "The monster! It's gone!"

Nordstrom's voice, from far away: "Goddam, I missed it!"

Even as Parker watched, they scrambled to their feet, shotguns at the ready, and ran after it, leaving darkness and the smell of gunsmoke. "Hey," he said feebly.

Winnie-the-Pooh barked in the distance.

"Oh, shit," Parker said. He thought fast. The monster had been hiding in a dead-end passage and had taken them by surprise. They might catch up with it, they might not. Meantime—

He scrabbled around and crawled farther from the light. "I'm coming, Winnie! Hold on!"

Winnie-the-Pooh barked several times, apparently

to lead him, and Parker hurried. Past the wide low passage, there was another room.

Circling it high up was a row of odd-shaped limestone shelves, all on a level. They were flat on top, with brackets angled down beneath, as if designed by an architect. The water had carved out the top part of the room, then found another passage below, and carved out the bottom part of the room. The thin layer of stone between them had finally collapsed, littering the floor with limestone shards. Uneasily, Parker realized that the same process could have undermined the current floor, which might give way at any time, dropping him into a deeper void below.

He hurried on to the tunnel, crawled on into the black-and-white void, never quite getting stuck in the narrow passages. Finally he found one too narrow to crawl into. Winnie-the-Pooch's bark came from deep inside it.

He shined his light in, shook his head. It went around a tight corner, and even if it opened up just beyond, he couldn't make it. Not even to the corner.

"Winnie!" he cried. "Winnie!"

An answering bark, and he thought he heard high, whiny, angry cries from beyond. Then, nothing.

"Winnie," he said, very quietly, and felt the sting of tears in his eyes.

A long time later he heard Evelyn Anderson's voice. The sheriff came quietly up beside him, peered into the hole. "Winnie-the-Pooch?" he asked gently.

"In there," Parker said, with a hopeless gesture. "I ain't heard a sound for quite a while."

Sheriff Anderson sighed. "Yeah. Well, the monster got away from us. Ran out past Gus, gave him a fright, but he's game; he called Renee and reported. God knows where it's got to; headed straight down for the river. Gus said it acted hurt, ran hunched over. He said you shot it a couple times last night."

"Yeah, I think I hit it oncet, anyways. How about Winnie?"

"Don't know what t'say," said the sheriff, and made to push his hat back. He'd lost it somewhere, and sighed again. "Still, the only hard part of gittin' out of here is the drop down to the mouth. I think a little dog like that could take the fall and not be crippled up. He'll be all right."

If the damn Smiglies ain't kilt and et him, Parker thought hopelessly. "Yeah," he said, sighing. "He'll be all right."

Listlessly he followed the sheriff out.

3

Jody "Hat" Stetson kicked a rock dispiritedly. He sat on a fallen tree trunk, surrounded by woods baking in the heat, on a hill overlooking the Osage near Monegaw Springs. Fire, gold, and graves occupied his thoughts.

Pore ole Joe.

According to the news reports, Joe Bumgardner had died from misadventure. Smoking while drunk. It was thought likely that whoever had dug up the empty Smithers grave—no doubt to look for the famous missing gold, ha-ha—had supplied the whiskey. But these people were not blamed for his death. Or even regarded as guilty of a serious crime; even the breaking and entering was not being taken seriously.

People were sorry for Joe and laughing at the grave-diggers.

Hat seethed, relieved that he was not blamed for

Joe, but smarting about the laughter—into which he'd
had to join, to allay suspicion. It had all come to nothing,
and now here he sat, no better off. At least this time
no one knew.

Beside him was a fishing pole, his ostensible reason
for being here, and near it a creel, containing a few
ounces of fresh marijuana leaves. Pickings had been
thin. Just my damn luck, he thought, aggrieved.

He hadn't been near a woman in weeks, and that
one was a dog who'd make it with anyone. Shirley
McGinnis he hadn't seen except in passing, at a
distance, since the night he'd gotten drunk and gone
to her house.

He thought wistfully of Nona Martens. He hadn't
seen her in nearly as long. He couldn't afford to eat
at the Night Owl, and he had become delicate about
going there to drink a beer or two, just to see her,
like a damn kid. How could he impress her as a cool,
suave, with-it dude, with no money?

Not to mention no friends. It was no fun hanging
out by himself, Nona or no. Poochie Dubret, Deutscher,
even young Billy Martens, all avoided him now. He
hoped the damn kid wouldn't talk about the Smithers
coffin job.

Nothing had worked out for him. Nothing. What
went wrong? Here he was, he'd been so many places,
seen so many things, he was good looking and young
and had a way with him. And no one wanted to know
him. The unknown gravedigger, ha-ha! A loser, Nona'd
called him.

If only the gold had been in the damn grave. *Then*
she'd'a come around. God, what a great ass she had.

Oh well. A few ounces of mary jane, sold in Clinchfield,
would buy him a night or two at the Night Owl, and
maybe stretch to a date. This time he'd hang around

till closing time. Maybe offer her a lift home, or something—something might work out, he thought, almost hopefully.

He heard a scrabbling sound, turned abstractedly to see, and stared. Two filthy kids scrambled out of a hole under the overhanging shelf where a wet-weather streambed cut the hillside. They were smeared with wet clay and had mean, pinched features on their sallow faces.

"You git outta here!" the first one shrilled, as soon as it saw him. It instantly scrabbled up a handful of rocks and dirt and threw it at him.

Taken aback, Hat ducked, feeling a pulse of anger.

"You git away, go-wan, git outta here," the two creatures yapped in their shrill, detestable voices. They threw more dirt and pebbles.

Furious, he stood up, dusting the dirt off. "Listen, you stupid kids, this is my mother's land and you're the ones—"

A crashing amid the dry leaves and sticks of the forest floor drew their attention. And Hat screamed with the kids as the wet-gleaming black monster burst through the trees, its eyes glaring crazily. It halted to stare at him, and Hat fell backward over the treetrunk he'd been sitting on. Immediately the monster turned its attention to the kids, who stared at it, their mouths open.

It boomed something in a snarling voice and charged.

The kids turned shrieking and tried to flee back to the hole. It caught them and Hat winced, shrinking down behind the log. There were two shrieks of fear and agony, one after the other, then a hideous ripping, rending sound, mingled with the angry shouts of the monster. Sick, trembling, Hat peeped under a root at the end of the treetrunk, and saw the Thing looming over the tumbled bodies. It tore loose something fastened with a string around its shiny black neck, and threw it down beside them, bellowing something Hat couldn't make out.

It then looked directly at Hat, irritatedly growled something, and stomped off through the dead leaves. Its footsteps faded into near silence along the old woods road that ran down to the river, where the leaves had been brushed away by tires.

Palefaced, Hat watched it go, sweating, his bowels loose.

Then he looked back at the kids. Two small bodies lay wrecked amid the leaves. Hat stood, his knees shaking, his whole body trembling faintly, and approached the bodies, drawn by a dreadful fascination.

They were boy and girl, he thought, very young and pitiful looking. Blood, was his first impression, splotches and dabs and puddles of blood all over them and in the leaves all around them. The next impression was the horrid warm shitty odor he'd smelled when cleaning fresh-killed chickens and squirrels and rabbits. Guts, their guts were showing where the thing's claws had slashed deeply into their thin bellies. The odd arm or leg was bent the wrong way.

Pale, he saw, looking at the faces. Very pale, bloodless. Skinny; arms and legs like pipestems, their knees and elbows bigger than the rest. Wearing old worn-out clothes so coated with dirt and clay he couldn't be sure of the colors. Worn-out sneakers. Holes worn in their jeans. Sharp white noses. Starved, he thought.

My God, it's the Smigly brats!

Hat numbly picked up a shiny object, gold among the dark leaves and blood-splotches. A sort of medallion on a tarry bit of string, rank with the musky odor of the monster. It was engraved with cabalistic symbols that meant nothing to him, but it gave him an immediate feeling of power and confidence. It cut right through the shock. Now we'll see, he thought. I'll show 'em all! And the gold, too, I'll find it, I'll have everything, just like on TV—

Rapt, he didn't react to the sound of scrabbling. Then a sneeze startled him and he turned, catching his breath lest it be the Thing.

A small dog confronted him. It was smeared with clay, and there was blood on its muzzle. Apparently it had come out of the same hole the Smiglies had. Now it approached the bodies, growling slightly, but halted at the odor of death. With that, all the menace went out of it, and it slumped tiredly. Then with a friendly wag of its tail, it looked up at him and whined. It was Winnie-the-Pooh, he realized.

"I didn't—" Hat cleared his throat. "I didn't do it, pup. The monster did it—"

Would anyone believe that a monster had done it? Or would they think *he* was the monster? Better to say nothing, he thought, pocketing the medallion. Tiptoeing back to the fallen tree, Hat got his rod and tackle, and went rustling through the dry leaves toward home. Behind him, the dog looked puzzled, shrugged, and made off for Monegaw Springs over the hill.

4

Justin Waley stepped out onto the porch of his old farmhouse, smiling.

Sue Weinberg cried, "Hi, swordsman!" as she struggled out of her little Honda. Opening the back door, she pulled out a rattan practice sword and a canvas bag containing her shield and armor. "I hope you're ready for lumps," she said, coming up onto the porch. "I just wish you'd practice more—you could be really good."

"I'm not a swordsman," he said, grinning. "I'm an accountant— I mean, an investment counselor." Taking the heavy bag, he led her through the house and out the back, toward the converted barn.

"You could at least join SCA." She pronounced it "skaw."

"I did, once." He'd joined briefly to learn the basics of swordplay. He opened the barn door and led her onto the polished hardwood floor.

The Society for Creative Anachronism was founded in the Sixties by fantasy and science fiction writers who wanted to get a feel for real sword swinging. Unlike the true Middle Ages, women in the SCA are allowed to fight, and Sue was a redoubtable swordswoman.

"Sir Richard showed me this, at the war last weekend," she said, sliding her sneakered feet tentatively on the barn's dance floor. "Watch!"

Hefting her shield, she stepped suddenly forward and cut sharply at an imaginary opponent. Apparently he evaded the cut, for she spun around with the force of her blow, her shield tucked under her chin. Digging a toe in, she completed the spin, stepping forward and continuing with the sword in a renewed cut, that apparently connected.

"Get it?"

"What's new about it?"

Sue sighed. "It's in the angle of the sword and the step. Watch again."

The difference was subtle, but the advantage it gave was striking. It took a couple of repetitions for Justin to get it. He pulled out his claymore for a two-handed version. Sue watched critically, offered advice, showed him again, and finally she sighed.

"You're as good as you're going to get without hours

of practice. That part's up to you. Oh, Justin!" She put her hands on her hips and looked up at him in exasperation. "You could be so good, if you'd only try!"

"Look, it's just exercise, okay?" Justin grinned down at her. At six feet one, he was eleven inches taller than she.

"Okay, get your armor on. Maybe if I give you enough lumps, you'll decide to practice."

Justin put on a shirt made of heavy quilting. It hung down to his knees. Over it went a chain-mail armor shirt, equally long; he'd made it patiently himself, out of black clothes-hanger wire. Plastic shin guards and a steel helmet completed his outfit. His small shield was a simple plywood buckler, painted black, quite battered around the edges.

Sue's outfit was a combination of plate and chain, with a bucket-like steel helmet, never fancy, and now battered. She faced him and grinned, hefting a rattan sword in a mail-gauntleted hand.

Justin's practice sword looked like a club. He wanted a replica of his claymore in length and weight, and if he had shaped the rattan into a sword blade, it would have been too light.

He gripped it in both hands and, crouching, approached Sue warily. She held her shield high, her sword overhead, ready for a cut. Fortunately she made it slow, this was merely a drill, and he was able to bring his ponderous blade around in time to counter. Sue kept increasing the pace, and Justin sweated to keep up. He had the reach on her, but small as she was, she kept getting inside his guard. Every time, she dealt him a thwack that bruised right through his armor and padding.

After an hour, both were panting and streaming with sweat inside their quilting.

"Enough," she said, stepping back and pulling off her helmet, to shake sweaty brown locks. "In a real fight, of course, you'd have been able to swing full force, and I wouldn't have dared take such chances."

"Who wants to fight?" he said, peeling off armor and helmet with relief. "I just want exercise. I bet your students don't give you any sass, though."

Sue laughed. She taught history in Appleville High School. The school board had had a special session to consider the possible Satanish paganism of a woman who put on armor and beat up men on weekends, but had found her not guilty after she cited Joan of Arc.

"Any boys who get snotty, I invite to a practice session, and beat the shit out of them. You'd be surprised how much they admire me for it. Boys are stupid. I'd resent anyone who showed up my macho pretensions like that."

"So would I, and I don't have any," Justin said. "Maybe that's why I refuse to fight with you. There's a fresh towel in the shower for you; you can go first."

"Oh boy, I need that. And I hope you have ale, as usual. Need to replenish my depleted fluids." As they trekked back to the house, she said, "Did you ever get around to making a scabbard for your claymore?"

"Going to see Ned Spengler in Oswego about it tonight, after I eat—I'm stopping by the Night Owl, or I'd offer you dinner."

5

"What is it?" Nona Martens asked crossly.

"Hat Stetson wants to see you again," Judy said.

"Tell him to go take a flying jump," she said, with restraint.

The Night Owl hadn't been open for an hour yet,

and Hat had already exceeded every record he'd ever set for obnoxiousness. He was half drunk when he came in, and worse, he had money. Not only had he eaten food—usually he just had beers—he had treated his friends, that nasty Poochie Dubret, and young Frankie whatever-his-name-was. Since the table was spending money for once, she'd had to render service, and as a result had a complete set of their fingerprints on her ass.

Hat had been bragging all evening about finding the Smiglies and leading the sheriff to them, and had described with relish the pitiful bodies lying in pools of blood dried black. Did he think that would turn her on? He'd been the center of a fascinated crowd. Thank God Billy wasn't around.

Nona had overheard enough of Hat's elephantinely secretive bragging to gather that he had spent the weekend gathering wild marijuana and had sold his pickings in Clinchfield for "plenty, man, plenn-tee." What he hadn't smoked. He'd be broke tomorrow, she figured.

"Tell him to go take a flying jump," she said.

"Hey." Strickland, one-third owner of the Night Owl, turned from where he was glaring at the serving trays. He looked sharply at her. "Don't talk like that about your customers, Martens. Get on out there and *serve*, hear?"

"But they've gone, they left their table," she said, peering out over the counter. "Where are they?" she asked Judy.

"In front of the building."

"Well, go see what they want," Strickland said.

"I know what he wants. He wants me to go out with him. Oh very well," she said tiredly, as he continued to glare at her. "I'll go have a word with the—with him."

After all, she thought moodily as she picked her way through the night spot, this damn job is the only damn job I've got. Hard enough to stay on old Strictly's good side, it's so small. God knows, there's plenty of younger women willing to take my place.

Maybe she could jolly Hat along so that he wouldn't get her fired, without actually promising to see him later, she thought tiredly. She pushed through the front door and found no one there. For a moment she had a leap of hope that they'd gone, but then she heard male laughter from the parking lot. Glumly she plodded around the corner onto the windowless blind side of the building.

"Ah, welcome to my parlor, little fly," said Hat, laughing, leaning on the fender of his pickup. Poochie and Frankie haw-hawed.

Nona tried to smile. "S-sorry, Hat. I can't come with you. I got a job, and I can't afford to lose it."

Hat straightened with an effort at suavity, but the motion revealed his drunkenness. "You keep sayin' that, darlin', but I know it's jusht a come-on. An' t'night li'l ole Jody Stetson's not bein' put off no more. So *you're comin' with me.*"

Lurching toward her, he had her before she could dodge. "No! Stop it, Hat! Poochie—Frank—"

But Poochie grabbed her and shoved her up against the truck. Hat alone, drunk as he was, she might have gotten away from, she thought. But not him and Poochie. She looked desperately at Frankie. He was looking a little perturbed, she saw.

"I'll have the law on you—all of you. I mean it—"

Frankie lost his grin. "Uh, hey, Hat—"

"Don't worry, Cowgirl," Hat said soothingly, groping her breast with one hand and fumbling for the pickup's door handle with the other. "It ain't against the law if she likes it, and it'sh our three words against her one."

Frankie laughed nervously and agreed, but before they could shove her into the truck, a gleaming black car came around the corner. They froze in hastily assumed casual poses, Hat hissing a whiskeyish threat at her to keep quiet. A tall lean balding fellow got out of the car, a regular customer. Unusual fellow for the night spot, ate food, drank little, and always wore a tie. Nona couldn't think of his name.

His gaze crossed them and he started to give them a polite nod, but he jolted to alertness when he saw her. There was a whipcrack tone to his voice as he said: "What's going on here?"

"Nothin', baldy," said Hat, making a show of pushing his dirty white cowboy hat casually back with his free hand.

"Waley. My name's Waley," he said sharply. That's it, Nona's memory cried out, that's just what he told me months ago.

"It's all off, it's all off," Poochie cried drunkenly.

"What are you doing with Miss Martens?"

Nona felt Hat jerk, offended by this. " 'What'm I doin' with Miz Martens?' " he sneered. "I'm takin' her home with me, what else, asshole!"

Waley's gaze locked with hers for a moment. He turned and opened the back car door, bent, and came out with a long flat package wrapped in brown paper. He held it menacingly, down at his waist.

"What's that?" Frankie asked.

"Curtain rods. Now, *let go of her and get away.*"

Hat looked over her head at Poochie, and roared with laughter. Poochie joined in, and even Frankie, nervously.

Waley ripped the brown paper across, reached inside,

and in a moment had whipped the paper off over his shoulder. He was holding a brightly shining sword. Nona had never dreamed that swords got so big.

The men gaped. "Jesus H. Christ," Poochie said reverently.

"A goddam *sword*," Hat said, just as astonished but without any reverence at all.

Nona felt his grip loosen as he stared, and she tore herself free and ducked away from them. "Run," she said breathlessly to the grimly advancing Waley, poising to do so herself.

Waley was holding the sword over his shoulder, baseball bat fashion. He looked at her and started to speak, but Hat barked with a different kind of laughter and reached for his back pocket.

"I'll show you how Indiana Jones swordfights—"

Nona opened her mouth to scream at Waley, but he'd evidently seen the same movie. His long legs were in motion before Hat finished his speech or his reach, the big sword whipping around in a gleaming arc. Hat's hand came back with a chromium glitter, but before he could raise the pistol, the sword connected with a meaty *chug*. Waley followed through, his stance that of a man who has hit a home run.

He had.

Handgun and gun hand spun together through the air to the mid-point of their arc. There they separated, the pistol coming down with a clunk, the hand with a sickly flap. It bounced over on its back.

Nona pressed her hand to her mouth.

Hat Stetson's face was suddenly shockingly pale. Unbelievingly he gripped his right wrist with his left hand, stared up at the gleaming sword, and fell back against the truck. He didn't stop there, his knees buckled and he slid slowly down the door to a seated position, leaning against it. Nona heard his sharp intake of breath, but he said nothing.

Poochie and Frankie were every bit as pale as he, and seemed about as sick. Poochie nearly fainted when Waley spun and pointed the big sword at him.

"You! Pick up that hand. Now!"

"M-me? Uh, please—"

Abruptly the big sword's point was at his neck and his eyeballs could have been raked off with a stick.

"Okay, okay, p-please—!"

Fearfully Poochie edged in front of Hat, wavered over to the hand, and looked at it.

"Pick it up! Don't puke on it, or I'll cut your guts out!"

Gulping, Poochie reached down and touched the hand's forefinger, started to jump back, looked at Waley, gulped again, and gripped it gingerly with thumb and finger. He looked at Waley again.

"Take it back into the kitchen and get it on ice, immediately. Nona, take him in the back door." He looked at the staring Hat. "Get it on ice, get you to Kansas City as soon as possible, they can reattach it. Better than a pair of hooks, anyway."

Hat turned a suddenly-hopeful look on Poochie, who nodded, still gulping convulsively. Poochie turned and looked at her.

Nona stepped forward and bent to pick up the pistol. A Colt Government Model Mark IV, she saw, chambered for .38 rather than .45.

"Don't get your fingerprints on it, but make sure it's safetied," Waley said. "Maybe you'd better empty the cylinder."

Nona shot him a quick glance. It was evident he didn't know automatic from revolver, but her respect was somehow heightened, rather than diminished, by this human flaw. "Yes, Mr. Waley," she said, hardly above a whisper.

"Justin," he said sharply. "My name is Justin." He turned to the others. "You follow Miss Martens inside. You stay here with Stetson."

"Is—is he gonna bleed to death?"

"Not from a transverse cut like that. Stay with him."

Waley—Justin—came over and put his left arm around her. The big sword sloped over his shoulder like a rifle. Nona looked up at him in gratitude, holding the pistol by the barrel much as Poochie held the severed hand.

"Th-thank you," she said, barely audible. She cleared her throat and spoke again, louder.

"Not at all," he said politely. "I want a word with you later," he added quickly.

Inside the kitchen, the sword and gun produced pandemonium, but not even the thin edge of blood on the sword caused anyone to drop a tray. The hand, following them in, did that.

To the popeyed Strickland, Justin said mysteriously, "Old Mac's back in town," in an ironic tone.

Strickland turned purple and ran out front. Justin took charge immediately, demanding their largest freezer bag, filled with ice. He ordered Judy to call Oswego Hospital for an ambulance.

A short fat man came waddling in from the front, wiping his mouth and putting on a brown hat. "Damn it all, I was off duty," he said plaintively. "And I already had a hard day." He wore a badge and was followed by a grim Strickland, who glared at Nona.

"Depitty Parker, Sheriff's Office," the fat man said. He paused next to them, and despite the kitchen odors Nona smelled colognes and deodorants over a healthy man-smell and a faint odor of sweat, not offensive.

When his hard brown gaze crossed hers she tried to pull herself together, realizing that she was still snuggled against Justin.

"Who 're you?"

"Justin Waley."

He looked shrewdly up at Justin, nodded. "Smithers and Waley?" Justin nodded. "Red Bud Hadley's new partner?"

With a startled blink, Justin nodded.

"What is that, a sword?"

"Replica Scottish claymore."

"Claymore." The deputy shook his head. "Thought that was a mine."

"It was named after the sword."

"You chop off someone's hand with it?"

"Hat Stetson's. Don't know his real name. He and this fellow and another boy got in some drunken fight out back and Stetson pulled a gun. Nona, show him. I had to disarm him."

"Dishand him, you mean," said Deputy Parker, glancing at the Colt. He took it with total disregard for fingerprints and looked at Poochie. "These boys gonna to dispute your story?"

Poochie had been looking sicker and sicker, though he was no longer holding the hand. He'd fastidiously shoved it down into a gingerly-offered bag of ice and put it in the fridge. He shook his head.

"How come you to be carryin' this claymore thing around? You do that all the time?"

"No, I was bringing it in to Ned Spengler to have a scabbard made for it."

"Whut was the argyment about?"

"I doubt if any of them remember. They were too drunk even for Miss Martens to make sense of it."

Nona nodded shakily. Poochie just looked at the floor.

Deputy Parker waddled with a surprisingly swift gait to the back door, went out.

"Get Miss Martens a drink," Justin said commandingly to Strickland.

Numbly the third-owner passed the command on to Judy, who poured her a couple of fingers of whiskey. Nona took it gratefully, realizing that she'd never needed a drink worse in her life. She offered to share it with Justin.

"No, thank you. However, I would like a diet Coke. My throat is dry," he said. He paid for it, and her whiskey. He would, she thought.

Deputy Parker waddled in grimly and said to Poochie, "Gimme your license."

Dumbly Poochie complied.

"You c'n pick this up tomorrow morning at nine, Sheriff's Office," Parker said, and shoved it into a shirt pocket that held another license. "Now, git."

Poochie got.

When an ambulance had come for Hat and gone wailing off on the hour and a half drive to Kansas City, and Deputy Parker and another deputy had finished questioning them, Justin escorted her out to her car. He'd squared Strickland, taking it for granted that no one would compel Miss Martens to work after the shocking experience she had had.

"I hope," he said, and paused to clear his throat. "I hope you don't think I'm taking advantage of your gratitude to press my case. But I—I have b-been strongly attracted to you since I first saw you here, five months ago."

They took three paces in silence, while Nona stared up at him, dumbfounded. "I-I hope you don't mind if I—if I, uh, invite you, uh, ask you for—"

In Nona's shaky condition, his bashfulness illuminated

the whole man. She saw at a glance a man competent in his own small sphere but nowhere else, totally at sea in most human relations, shy, lonely, and unloved. Why some smart woman hadn't snapped him up years ago—his heart was going cheap, just a little affection, that was all—

"A date?" she said.

He nodded, apparently too tongue-tied to speak.

This shock on top of all the evening's shocks was almost too much. Nona barely managed to choke back laughter. After a moment, she said simply, "Y-Yes, J-Justin," and leaned against him.

He put his arms around her. Holding her tightly, he said, in a dreamy, satisfied tone, "I'll never have to eat that awful food again."

And she burst first into hysterical laughter, then into tears.

Chapter Eight:

Chances Are

1

Angie Smithers McKay was wearing very tight fawn pants and a tan rayon blouse that broke into a froth of white lace down the front. Justin Waley had observed, as she led him to seats in the living room, that the pants did full justice to a figure which at worst could be called womanly, and at best, full-figured. When she seated herself just in front of him and leaned anxiously forward, the observation was redoubled.

"Such a terrible thing, Justin," she said. "Such a shock—to find him there," with a gesture of her head toward the kitchen. "I had to have all my things cleaned! And, oh, I'd just had the *worst* quarrel with that damned Paul Gibson! I wasn't about to invite him in—but I wish I could've seen the look on his face when he realized Bernie had walked! I just know Paul had something to do with it—his death, I mean."

"Everybody seems to think so, Mrs. McKay—"

"Oh, please, Justin—Angie."

"Angie," he said hastily. "But so far there's no proof. I've talked to Sheriff Anderson and Deputy Parker. They don't have anything to go on yet, but they're still investigating. And Paul Gibson is Number One on their list."

"And I'm Number Two, aren't I?" she said in a small voice, putting her hand on his knee.

Justin repressed the temptation to squirm. "Well, yes," he said reluctantly. "It's too obvious."

"It's classic," she said wryly. "Everybody thinks so. I-I th-thought—" Her voice broke and she stood up suddenly and looked away from him. "I th-thought I had friends, but no one believes I'm innocent!" It came out as a wail, and despite himself Justin's heart hurt. "All my friends are g-gossiping about me and that n-nasty Paul G-Gibson. . . ."

Then her knees unlocked and she folded up and came down into his arms, sobbing, rooting her face into his chest. Justin was taken by surprise, and apparently so was she. He patted her back and made awkward soothing noises.

"Oh, Justin, you're the only friend I've got, except my family," she said, when she finally caught her breath.

She tipped her teary face up at him, then hid it again. He knew she'd never have wrecked her makeup like that for an act.

"The Smitherses never really had any friends in Oswego," she said against his chest. "W-we're the johnny-come-latelies. Y-you know before the Smitherses, there were only three families in Oswego. The Meiklejohns never accepted us. Never! Now they're all saying what else could you expect? Oh, Justin, you're our only friend, and n-now even you're leaving us. S-starting your own company and leaving Uncle Bill alone. Justin, are you

my friend? What do you really think of me? Be honest,"
she said, muffled but pleading.

Justin shifted his weight, feeling tortured, but spoke
with strangled honesty. "Well, what I was really
thinking just now was that this is a good investment
opportunity for me. Sorry," he added, as she looked
up dumbfounded.

Her tear-streaked face broke into radiance; she burst
out laughing. Justin had never liked her so much. "I
asked for an honest opinion! You're probably right;
the Smitherses really need you now." She looked
wistfully at him for a moment. "I need you too."

Justin met her gaze for a moment, but bells inside
him were ringing. This was not the kind of woman he
wanted, he realized. He didn't have time to put it into
words but in a few flashing images of her as wife and
mother he realized she didn't fit in his world. Social
success and flirtatious amusements were her ambitions,
not motherhood.

She pulled away and touched her face with a square
of frilly cloth. "I'm sorry. I've made a fool of myself."

"Oh, well, I don't blame you for breaking down,"
Justin said hastily.

She rolled her eyes sideways to look at him. "I meant,
the way I've been hustling you, trying to inveigle you
into our rotten family's affairs." She sighed. "Even
today, when you agreed to come see me, I've been all
in a flutter. I guess I was hoping you'd leap into action
with your big sword and solve all our problems."

Justin moved fretfully at mention of the sword; he'd
gotten entirely too much attention for defending Nona.
It had even been mentioned on national TV news,
though he'd managed to avoid being interviewed or
photographed. All they'd got was a clip of him ducking
into his office.

Angie sat hunched, looking forlornly away from him, seeming old—or was it the ruined makeup? He hesitantly raised his hand, laid it against her back, and she looked sideways at him.

"What should we do, Justin? The Smitherses, I mean."

Justin thought about that for a bit. "Well," he said hesitantly, "one thing the family can do is what the McKays have done—renounce all claims to the gold and leave it for whoever finds it." He cocked an eyebrow. "Much of the talk centers on the belief that Bernie was killed, somehow, for the gold."

She thought about that for a moment. "You've obviously never been rich," she observed. "Giving up claims to money or land is not something that rich people naturally think of. But I believe you're right; it'll help. I'll mention it to the family—I know Uncle Bill will take your advice. And Uncle Albert isn't around to object," she added grimly. "What about me? What can I do about the talk, about Paul and me?"

Justin hesitated. "I don't know, short of proving your innocence. And I don't know how you can do that. Sit tight and wait, is the best I can say."

Angie nodded, pouting a little in disappointment. "That's all?" Then she looked guiltily at him and smiled faintly.

"You're too nice a guy, Justin. I'm still playing on you. On your sympathies now." She looked away, dabbed at her eyes again. "I think I lost something worth a lot more than Uncle Bill's agency, or Uncle Albert's gold—or the Smithers's social position."

Despite his decision not to get involved with her, Justin felt a pang of sorrow. Under other circumstances— what a woman she was—oh well. Oh hell.

"But you're right," she added, more firmly. "This *is*

a good investment opportunity for a new counseling service. Because the Smithers family desperately needs help. And," lowly, "I need a friend."

Justin put his arm around her. "You have that, at any rate. And I've spoken to the Sheriff about your breaking up with Gibson before the murder was known, though of course they can explain that. Still, I've told them I think you're innocent, for what it's worth."

She sighed against his shoulder. "Thank you for that, anyway." After a moment: "I invited you here meaning to tease you and toll you into helping me—us." She stirred, looking up at him. "No more games, Justin. If you want me, you can have me. A forlorn woman is easy," with shaky humor.

Justin patted her. "I was never as attracted as I am now," he admitted. "But—"

"I didn't think you were seeing anyone."

"I have a date for Saturday—first date—I hope—"

With a swift intuitive leap, she said: "That waitress?"

After a moment: "Yes."

After another moment: "Let me know how it goes, okay?"

"Yes," surprising himself.

"And, I hope it works out." She sighed.

2

Deputy Rod Parker looked up when Judith Lamour said excitedly, "There he is! Justin Waley!"

The tall lean birdlike fellow strode like a stork past their booth in Bracher's Restaurant. His thin harsh features were suddenly transformed by a smile as he bent over beside a booth farther back. Parker could

just see red hair over the top of the booth. Nona
Martens, he supposed—nea: lady, not to mention sexy.
Apparently Waley was seeing her, after having saved
her from that bastard, Stetson. There'd been a report
that last night her car had broken down, and he had
come out and had it towed in.

"Doesn't he just look like a downy little chick when
he smiles?" Judith said fondly. "I know Nona—I used
to part-time at the Night Owl. She's all right."

"Can't say as I ever thought of him as a chick, Miss
Luhmoor—Judith," Parker said. "I seen that sword
of his."

"Oh, yes, I wanted to ask you about that! You were
there?" She looked eagerly at him, bright-eyed.

"Yeah, but I didn't see him take off Stetson's hand.
I was chowing down, inside."

"He saved her from those boys," she said, so impres-
sively she paused with spoon in air. She had eagerly
agreed to meet with him after work but had only
allowed him to buy her frozen yogurt.

"Unofficially, right. Of course, officially it was just
a quarrel, but—" Parker nodded sagely and sipped
his coffee. "We been keepin' an eye on Doo-bray and
Cowgill, since then."

Judith pouted a little. "I used to go out with Bob—
Dubret, you know. I never would have guessed he'd
do such a thing!"

"Me neither. Tell you the truth, I don't reckon he
would, ordinarily. Don't think he's got the guts. Though,
you know, if he was sure he could git away with it, no
tellin'."

She nodded emphatically, her curls bobbing. "It was
that damned Hat Stetson! He'd do anything!" she said
around a mouthful of yogurt.

Parker nodded. Sheriff Anderson and he and the

other deputies had had several serious conversations about Stetson.

"Do you think they're the ones who dug up old Mr. Smithers' grave?" she asked. "The Baptist grave, I should say; the family sold it back to the church."

"Yeah. Not that I think you'd likely know anything, but why on earth would anyone dig it up again? There's nothing in it, not even Smithers. I hear they threw his ashes out of a airplane. Cheap, I call it."

Judith smiled demurely. "Oh, no, that's often done with ashes. As for the grave, I think somebody was looking for the missing gold." Her eyes sparkled, bright brown.

Parker nodded. That was the obvious thing everybody thought. "Somebody thought he took it with him? When he wasn't even in the grave?"

"Well, afterward, I got to thinking about it," she said. "And you know, Rod, I can see how someone might think that. See, the grave was dug when he was first took bad sick and the doctor was sure he had only hours to live. He was the kind of guy who always had to be in control, even at his own funeral."

Parker laughed and she giggled.

"Right!" she said. "He knew he was dying, so he ordered the grave dug. Then he got better. Now, if they thought he snuck out there during the week the grave lay open— See?"

"Yeah. Could he have?"

Her expression changed to amused contempt. "Hell, no. He was too sick even to come down and pick out his casket. I mean, the month before he died, or maybe it was six weeks, he came in and looked at them, but he couldn't make up his mind. We thought he'd come in when he got better, but he wasn't *that* much better. So he had us send out our three best caskets for a day, so he could choose one."

Parker was fascinated. "What a pickiunus ole bastard," he said. "So he picked a coffin then?"

"No. I heard Mr. Culter grumbling, because he had an offer on one, and went ahead and sold it. He expected to hear, during that last week. But Mr. Smithers died, and Mr. McKay, the one that was murdered, came and said, Give us the copper one."

" 'Cause that was the most expensive one?"

"I guess. It's the Smithers family you know, have to be as high toned as the Ikles and Blanchards and Meiklejohns."

Parker nodded, spoke thoughtfully. "Anyway, we figure whoever dug up the empty grave didn't find any gold. They prob'ly left in a hurry when the church caught fire, and there's no gold coins scattered around. Not that we got much on 'em. The damage to the cemetery is slight, except for one thing."

Judith nodded eagerly, her curls dancing. "Arson!" she said eagerly. "And maybe murder—they didn't want that poor old drunk to talk."

Parker was startled. "Oh, the church burning? No, we figure that was prob'ly an accident. Old Joe Bumgardner— They let him sleep there; he's a old drunk with no money, like it said in the paper. Those Babtists are nice folk, they're mostly pore theirselves."

"But he'd seen them!"

"They expected to cover their tracks. Wouldn't have been any reason for him to testify. Thank God I wasn't there when they found him," Parker added. "Not a pleasant sight. I hope he was passed out when it happened. Anyway. They had insurance, and the building's no great loss, it wasn't even very old, not like a historical landmark, you know."

"Then—what you're really concerned about is the breaking and entering—the shed?"

Parker grinned. "You got it, Judith," he said, daringly using her name. No frowned lightning struck.

She shook her head decisively. "You can say what you like, but I think it was those boys again. After all, they know their way around the cemeteries. They know about the shed, and the tractor."

Parker nodded slowly. "A good startin' point," he said. "We been lookin' into them from the beginnin', of course. But we got nowhere."

Judith nodded thoughtfully, then shrugged and changed the subject: "Just how big is Mr. Waley's sword?"

"A good five foot long over all. Guess the blade must be three, three and a half feet. *Biggest* damn huntin' knife I ever seen."

Judith laughed, and having cleaned her dish, scrupulously licked her spoon. "That was nice—thank you." Cocking her head and with an impish grin, she said, "Know what 'hunting knife' is in German?"

Parker shook his head. Regretfully, he realized that the interlude was coming to an end. Afterward, for him there was nothing but Ma's shopping—and Ma.

"Fahrtenmesser!"

He blinked, and a moment later joined her in laughter.

"It really means 'journey knife,' because in German, 'Messer' is knife and 'Farht' is journey." She spread her fingers across her face in pantomimed embarrassment and giggled.

"Same as in English," Parker said without thinking. "I generally take a journey after—" He stopped and felt his ears turning red.

Her laughter was delighted and unembarrassed. "Oh, Rod! And you feel like taking a journey now!" She cocked her head and surveyed him, bright eyes dancing. "You'll prob'ly never invite me out again. If I don't stop embarrassing you!"

"It's not that," he mumbled, looking at his empty plate. He couldn't remember what he'd eaten.

She put her elbows on the table and sparkled at him. "You think I'm here just because I want all the dirt," she said. "Never occurred to you I agreed to see you because I might like you, Rod?"

It hadn't, and his startled look must have made that plain.

She laughed and said, "Well, think about it. Like, think about calling me up sometime even if you can't think of any official business with me! I'm not seeing anybody just now, so I'm home most nights. And of course weekends."

"Uh—uh, yeah. Right." Parker opened and closed his mouth. The idea that a woman, especially one as attractive and popular as Judith Lamour, might be interested in him was not only surprising, it was frightening.

If you have someone's good opinion, you have so much more to lose than if you don't.

"You'd never go out with a guy like me. I mean, I'm such a lump, such a—a troll," he said, sweating, then fearful because he was sweating. He wished he could wipe his face; he wished he had put on more deodorant.

She opened her eyes wide. "Oh, Rod, what do you know about what a woman likes! *You* can't tell—only by asking! Let me help you." She put her pointed little chin on her interlaced fingers and looked archly at him. "Ask me what I'm doing tonight!"

Parker's heart stood still for a moment. Fearfully, gulping, feeling that he was being set up for a cruel joke, he mumbled, "W-what are you doing tonight, J-Judith?"

"Tonight I can't come, because I'm visiting my mother and sister," she said. "And tomorrow night I'm having a perm." She fluffed her hair. "You see how I spend my evenings! But try asking me about Saturday."

Parker had unconsciously leaned toward her. There were dimples at the ends of her smile. Her eyes were the richest, brightest brown he'd ever seen. They sparkled. Her smile was not impish at all; she wasn't making fun of him a bit. Dizzily he thought, she really *does* like me!

He couldn't understand it.

"Uh—how about Saturday?" he managed at last.

Her smile widened. "That's a *wonderful* idea, Rod," she said. "I have the whole day and the whole night free; how's that sound? My hair will be fixed up, I'll take a bubble bath, and I'll break out my best perfume. Haven't touched it for weeks."

When she left, with a last sparkling wink at him, Parker's eyes had tears in them. He felt utterly conspicuous, as if everyone was looking at him. But he couldn't stop grinning.

Like a idiot, he thought. He went on grinning.

3

Justin Waley strode eagerly through Bracher's, peering at the booths in the dimness after the midsummer blast of light outside. There she was, her hair red over the back of the brown leatherette booth. His heart jumped up and he stepped forward swiftly, feeling a dread anxiety until she glanced around, caught his eye, and said, "Hello, Justin."

She smiled politely. He felt his own face wrenched by a big sloppy smile like a puppy's. "Hello, Nona, I hope I'm not late."

"Oh, no, I just got here a minute ago."

"Good news," he said, as he seated himself. The waitress had been by; there were two red-covered menus on the table. He picked one up. "Red Bud Hadley is taking two weeks off from his job and we'll open our office in Clinchfield on Monday. We've already rented one, just off the Square. His wife Margie will be our receptionist."

"Oh, that's wonderful." Politely.

"After the two weeks, we'll have to decide what to do—take turns, probably, on alternate days, or have Margie hold down the fort when we're not there, or just what."

"Yes."

Justin glanced at her. There was a note of strain in her tone. Also in her expression. "Is everything all right?" he asked anxiously. "Is your car okay?"

"Oh, yes. Uh, I, uh, I j-just wanted to thank you for helping last night—"

She was so serious that he had to minimize his smile. He hoped that didn't turn it into a smirk. "Oh, no problem. I was glad to be of help," he said, pretending to glance at his menu. He had been more than glad, he'd been delighted. To be turned to for help by *her*—

She was looking at him anxiously.

Justin studied her expression for a moment. Doubtfully he said, "Was *that* worrying you?"

Nona looked down, then wryly up at him. "Most men resent being woke up and having to go out in the middle of the night. I thought—you might not want to hang around a woman who—"

She was really worried about that, he realized. Justin

managed to keep from laughing, but she stopped in mid sentence, looking at him. He thought quickly for some way to reassure her, and said, "I can't wait for Saturday."

At her uncertain look, he added anxiously, "We have a date—remember?"

Nona blinked. After a moment she propped her chin on her hand and looked back at him, and all the anxiety was gone from her expression. It was fond, and warm, and—sultry. "Yes indeed we do." She smiled slowly, meaningfully. "Eat lots of meat."

He'd never noticed before just how warm and husky her voice was.

The plump older one of the restaurant's two waitresses appeared at his elbow, smiling maternally at him as she always did. "Ready to order?"

Down the row of booths, Parker, that shrewd competent deputy, was standing up. A girl had been in the same booth with him, a perky little thing with an impish smile; he knew her from somewhere.

Justin wondered if his ears were as red as Parker's.

4

It was a funeral. Culter's funeral parlor, with the Smithers family solemn in the uncomfortable pews. Bernie McKay observed the scene dreamily for a time, from several angles, before he realized that he was dreaming.

It's Uncle Albert's funeral, he thought. I'm dreaming of the funeral again, and any minute the damned old man is going to sit up and give me the finger.

But it wasn't the coffin his dream image focused on. It was his wife, Angie. She sat there, pious as a nun; butter wouldn't melt in her mouth. And all the time she was two-timing me with that asshole Gibson, he thought angrily.

But why aren't I sitting next to her?

Well, it was a dream; he never saw himself in dreams. Nobody noticed him wandering around the room, but that was normal. It seemed a pretty pointless dream. Uncle Albert never did sit up. Bernie was rather thankful in fact to note that the coffin was closed and firmly latched.

Finally he got bored and left.

Bernie was back at his house, and it was night, and Gibson was there. He was talking angrily to Angie. Furious, Bernie shouted at them, but they ignored him. Angie's pale face was as cold and hard as if it had been carved from snow. She kept shaking her head, not at Bernie's shouts—she seemed unaware of him—but at Gibson.

Gibson was also angry and upset; he kept urging her and Angie kept refusing. *Bitch,* he thought, *now you turn nun. Go ahead, get it on with him—I'm dead; should I care?*

Dead? he thought.

My God, yes, I'm dead. I must be a ghost. So this is what it felt like; this is what Uncle Albert felt.

Experimentally he moved around and found that it was true; ghosts could go through walls, and zip from place to place instantly. Not only could he not touch walls, he couldn't touch anything. Also, things were dim and vague and dark, like vision in some dreams. Indeed, he seemed to inhabit a dream world. Like a dream, it had laws and limitations.

One limitation he found immediately: he couldn't simply go out and walk down the street. He was bound to certain places, or certain people. He could follow

Angie around, he found, though not everywhere she **went.** He could haunt his house, and once he found **himself,** puzzled, at the Methodist cemetery. Twice he found himself at the strip pit where Gibson had killed him, and once he partly retraced the odyssey he had taken through the woods after he came out of the water.

Again he found himself back at the funeral. Again he was back at the house, watching a bitterly silent Angie watch a bitterly angry Gibson drive off. Then he was in a place he did not remember ever seeing, a dim dark room mainly inhabited by Gibson, drinking sourly out of a bottle. To his fury, he saw one of Angie's medals on the little table beside Gibson. These were silver Bicentennial medals she'd bought from a coin dealer—they'd been made by a private mint in '76. She'd had her name engraved on the scrolls carried by the florid eagles and had given them to "a choice selection of special friends." Bernie hadn't received one.

"Give me that medal!" he cried, and tried to grab Gibson's throat. He couldn't touch the other. Neither could he touch Angie's gift; his hand went through it. Giving up on it, Bernie shoved his face in front of the other's, yelling, "You don't rate it, you fucking gigolo! Give it back!" Gibson frowned at nothing and petulantly tipped his bottle up again.

Bernie's chest felt tight; he felt unshed tears in his ghostly eyes.

"She never cared for you; never mind that cheap toy, she just wanted to fuck you!" he said, gesturing wildly at the medal. "She never cared for anybody but herself," he added, bitterly.

Still Gibson sat drinking morosely, not seeing or hearing him.

That made Bernie anxious. Thinking strongly of Angie brought him back to her, trudging up the stairs to their bedroom. She didn't see him either, or hear his loudest shout.

If these two couldn't see him, who could?

As he was thinking this, he let go mentally of the scene and wandered through dark and light areas for a time, tasting fear. Then he found himself at Mount Pisgah Baptist Cemetery. There was the grave he recognized from the funeral: Uncle Albert's grave. Fearfully he approached it, half expecting, as in a nightmare, Uncle Albert's decaying corpse to come clawing out of it.

No, not the corpse—it was Uncle Albert Smithers himself he found bending over the filled-in grave. There was no headstone, and the hole was utterly uncared-for, Bernie noticed. Uncle Albert was weeping over it.

Weeping!

Bernie hesitated, tempted to wish himself back to Angie's bedroom. But he couldn't resist the spectacle. Uncle Albert wept and wailed under an uncaring sky, and no one heard but him.

What's he weeping for?

A few broken sentences enlightened him. The gold. It was his stolen and now lost gold the ghost of the larcenous old man wept for.

"Old fool!" Bernie said. "If you hadn't been so intent on robbing me, and had spent the money, you'd have gotten the good of it while you were alive. Now you couldn't use it if you found it."

He snorted with amusement. Half of the bewept gold was his, but he didn't give a damn.

"Uncle Albert!" he hollered. "Hey, Uncle Albert! If you find it, you can have my half too! Don't spend it all in one place!"

Uncle Albert heard neither his jeers nor his laughter. When his amusement was spent, Bernie stood looking sadly on at the spectacle: all that was left of a human being, reduced to a set of simple reflexes—to a posture of weeping for the unattainable. A slow chill settled over him.

"There but for the grace of God go I" did not apply, he thought, alarmed. It was more a case of "Why, this is Hell, nor am I out of it."

The same Hell gaped for him.

Bernie had read long ago of experiments in sensory deprivation. Subjects who were not allowed to see, hear, or feel anything went mad. And a ghost couldn't feel anything, couldn't touch anything except maybe a couple things, and could only see a certain few scenes.

With Bernie's death, Uncle Albert had lost the only person who could interact with him. There was nothing left for him but the memory of his gold. By now it too was probably a pretty vague concept to him.

A sensation as of goosepimples stirred over Bernie. Eventually, he thought, Uncle Albert would fade out to a mere moan, a sigh, a movement of air. He stared in horror at the ritualistically weeping spectre.

You today, me tomorrow, he thought, prickling.

The burning fiery furnace of Hell was preferable to this.

Forever—or until Bernie faded away—feeling nothing, smelling nothing, tasting nothing, hearing little—and unheard, unseen, untouched—until his mind gave way to blessed madness and he became a mere crotchet, an unheard sound of raving or weeping or muttering. . . .

The dark cemetery with its dark occupant faded and Bernie approached a pool of white light. The room was dark, lit only by a fluorescent desk lamp. Paul

Gibson crouched over the desk, his head almost under the lamp, looking with bitter satisfaction at a set of glossy Polaroids.

The pictures seemed to leap up before Bernie.

Pictures of Angie, nude. Angie, wearing heels and hose and a saucy look. Angie, looking demurely at the camera with that high-class, haughty look she used to cow him with, sitting bolt upright and stark naked. Angie, in black hose with lace garters, her legs open for the camera, laughing with an expression she had never used on Bernie. She'd refused to pose for him—with that same haughty look.

"You bitch!" he cried, raging, stung. "If I could kill you—and Gibson too, you bastard! I'll get you—I'll get you both—fucking like dogs, right under my eyes— I'll get you—and you killed me, you fucking shitheap, I'll get you for that, too— Police! Murder! Help, police!"

Where the hell were the cops when you needed one? Where was that one who was at Uncle Albert's funeral? With the thought, he was back at his own funeral, Angie sitting up straight and dry-eyed, the brave widow, Gibson nowhere, ha-ha, a joke on him! He got nothing, the son of a bitch. Where was that cop? White Man, or White Face or whatever his weird name was. . . .

"You bastards," Bernie said silently in the darkness. "I'll get you, find someone who can see me and *I'll get you*—"

Paul Gibson turned away momentarily, burying his face in his hands. Bernie couldn't help it—he reached out and touched one of the pictures of Angie, though he knew he couldn't actua— He started. He felt glossy paper. He could! He could! Apparently, if it was a thing connected to Angie's cuckolding him. . . . My God, he thought, hastily drawing back his hand before Gibson noticed, just you wait until you fall asleep, you bastard! I've *got* you!

5

The diver came out of the murky water and pushed his mask back. "Okay!" he called, jerking one thumb up.

Deputy Rod Parker passed it on to the guy on the crane, who was already gunning his engine. The cable wound up and the murky water began to move. The diver got hastily out.

Parker, the sheriff, a couple of other deputies, White Bird Hadley from the Oswego cops, and the workmen stood around, watching. The dark water parted and there was a metallic gleam. Red-brown, Parker thought, that's gotta be it. The Cadillac came slowly out of the strip pit, the crane engine roaring as the load came on it.

The man on the crane waited while water poured from the machine, then swung it slowly toward the bank. He set it down carefully and killed his engine, lit a cigarette.

The sheriff and White Bird went over to the car, Parker following.

"Key still in the ignition," said White Bird immediately.

Evelyn Anderson reached in, clicked it back and forth. "Turned on, too. Looks like it was driven into the water at low speed."

"Not by McKay," said Parker. "Coroner said he was unconscious before he drownded."

"Right, well, we knew he was murdered," White Bird said. "Killer sapped him, stuck him in his car, and let it run into the pit."

"Estes saw only one man in the Cad when it turned in here," the sheriff said. Estes was a farmer who'd happened to be driving his tractor by at the time; he was in the crowd now. "McKay could've been sapped somewhere else and driven here in his own car. I doubt it, though. How'd the killer get away, without a car? No, I make a guess the killer set up an appointment with McKay."

"An appointment here?" White Bird asked.

"If they both wanted it kep' secret," the sheriff said.

"Hmmm," White Bird said. "Maybe McKay found Smithers's hidden gold, and didn't let on. If someone learned that, especially if they knew where he'd put it, they might have knocked him off for it."

Parker stirred impatiently. "Well, these complicated theories sound good, but one thing we know is, McKay's wife was seen with McKay's assistant a lot, before and after he was murdered. Gibson. He wouldn't of been the first guy to marry the boss's widow. No way he could guess she would drop him after the old guy was croaked."

Anderson nodded; after a moment, so did Hadley, reluctantly. "You're right," the sheriff said. "The only solid thing we got to go on is Gibson. And it's sure he don't have the gold, or he would've been long gone."

Parker shivered a little, looking at the surging, murky water. All too clearly, he imagined the rotting corpse clawing its way up the bank, tearing at the clayey soil with its bloated fingers. Seemed every investigation lately involved something eerie; what was eating St. Claude County?

Even the Smigly brats stabbing old man Hennessey with a damn pitchfork turned into a weird tale. First the brats went feral, then Parker found Clothilde Smigly praying to a damn mean idol, then they stirred up some strange monster while looking for the brats.

It was still in the tributaries of the Osage. Occasionally they got reports from frightened fishermen.

And then when Hat Stetson reported the Smigly bodies and the sheriff and Nordstrom went out to bring them in, the elder Smiglies blamed them. Parker hadn't been there when the parents came in to identify the bodies, but the sheriff had, and he said they were quiet, but plainly mad. Jake's paranoia sure must've been confirmed, Parker thought.

Apparently Clothilde had stopped weeping long enough to glare at Anderson. She'd mumbled something about getting even. Anderson had shrugged, when repeating it to the deputies. Privately he had consulted Parker about it, asking him if he thought she'd sic her juju stone on him. Parker was proud to have been consulted, but had no idea.

"I'm wearin' a cross, and I'm a born-ag'in Christian," Evelyn had said resignedly, shaking his head. "I figger that should count for something."

That or something had, so far. But Parker had no such comfort, and slept uneasily. He'd helped drag the brats away.

He jumped at a clutch on his arm. It was White Bird Hadley, staring at the strip pit. Parker followed his gaze back, his breath coming short, seeing again his vision of McKay clawing his way out. Bits of old black leaves and trash drifted to the turbid surface and sank lazily; ripples lapped against the bank.

"My God!" Hadley said, staring at the water.

"What?" "What is it?" they asked.

"McKay! McKay, crawling out of the pit. Don't you see him?"

"No!" Parker said.

"Must be a ghost," said the sheriff. "Don't see a thing. You, Parker?"

"Not a thing," Parker said, sweating, feeling pale.

Hadley said, "He's comin' over here. He don't look dead—wearing a suit. It doesn't look wet. What?" He stared at nothing, then looked at them. "You were right, Parker. He says Gibson hit him on the side of the head. He says they came here to consider buyin' the pits for a development. He says Gibson was playing around with his wife. What?" He listened for a moment, turned back to them.

"He says Gibson has his good luck piece. It's a silver Bicentennial medal put out by a private mint, with an eagle on it like on coins. It has his wife's name, Angie, on it. He says she gave it to him for their anniversary several years ago. He says he never went anywhere without it."

The sheriff looked at Parker, looked back at Hadley. "Right. We'll pick up Mr. Paul Gibson for questioning. Where's the medal, in his apartment?"

White Bird opened his mouth, closed it. "He's gone!"

"I'd say he told us enough," Parker said. "Too bad ghosts can't testify in court."

6

"Come and get it before I throw it out!" Nona Martens called.

Justin and her son Billy came into Justin's big old kitchen, Justin smiling at her, Billy sullen. It was Saturday night, but he'd had no place to go and no one to go with, so it wasn't that.

"Hope you like it," she said, setting a roast on the table.

Billy grunted as he sat down opposite Justin.

Justin hadn't seemed to notice his attitude all evening.

Well, maybe they'd moved a little fast for the boy. They'd moved their date up to Friday night, last night, she'd called in to work; Strictly Strickland must still be furious—and she'd spent the night with him. Already she was thinking of Justin as "her man"—and he'd urged her to move in with him. Nona was amazed that Justin had overcome his shyness so quickly—but she'd certainly encouraged him, last night, singing "Chances are/Your chances are awf'ly good."

He had taken her advice about eating meat.

Billy accepted roast pork ungraciously. Nona looked at him nervously. "Dig in, boys. I hope you like the roast, Justin. It's the way my mother used to make it."

He tasted it and nodded in approval. "My mother will want to meet you as soon as she learns of you," he said. "I'll call her tomorrow, if it's all right with you."

Rather breathless, but game, Nona nodded.

"She'll be pleased that I have someone looking after me," Justin said. "But I warn you, she'll insist on giving you all *my* favorite recipes! Here, Bill, have some of the corn."

Billy grunted again, hunched over his plate, not looking up. Sulkily he slopped creamed corn onto his plate.

"For canned corn, it's not bad," Nona said hastily, smiling brightly at her son but feeling angry. He was doing his best to spoil the evening. Outside, distant thunder boomed as a storm worked across the sky toward them.

"I was raised on canned corn," said Justin. "Of course, a lot of it was canned by my mother. Incidentally, I have a beef, a hog, and a dozen chickens coming along. A farmer named Hatterson is raising them for me, and the locker plant will slaughter and prepare them, except for the chickens. I have to take care of them, but my mother helps."

"What do you do, chop their heads off with your sword?" Billy asked sourly.

Nona glared at him, but Justin said, pleasantly, "No, nobody's that fast. Besides, might ding the blade. I just cut them up and freeze them, nothing fancy—there should still be a couple in the deepfreeze," he added to Nona. "With a family, now, I need to think about increasing my order for meat."

Billy looked as if he might say something more, but Nona spoke quickly.

"You get your meat real cheap, living in the country, if you can afford to," she said. "I see a space out back that would make a good garden, too. You don't garden?"

"No, and I know I should do some things. But let's face it, you can buy frozen snap beans for a tenth the cost, in time and trouble, that you can raise them. So I don't let it bother me so much. Of course, for cucumbers, melons, tomatoes, and the like, gardening would be cheaper."

"Not to mention better!" Nona said. "Well, next year we'll have to take a look at that plot," she added with pleasure. "I'm an avid gardener, and quite a good one, too. And I want to prune your roses tomorrow."

The meal continued pleasantly on their part, but with the continual strain of Billy's attitude. Nona mentally revolved words to use on him. She sighed. It was natural for the boy to be jealous; he'd never shared her with anyone since his daddy left, and he was just a little boy then. They'd really depended on each other.

Boylike, he wanted to be a man, independent, but he wanted her to still be his momma.

They sat for a bit after the meal, snug inside as the storm worked up outside, and Nona finally got up to do the dishes. Rather to her surprise, and considerably to her pleasure, Justin didn't march off into the living room as all the men in her life had done. He got up and helped.

She said, "I really do want to meet your mother. She raised you up nice."

Justin laughed. "I've always enjoyed doing dishes. But I'll wipe—I know where I want things put. Old bachelor, you know, set in my ways," he added apologetically.

Billy sat like a bump on a log, refusing to leave them alone together, refusing to take part in the camaraderie. When the dishes were done, Justin turned to him.

"Bill, I wonder if you'd help me this evening."

An inarticulate grunt.

Justin smiled. "Maybe you know I exercise in the evening by swinging a heavy sword around. It's good exercise, but every now and then I need a refresher in the real thing. Wonder if you'd agree to join me in a mock battle with practice swords?"

Billy's interest overcame his sullenness, Nona saw. His ears practically perked up. She'd seen him looking swiftly around the living room when he arrived, presumably for the famous sword.

"Guess so," he said gruffly, pretending to be surly still.

They went out to the barn in the watery pre-storm light. Not having been invited, Nona hesitated to follow; she knew Justin felt uncomfortable at being watched while exercising, though he'd showed her his sword readily enough. She bustled around the house instead, dusting, straightening, keeping herself busy.

From time to time she looked anxiously out the window.

The storm had broken with a savage glare of lightning and burst of thunder. The trees bent to the blast, showing the pale undersides of their leaves. Blue-black darkness came on under the raging clouds, periodically relieved by blue-white light so intense it froze the wildly-waving trees. Thunder rattled the windows.

She would have given anything for a peek into the barn.

After about forty-five minutes "her men" came running laughing back through the blast, arriving sopping wet and with their hair sleeked to their heads. Justin's skull rose nobly above his brows, like Jean-Luc Picard's, she thought fondly. Billy looked like a miserable drowned rat.

"Get those clothes off!" she cried. Water was streaming from them onto the kitchen floor.

Justin laughed shakily, shivering with the chill, and peeled out of his shirt. Glancing hesitantly at her, he kicked out of his shoes and slid his sodden pants down his slim white legs. Billy stripped without hesitation, gasping several times in obvious pain.

Nona gulped at the sight of his arms and ribs. Blue and black bruises were all over them, darkening moment by moment. Justin, she saw, had some as well, though by no means as many, or as bad. Billy felt of his ribs, wincing and grinning ruefully.

"I'll fetch some jeans for you," Justin said to him. "They'll be too long, but they're dry. And a shirt."

Nona hurried to the linen closet and brought out towels.

"Thanks, Mom," Billy said, wrapping his shivering frame in one. He grinned at her. "That rain is cold!"

"Yeah," she said breathlessly, picking up their clothes. She stepped into the washroom next to the kitchen, emptied all pockets, and tossed everything into the dryer. "Have 'em ready for you by the time you're ready to go home," she said.

"Thanks, Mom," he said cheerfully, sliding into Justin's clothes.

They all sat drinking coffee while the clothes dried and the rain tapered off and stopped. The clouds remained, outside, but inside the house they were gone. Justin and Billy talked of handguns and Nona sat silent and astonished, watching them. Handguns, it turned out, were an old passion of her son's. Now he was respectfully asking Justin's opinion.

"Don't know much about guns. I'm not even any hand with the sword, not in real combat," Justin said. "Yet it took years to get where I am with it. But guns are easier to learn, I understand. It'll take lots of practice. That can be expensive, unless you're using a .22. You might consider investing in a reloading kit."

"I need to git me a good, stiddy job," Billy said reflectively. "Somethin' that pays better than doin' odd jobs."

Hallelujah, hail Columbia, Nona thought, dumbfounded.

By the time Billy left, it was clear that he had determined to be as good with a pistol as Justin was with a sword. Nona said goodnight to him, still stunned, and turned questioningly to Justin.

He grinned. "Takes a boy to know one."

Chapter Nine:

On the Bayou

1

"Hey, Hat, good to see you!"

Jody Stetson, just off the Trailways bus from Kansas City, had wandered into the narrow, cavelike Bus Stop Cafe with the vague intention of getting a cup of coffee and a piece of pie. They were the only decent things to be had in the place, if you weren't too fussy about your coffee. The hookers had moved out to Highway Thirteen long ago, when the truckers stopped coming into Oswego.

"Yo, Greathouse," Hat said to the plump youngish man who had called to him. He joined the other in his dimlit booth, also inhabited by two fat bleached blonde girls, one with a big nose. George Greathouse he knew, and the big-nosed girl: "Hi, Sadie." They were types he'd known all his life. Hat took off his white cowboy hat with a small flourish, smiling with easy charm at them, his wariness hidden.

"Oh, you're the one got his hand cut—"

Sadie jabbed the speaker in the ribs and quickly said, "We're rilly glad to see you back, Hat. Never thought you'd bother to come back to this one-horse burger." But she too was looking at his right hand.

Hat's tension eased. They were curious, awed, uncertain, but not repelled. For once he was the hero, or at least the center of attention. The one time in his life he made the news, Waley, damn him, got all the publicity. All Hat got was three seconds of them wheeling his ass into Research Medical in Kansas City. He held his hand up and showed them the still-pink scar around the wrist. They oohed and aahed.

The elderly waitress appeared like magic. "Hi, Hat," she said, staring at his hand.

"Don't high hat me," he said, smiling—it was an old line with him. "Coffee and coconut cream pie, Betty."

"Sure, Hat." She tentatively touched his hand. "It feels normal. How does it feel to you?"

"Like it's asleep," Hat said. He stroked it with his left forefinger. "The skin feels almost normal, most places—I can kind of feel things, and I can feel hot and cold. But inside, it's numb. Like it's asleep, but not tingling, you know?"

"But can you use it?" Sadie asked.

"Not very well, but it's a lot better than a pair of hooks," he said. "I'm learning to use my left hand for anything that needs fine control. But I can still eat with it, if I'm careful."

"Does rubbing help?" the other girl asked, taking it and trying.

"No, the nerves themselves are cut. I'm just lucky they were able to match up and sew as many back together as they did. At least I have a lot of control." Hat demonstrated by picking up a paper napkin that was lying flat on the table, with a little fumbling of his numb finger and thumb.

"You really grew back fast," said Greathouse. "I thought it took longer."

"Usually it does," said Hat. "Doctors were surprised."

It had something to do with the weird gold medallion the black monster had thrown down beside the Smigly brats. Hat hadn't told anyone that when he held it, his hand felt normal. He could feel it, and feel anything that touched his hand. This gave him hope it would yet recover fully, with the help of the medallion's magic. He slept with it in his hand.

"Wow. You were really lucky," said Sadie, awed. "He could've taken your head off just as easy!"

"Be a lot harder to sew that back on," said Greathouse, haw-hawing like an idiot.

Hat's mood darkened, but the return of Betty with pie and coffee distracted the others. Apparently nobody noticed his momentary rage.

No. He hadn't forgotten Justin Waley and his fucking sword. Or Nona Martens.

Hat had unfinished business in St. Claude County.

2

Deputy Rod Parker had never done anything he was prouder of than to escort Judith Lamour into the Night Owl. At the same time he was embarrassed; he knew everybody would laugh at the idea of him out with her. Judith, for her part, was totally unselfconscious; she greeted her old friends among the waitresses as brightly as ever.

"You know Rod, don't you? Deputy Rod Parker!"

"Yes, Rod comes here a lot."

They'd never called him by his first name before; now they were all smiles.

"Give us a booth at the back," Judith said. Seated, she shook her bright curls and looked around eagerly. "Oh, there's Maudie Lewis, and that guy she's going with now." She waved. "And Lonnie Meiklejohn and his cheerleader from Appleville. She's too young for him." She didn't wave.

"Oh! It's Jody Stetson!"

Parker looked around grimly. "Yeah, we got word a coupla days ago that he's back in town."

Stetson met his gaze with his own lowering one.

"Don't like me much," Parker said. "Never will. 'Fraid I wasn't very sympathetic when he got his hand cut off." He shrugged. "One more troublemaker for us to keep track of."

"Do you think maybe he's learned his lesson?"

Parker thought about it. "Prob'ly not. Guys like that, they start actin' one way when they're young, they never grow out of it. Maybe a bad enough shock, like, would change 'em, but most likely, the way they *handle* the shock is to go back to their old way of thinkin'."

He felt as if he were struggling uphill through mud, putting his feelings into words. "I mean, if it was a tornado that give 'im the shock, it might change 'im. But a guy, in a fight, no way. To feel right about hisself, he's gotta say, well, he cheated, I never had a chanst, next time I'll show 'im, I'll show 'em all. See what I mean?"

Judith nodded. "I guess I do. I was hoping he'd be different, but you're prob'ly right. You're a lot smarter than you let on, Rod, to figure him out that way!"

Surprised, abashed, he said, "Well, that's just common sense. Anyway, he's behavin' hisself right now."

The waitress showed up and they made selections.

Sipping her water and nodding at a table across the room, Judith said, "Have you heard about Lonnie Meiklejohn seeing the monster in the river?"

Parker set down his coffee cup. "I ain't read the last reports. The monster's been seen so many times and places, we don't b'leeve the reports, anyway."

"Good thing it only comes out at night, or it'd scare off the fishermen down from Kansas City. Are you trying to capture it?"

Parker frowned. "Well, it scares people, but the only thing we think it done is kill the Smigly brats, and we'd have trouble provin' that. It may look like a wile animal, but Sheriff Anderson has put out the word that it's prob'ly got human rights. I shot at it in self-defense, but it might not be legal to go out and gun it down like a dog. As for catchin' it—" He shook his head.

There'd been a couple of expeditions into its former lair in Monegaw Cave, one of them sober, but it had apparently never gone back there. The reports they were sure of always placed it in or near the river or its tributaries.

"But hasn't it killed chickens and hogs—?"

"Plenty of claims, but no proof. Not even footprints. Evelyn thinks it eats fish."

Their sandwiches came. When he had taken his first bite, Judith looked mischievously at him and said, "So you arrested Paul Gibson."

"Sheriff Anderson and White Bird Hadley did."

"Did he do it?"

" 'Cordin' to what the ghost tole White Bird. Gibson had this coin thing McKay's wife give him. Kind of a good luck charm. A silver coin with their names on it. McKay tuck it ever'where with him, I hear. His wife identified it and confirmed she give it to McKay. She almost fainted when she seen it."

"But Gibson denied everything? Do you have any other proof?"

"It's all a game to you, ain't it?" Parker said, grinning at her. "Yeah, we got evidence. Testimony that Gibson was seen with Miz McKay. Her admission that she thought he was a good guy and that she was pushin' McKay to make him his pardner. She said he proposed to her after the murder, but before the corpse came back. Said she turned him down."

"So his motive for the murder was, he expected to marry her and be made a partner in the real estate business?" Judith asked eagerly.

"Yeah, she bein' the owner of what was left of the business, she could've done that," Parker said. " 'Course he denies everything. Says she give him the luck charm with her name on it last Christmas, denies proposing to her, everything. When we told him the charm has 'Love to Bernie' written on it, he said we was lyin', tryin' to catch him out." Parker shrugged his big shoulders. "What else could he say?"

"Could *she* have done it—Angie?"

"We looked into her when he disappeared," said Parker, shaking his head. "We had a witness that saw her at her house after McKay left—witness saw McKay drive off—and Miz McKay talked to her thirty minutes or more after McKay was gone. What's more, her car was in the drive most of the afternoon. She did go shopping in Yost's department store, but that was later."

"And Gibson?"

"He left the office right after McKay did and didn't git back for two hours. Nobody thought anything of it at the time, because he was in and out all the time. But he had time to git to the strip pits, do it, and git back."

Judith sighed in something like rapture. "Wow. I

remember him from school," she said. "He was three years older than me and never noticed me. Not that I thought he was so cool, I mean, we all knew the Gibson family. But I knew him! And now he's under arrest for murder! Wow!" she added happily.

Parker couldn't help laughing. "I'm glad somebody gits a charge out of it."

Judith smiled meaningfully at him. "I told you once, Rod Parker. I don't go out with you just to hear the gossip. You just wait till you take me home. You're going to get a surprise!"

Parker felt a thrill of total happiness go through him. He had never felt so little like an unwanted troll in his life, so that when he put his hand over hers, he was startled that his was so plump.

"Or maybe it's me that'll get the surprise," she murmured.

3

"That'll ruin a three-dollar bill," Hat Stetson said, with a weak flash of his old wit.

The young waitress smiled dutifully, writing down his order. The Night Owl roared and boomed around them. He didn't know her, and she didn't seem to recognize him. Hat stopped himself from asking about Nona Martens; he hadn't seen her tonight.

"Been here long?" he asked.

"Couple weeks," she said. "Summer job." She left, hips switching enticingly, without a glance back.

God, was she still in high school? Prob'ly jail bait. No, the place served liquor. College, maybe. Her smiles were purely commercial; she had looked at him with complete disinterest. Even as he watched in dismay,

Hat saw her turn, her face transformed by a real smile, to wave and call to pimply friends in a booth by the front window. Kids her age.

Hat was ten years older than she. Suddenly he felt elderly. He wasn't the with-it young dude anymore—far as they were concerned, he was out of it, an old fart pretending to be young still.

College kids, he thought with envious contempt.

A short fattish man walked by with a slender young woman whose head was covered with bright brown curls. Hat almost knew her. They were seated and he remembered: she was that girl Poochie Doo-brett used to go out with. Then she drew her companion's attention to him, and Hat was startled to meet the grim gaze of Deputy Parker. He met Parker's penetrating glance sullenly, but was relieved when the other looked away. For a moment he'd been afraid Parker would humiliate him by coming over and shaking him down.

Fat bastard. Hat hoped Parker wouldn't get on his case, now they knew he was back in town. He was going to have trouble enough with his plans, without the law watching him.

Damn him. Hat reached into his shirtfront, felt of the medallion. Maybe, when he'd taken care of Nona Martens and that showoff bastard Waley, he could think about Parker.

A redheaded young man came in, his face covered with freckles. In the harsh light of the Night Owl, Hat was uncertain. Then the other turned a little, revealed himself to be older—Cowgill. Frankie Cowgill.

Hat started to wave and call to him, hesitated. He'd had to gather his nerve to come here tonight, and it had been an actual relief to find no one here whom he knew. No one recognized him, it seemed.

Officially it had just been a drunken quarrel that

nobody remembered anything about. Officially there was no hint of any threat to Nona Martens. Officially Hat had just pulled a gun when Waley tried to break up the fight, or maybe had pulled it on his friends. Officially Hat was nothing worse than a drunken redneck stumblebum.

Unofficially, he could guess what everybody thought, and their contempt.

So now he was hiding out in a back booth with his trademark cheap white cowboy hat lying hidden on the seat beside him. But surely Cowgill—?

Before he could make up his mind, Cowgill recognized him, waved, and came back to his booth.

"Hey, Hat, good to see you." He held out his hand.

"Cowgirl!" Hat took his hand and was touched when Cowgill shook, then nearly dropped his hand.

"Uh—I hope I didn't—? This is the one—?"

"Yeah, this is the one," Hat said easily. "No harm done, it's still good fer shakin'. Not so good at pickin' up checks." He showed the scar.

"I still have nightmares about it flyin' through the air," said Cowgill solemnly.

Hat grinned his practiced boyish grin. "Me too."

Cowgill laughed suddenly, whacked him on the shoulder, sat down. "Good t'see you back, Hat. I heard you was in town ag'in and come by a couple times, hopin' you'd be here, but you wasn't."

"Yeah, well I don't git around much any more," Hat said, almost maudlin. He was still smarting from the waitress's youth and disinterest. Somehow it was a betrayal, that anybody should grow up young after him.

And damn if she wasn't coming back.

She smiled her professional smile at Cowgill, nodded at his order—like Hat's, just for beer. It was a relief to Hat that she was no friendlier to Cowgill than to him, though the redhead knew her name.

"She's maybe gonna marry my cousin," Cowgill said, when Hat asked about her.

"Oh."

Nothing doing there, then. Hat didn't admit it to himself, but it was a relief that he need not try. He couldn't lose if he didn't ask. Besides, he told himself, he wasn't interested in her, young or not.

"Nice ass," Hat said dismissingly.

He looked around the Night Owl, hoping to see Nona Martens. He wasn't going to ask about her, though. Especially not in front of Frankie Cowgill, who would have helped him carry her off.

No sign of her.

Cowgill was babbling something about having seen George Greathouse, who'd told him Hat was back in town.

Hat looked at him. Hat was as sensitive as a newly bashed finger about people's opinion of him, especially women. But it'd been weeks, and he had a yen like he'd never had, even when he was in the Army in Germany. Delicately he asked, "Seen Daffy Greathouse lately?"

"Haw, haw! No. You ain't heard? Daphne run off with a trucker two weeks ago. George says his mother got a poce-card from her from Pomme deeTarr, and that's all they know."

"Oh."

Too bad; Daffy was a pig, but she was the easiest lay in St. Claude county. Oh well, save it for Nona. Concealing his disappointment, Hat looked up with a smile as the waitress brought their beers. Ignoring his interest coolly, she took their money and departed.

Well, fuck her. And Nona. And Waley.

Yeah. He'd like to fuck 'em all. But how?

"Hey, Hat, you know Bernard Kieffer?" Cowgill was saying. "Says he ain't been coon huntin' in ages. I told 'im it was way too early for coon huntin', but he said damn if he cared, he'd just like to git out with the dogs."

"Yeah?" Then Hat came alert. He took a gulp of his beer to hide it. Hunting? —And Hat needed an alibi.

"Wouldn' mind a run with the dawgs m'self," Hat said with studied disinterest. What was the name of that hunting friend of Cowgirl's? And maybe he could get Mike Yost in on it, if his damn wife didn't keep him in, like a baby. "You know anyone's got good coon dogs?"

"Oh, hell, yeah, I know a coupla guys that got dogs. Too bad about Knuckles, you heard about him? Killed by the damn Smigly brats. And Ben Masters hadda sell all his. But the Griersons'll be glad to come, and they got good dogs."

"Blue ticks, black and tans, or what?"

"Blue ticks, and real sweet-mouthed, from what Ben says. I know he'd love to come along. We c'n go up Woods Chapel Road, that's good 'n' wild."

"Naw, I figured on that stretch up Little Monny-go Crick," Hat said. It was only a couple miles from Nona Martens's trailer. "Fulla coons. Git into it from the west, them back roads out of Laurie City. How's that sound?"

"Sounds like a winner."

"Good. How 'bout Sattidee?"

"Yeah. Sattidee." Cowgill lifted his beer, grinning hugely.

Hat lifted his, grinning also. He drank to Nona Martens, nude, tied up, and totally submissive. He drank to Justin Waley groveling abjectly at his feet. And himself with a perfect alibi—the hunt would go on all night.

4

Justin Waley smiled. Angie Smithers McKay smiled back, admitting him decorously to her house. She was wearing—to his relief—a modest summer dress, loose, light, and concealing. Her smile was genuine, but anxious.

"Good news," Justin said, when the door was closed. He reached into his inside jacket pocket and pulled out an envelope.

Hesitantly, glancing at him, she took it, looked at it. Justin had studied it himself. The postmark was the city's, from yesterday. The envelope was stuffed. She opened it and pulled out a thick bundle of glossy photographs. Negatives spilled out, fell to the floor.

"Oh!"

They were nude shots of Angie herself. She turned a frightened glance on him. "Oh no! These will prove that Paul—that I—that—"

"Not any more," Justin said, smiling tightly.

"Where did you get them—?" Faintly.

"In that envelope. It came in the mail."

"But—who—? Who—?"

"There's a note with them."

Taking a trembling breath and sitting down suddenly, looking much older, Angie spread out the pictures and found the note. She paled as she read it.

Justin — These will prove that bitch was getting it on with Gibson You can get a conviction with these Bernie.

She stared at him, her eyes ringed with white, face stark. "Bernie!"

"Yes," Justin said with great satisfaction. "We know his ghost was walking—White Bird Hadley saw him at the strip pits, you know. It seems he searched Gibson's house before the authorities did, and foolishly—if he wanted you convicted—mailed these to me. Even if someone wanted you convicted, there's no way now these would be evidence. Ghosts aren't too bright."

Justin shrugged, amused. "Poor stupid vindictive Bernie. You could destroy them, of course. I thought you might like to keep them. Someday you may be pleased to remember how you looked, when young and beautiful."

"But—I mean—wouldn't people know—couldn't they tell—? If they searched my house and found them—"

"Well, there's none of you with Gibson. Mostly they're against neutral backgrounds; a white curtain, and is that a pale blue sheet? You could say you posed for Bernie. Or of course you could burn them, though I wouldn't start a fire in this weather. It might cause talk."

Angie sat recovering, just breathing. "My God. You don't know how worried I've been about these. When they didn't find them, I was afraid that Paul had them hidden away, so if he lost his case he could plead guilty, turn state's evidence, and blame me for everything on appeal."

Justin picked up the negatives and methodically put everything back in the envelope. "I was tempted to keep these, but my future wife wouldn't approve. But even if these *had* turned up, it wouldn't be enough to free Gibson and convict you. Not with the commemorative coin you gave Bernie in his possession."

Angie was still pale. She looked at him and her eyes were large in a face that had gotten noticeably thinner since finding Bernie's rotting corpse in her kitchen. "Justin—I have to tell you. Paul's right; I *did* give that coin to him, and the chain it was on. I gave a number of them to my friends, b-but I never gave one to Bernie. H-he had quit being a friend by then."

Justin was startled. He closed his mouth, then said, "But—it says *To Bernie with Love* in fine script! According to the picture of it in the paper—"

She lay back in the chair, looked at him wanly. "Yes," she said, almost too low to hear. "That's what it says *now*. Is it any wonder I almost fainted when I saw it?"

"*Bernie?*"

"Must be, must have been. It just said 'Angie' before, like all of them. There was room for a short inscription in fine print, though. If he could write that letter—?"

Justin started to laugh. "Bernie! Damn his vindictive hide! But I can't blame him; Gibson might've got off, with no better evidence than we had otherwise. There's no doubt in your mind that he's guilty?"

"Oh, no, not after the way he acted, before anybody else knew Bernie was dead. Sure that he was getting me and the agency, both. But Justin, what if Bernie's ghost accuses me, starts talk—?"

"Not without evidence," said Justin confidently. "It's only a ghost; its testimony is not evidence. Furthermore, adultery might be a crime, but it isn't murder. What's more, Bernie was no better than you in that respect."

"I know. So you're not worried about the ghost—?"

"If it makes trouble, you can get a court order for an exorcism easily enough." Justin shrugged coolly.

"I guess you're right." A faint radiance came to her pale features. "I'll put these away in some private place;

not that Paul will think of me having them. And,"
getting up, "why don't we drink a little toast to the
memory of Bernie McKay?"

Justin followed her willingly. "A thank you and a
farewell to you, Bernie."

5

The sun was blindingly bright and hot, but Saturday
wasn't far away.

Hat Stetson was pumping up a tractor tire for a
farmer, working for peanuts again. In front of him was
a crumbling, massive barn, its red paint mostly
weathered off, used now only as an implement shed
and for parts storage. At his feet was a homemade
compressor, rigged out of a refrigerator motor and
pump. A rubber hose ran from it to the valve at the
bottom of the tire.

Hat leaned idly against the tire, his left hand on the
upper edge of the huge rim, as high as his shoulder.
The little compressor chugged and chugged and
chugged, the tire hissed as its great tube slowly, slowly,
filled.

Hat waited with the patience of a man paid by the
hour. He stared off into the distance past the ancient
ex-barn, brooding. In his vague imaginings, images
of Justin Waley, Nona Martens, revenge, and gold all
danced together.

Pow! A sudden loud pop as the bead of the tire
jumped out of the rim's bottom trough. Hat looked
around resignedly. The tire wasn't half full. The rim
had a wide, shallow trough for the tire and tube to fit
into. In the bottom of this trough was another, deeper
and narrrower. In the bottom of it was a third. The

expanding tube had just forced the loose bead of the tire out of the central trough and into the second one. The compressor chugged away at his feet.

Hat's mind went back to Nona Martens, nude and subdued. The image no longer tightened his pants as fantasies of her had long done. That had changed in the hospital. Oh, he'd fuck her all right, every which way there was. But the savage satisfaction he felt at the thought of her helpless in his hands pleased a deeper, more primal, and altogether darker part of him than his crotch. . . .

He'd show her, he'd show them all! Laugh at me, will you, cut off my hand, huh?

He fingered the gold medallion inside his shirt with his right hand, feeling its warmth and hardness. His hand felt normal while touching it. But when he reached over and touched the steel rim, it was numb. Some day, it wouldn't be. Getting even with Nona and Waley would help; he could tell. Water the growing plant with blood.

Everything'll be different then. He thought of the young waitress in the Night Owl, who had looked at him with cool indifference. Everything.

Grimly, he thought, And I'll have the gold, too.

For the thousandth time he cursed himself for not being able to guess where the gold was. For the thousandth time he cursed old Smithers for hiding it so well. Whenever he touched the medallion, he *knew*, he positively *knew*, that the gold was still waiting for him. Somewhere.

Yeah, he thought grimly. He gripped the cool steel rim idly with his left hand. I'll have the gold too. Figure out where it's hid. But I'm not waitin' for it. I'll git even with Waley first, if it's the last thing I do. And Nona. He had it all worked out.

Fix it so's it looks like he's the one did it to her, yeah. Everybody knows they're dating and he's kinda weird. Go to her trailer first, work her over. Hurry to Waley's house—Hat had swung by there this morning, checking out the location—shove a gun in his face, roust him out of bed, handcuff him. Fuck her one last time while Waley's watchin', then chop off her head with the sword, and shoot Waley with the pistol. Get the cuffs off him, put the gun in his hands so it looks like he—

Pow!

"Aaaaah!" Hat cried, and jerked his left hand. Too late; he only succeeded in making the bruise worse.

The heavy tire's stiff bead had finally been forced over the lip of the second trough, and it had slammed with crushing force against his fingers. It hurt like a son-of-bitch; it was like having a car door slammed on your hand. Tears of pain started from his eyes. Hat tugged again, despite the pain; a trickle of panic went through him at the relentless chugging of the compressor.

Panting, he reached for the tire valve, for the knurled brass collar where the compressor's hose tip was screwed onto it. It was too low, hung up as he was. He barely touched it with the tips of his fingers—or thought he did, he couldn't tell. He probably couldn't twist it even if his hand wasn't numb.

The tire pressed with ever-increasing force against his fingers.

"Shee-yit!" Hat yelled. He was too proud to yell for help, but a secret, childish part of him hoped help would hear his cry and come. "Fuckin' goddam bitch!"

If anyone heard, they didn't recognize his cry as a plea for help, despite the scalding urgency pain put into it. And still the compressor chugged. The tire made no further sound, but despite the pain, despite

even the spreading numbness, Hat could feel the
pressure increasing. Am I gonna lose *this* hand too?
he thought in anguish.

"Damn that fuckin' barn—" Nobody could see him,
back here where the old tractor was commonly parked.

Frantically Hat reached for the rubber hose with
his toe, raised it to his right hand. It throbbed distantly
through the numbness to the beat of the compressor.
He jerked. But it was fastened to the compressor's
nipple with stainless steel hose clamps; all he did
was tip the compressor over. That didn't help. He
whimpered, desperate. Pull up the slack in the electric
line and unplug the compressor—?

No, he remembered that the extension cord was
knotted around a spike in the barn, to prevent it coming
unplugged accidentally.

He was going to lose his *fingers* here if he didn't—
Cut the hose!

Panting with relief, Hat dug for the knife in his pants
pocket. Because of his growing left-handedness, he had
taken to carrying it and his keys and change in his left
pocket. Twisting around, he drove his numb right hand
down into it, face contorted in a frozen wince. After a
seeming eternity, he pawed a handful of stuff out and
lifted it to eye level. Carefully he dropped item after
item, leaving only the knife. He almost dropped it, too—
panic scalded through him—but he caught it, numbly.

He held it before his eyes. Sweat dripped into them.

Hat blinked the sting away, looked anxiously at the
knife. Now his greatest fear was that he would drop
it—if he did, he could never recover it. After a moment
that seemed a long time, he figured it out. He put
the knife in his mouth, clamped down on it with tooth-
bursting force, and clawed the blade open with his
right thumbnail.

His hand trembled so when he gripped the handle, he almost did drop the knife. And when he tried to cut, the tough rubber hose repelled it, again almost causing him to drop the knife. Never had his numb hand felt so weak. Then with a sense of relief like that from constipation, the knife went through the hose and air began to whoosh out of the tire.

Hat hung, eyes closed, as the pressure eased. Finally he was able to pull his fingers out. He didn't want anything more out of life, at that moment. Revenge, gold, women, respect, fast cars and all—none of them could ever mean more than the simple act of slipping his hand out of that crushing trap.

Sitting slumped, back against the wheel while the compressor chugged easily on, Hat held up his bloating fingers. Gingerly he attempted to wiggle them and was amazed and delighted when they moved. Maybe he wasn't going to lose them after all.

But now he'd have to explain what happened, listen to all the jokes and laughter at him—

Even as he thought this, he heard someone speak, coming around the barn. A laugh, a half-whispered reply, a giggle. Mutterings, speech and answer. Old Joe, of course, he did odd jobs for the family—

Hat's hair prickled all over his head; his eyes bugged out; he could feel his skin going pale. Joe Bumgardner—Joe, who'd maybe screamed and cried for help while Hat grubbed unheeding in an empty grave for dirty gold. . . .

The muttered conversation moved along the barn under the bright summer sun, casting no shadow. Hat tracked the ghost's movements by ear, but saw nothing. If it saw him, it did not speak to him. It spoke only to itself. And so speaking, it passed through the door and was lost in the darkness of the barn.

Hat drew a deep breath, cradling his hurt hand against his chest. He felt that his eyelids were drawn back as far as they could go; he shivered with fear even as the sweat ran down his ribs from his armpits.

For the first time it occurred to him that revenge might work both ways. "I didn't mean it, Joe," he said hoarsely, shivering.

The ghost's giggling voice muted into menacing silence.

6

Deputy Rod Parker put down his pen and stretched, listening absently to the TV news account of a woman in New York who was accusing a vampire of date rape. She had filed charges of murder, molestation, and infection with a sexually transmitted disease. "He never told me he was a vampire," the announcer quoted her.

"Oswald Hillis, attorney for the accused, denied the charges," came the bland voice of the announcer. " 'Mr. Rampling would never infect anyone unwillingly. It was a consensual act,' Mr. Hillis said."

"Yeah, I bet," said Gus Snyder.

The small black boy sat flipping over the pages of a car magazine in the sheriff's office while Parker sweated over his reports. They were going fishing after Parker got off work.

With a burst of laughter and a thumple of boots, Deputies Nordstrom and Harris came in, to leave their cruisers and check out.

"Where's the sheriff?" Harris asked.

"He ain't in," Parker said.

"Heya, Snyder," Nordstrom said. "That's *my* chair.

You put your little black ass anywhere you feel like, izzat it?"

"Betcher pale ass," came back Gus pertly.

"Gonna hafta knock your block off one 'a' these days," Nordstrom said, grinning.

Parker was on his feet. "You let him alone!" He felt the reddening of his face, the blazing of his own eyes. "You lay a hand on him, I bust your ass!"

Nordstrom stared at him. "Hey, man, I was just—"

"Gus's my buddy, an' no one shoves 'im around, you got that, Nordstrom?"

Parker was up against the big Swede of a deputy, but couldn't get in his face on account of Nordstrom was so much taller. Nordstrom recoiled, more astonished than anything. Parker felt himself on such a hairtrigger that any other movement would've started the fight. He followed the big man up, opening his mouth—

Gus tugged on Parker's arm. "Hey, hey, Parker, he's just funnin', it don't mean nothin'. I known him since I was so high!"

"I don't give a shit! You lay off him, Nordstrom!" Parker's voice caused the weathered windowpanes to rattle slightly behind him.

"Hey, man, all right, all right. No one ain't touchin' 'im." Nordstrom backed and waved his hand pacifically. "See you around, Gus. C'mon, Harris."

Still angry, Parker took a couple of steps after them, but the door closed behind them. Their outlines vanished from the frosted glass, and the anger from Parker's clouded mind. He glimpsed Renee, the dispatcher, peering in astonishment out of her office.

Parker turned, feeling foolish.

"Wow," Gus said. "You backed down *Chuck Nordstrom?*"

Belatedly Parker remembered that, before becoming a deputy, Nordstrom had had a bad rep in Monegaw Springs, where toughness was taken for granted.

"Unh," he said.

Gus was looking at him with wide-eyed admiration.

"It's not like that," Parker said, his mind starting to work again. "He wasn't *scairt* of me. Brawlin' on the job would be bad for him. He's got a wife, he needs his job. He ain't no *kid* no more, you know? He ain't gotta prove nothin'. Get me? It's like I really took advantage of him."

"Hey, yeah, I get you an' all that, but he didn't stand up to you, he could've at least explained, you know, but he *backed off*! Right?"

Parker sighed. He reached out and mauled the kid's short-cropped head. "You got a lot to learn, Gus, but so did I. I was a lot older'n you when I learned it."

"Rod!" said Renee. The Sunshine Girl stepped out of her cubicle, startling Parker. "We just got a call from Jake Smigly—he said a monster is out there in the woods by his house! His wife ran out to fight it off. I notified the sheriff. He wants you to join him there."

"On my way," Parker said instantly, grabbing his hat and a shotgun. He wondered if Evelyn had asked for him personally, or just whoever was in the office.

Another monster, he thought, slamming his car door and twisting the key. Or was it the same? And Clothilde had gone out to fight it off?

"Hey!" he said. Gus had piled in through the opposite door. "You cain't come!"

"I was in on it from the beginning, and I wanna see it out!" Gus looked at him pleadingly. Tough guy though he acted, he was still a little boy. Wants to see the circus, Parker thought.

The engine roared while Parker looked at him. "If anything was to happen to you, it'd cost me my job," he said.

Gus nodded soberly, but still pleaded with his eyes.

"Still, you do what you're told, and you got a good sensible head on you. Yeah, you can come, but you may have to stay in the car."

Parker made good time till he turned off on the rough back road that led past the Smigly place. Even then he was in so much of a hurry he kept bottoming out. Gus held on grimly, or he'd have been bounced around like a brown M&M.

The sheriff's cruiser was parked before the littered yard of the place. Parker slammed to a stop behind it and hurried to the house, Gus right behind him. The hounds were all cowering on the porch; they moved aside apologetically as he opened the door.

For once the Smiglies weren't sorry to see cops. They sat solemnly around the room, looking at him and the sheriff. Evelyn Anderson turned as Parker entered, and frowned at Gus.

"Just got here a minute ago. Jake says the kids saw the monster tear past and the dogs all came running and tried git into the house. They don't know where it is now. Mrs. Smigly grabbed a cleaver and ran out. Jake says he won't come with us."

"You never seen it, Mister," Jake said blusteringly. "It was big and black and shiny and mean, and it wasn't natural. It's evil, that's what it is!"

"It don't seem to be around now," said the sheriff.

"Sounds like the one from the cave," Parker said. "Anyway, I c'n guess where Miz Smigly is—c'mon, Evelyn. You stay here, Gus."

He gestured with his shotgun and hurried out onto the porch, past the shivering dogs, and around the house, Anderson right behind him with his rifle at port. On the winding path back into the woods he tried to hurry without making noise.

"This the path out to the idol?" the sheriff asked, low-voiced.

"Yeah. Dammit, Gus, git back to the house!" But you can't shout in a whisper and Gus continued to follow them ten yards back. "Shit!"

They were soon at the clearing, and Parker's breath came short even before he came in sight of it. He forgot about Gus. He felt as if he were walking into a humming cloud of bees, except that it wasn't bees buzzing around him.

Sudden stark terror washed over him, panic fear of the monster. Then it was gone, burned away by murderous rage against Clothilde, who got them out here. He'd like to kill her! But that gave way to anger at the sheriff, who blundered into him when he stopped. He looked back, ready to snarl *Watch it!*

The sheriff's pale, sweat-covered face checked him.

"Jesus," Parker whispered. "What's goin' on?"

"Must be the idol," Evelyn murmured. "Makin' me crazy." Gus peered past him at Parker, popeyed.

"Yeah." Parker tried to get a grip on himself, feeling the sweat start out from every pore. He inched his way into the clearing, fighting off panic and rage, hate and fear.

Clothilde lay sprawled across the center of the clearing, a pile of dirty clothes, obviously dead. The sight of her triggered a raging satisfaction in Parker. He felt that he was glad he'd killed her, remembered with pleasure her flesh coming off in strips under his claws—

Parker took a breath, shook himself like a hound.

Anderson made a choked sound of rage and whipped

up his rifle, but caught himself. The monster lay beyond Clothilde. Parker almost panicked at the sight.

After a moment it became clear that it was dead also. Flies buzzed around both bodies. Parker stepped forward slowly, pulled powerfully by a raging satisfaction the sight, sweating in the still, hot, summer air.

They stood looking at the woman for a moment. Parker couldn't decide if she had bled to death from her torn throat, or if her neck was broken. He looked with savage satisfaction at the monster. Her fighting technique had not improved; she had evidently flailed away with the cleaver ineffectually. There were cut marks all over the creature's head and shoulders, but none looked serious. Still, the thing was dead.

Of what?

"What's that smell?" the sheriff asked, voice strained.

Parker had smelled it too. He'd thought it was just the monster's stink. No, it smelled like rotten meat. He put one foot on the monster's shoulder and cautiously rolled it over.

"My God," he said, retching. Evelyn Anderson grunted.

There was an old wound in its belly, gangrenous now and swollen hideously.

"Must be where you got it with your handgun, when you first saw it," Evelyn said, thumbing his hat back and wiping his brow. "Nice shooting, taken by surprise in the dark that way. But what a tough critter, to've lived all this long."

"Yeah," Parker said, hushed. "Look! It was after Clothilde's idol and she was tryin' to stop it!"

The instant he said that the unnatural emotions in the clearing swooped on him again, and he realized that while he was thinking, they had faded to the background, a mere jumpiness. Now he felt a wash of panic at the notion of the idol's destruction, then rage.

"It was tryin' to smash the idol," said Evelyn, stooping over the smashed clay. "What is it; sumpthin' she made herself?"

"I guess. Wait, what's this?"

Parker kicked the remains of the idol apart, ignoring the moment of panic the action brought, and they looked at each other. "Thunder egg," Parker said. "A big 'un." Grapefruit size.

"What is it?" Gus whispered, tiptoeing step by fascinated step into the clearing.

"Geode. Kind of a hole in the rock that's seeped fulla quartz crystals," Evelyn said, wiping his face distractedly. "Real pretty when you cut 'em open and polish 'em up."

They stood looking at it. It seemed to be the center of the swirling hateful emotions in the tiny clearing.

"Loan me your shotgun," the sheriff said grimly. Parker traded it for the rifle. The sheriff put its muzzle to the rock and pulled the trigger. Panic swirled so high Parker almost choked, but he held rigidly still. The shotgun made its throaty *booom* and the geode flew to pieces, its interior gems sparkling in a shaft of sunlight.

Instantly the emotions flared up into a fury, like suddenly becoming a homicidal maniac, then turned to pain and fear. They drained away.

Parker looked around, looked back at the sheriff, who seemed as awed as he. Gus shook his head in comical surprise. Wonderingly, Parker found that it was still suffocatingly hot in the forest, hot now with no more than the normal summer's heat.

"Thank God it's dead," Parker said, mechanically exchanging the rifle for the shotgun. "I felt—"

The sheriff jumped as high as he did at the sound of a voice behind them. They whirled, guns coming to bear, but saw nothing. A male voice laughed, spoke again in a sort of muffled half-whisper, giggled, and spoke again, louder. It was approaching through a section of heavy brush, across a drift of crisp dead leaves and dry twigs, but made only speech sounds.

"What the hell?" Anderson asked. "Jake, that you?"

The voice didn't respond. It whispered loudly to itself, giggled, repeated itself, and giggled again.

"Why, it's old Joe. What's he doin' here?" Parker asked.

"Joe—*Bumgardner*?" the sheriff asked, the pitch of his voice climbing on the last name.

"Unh—" Parker's back crawled; he felt himself pale.

"He's *dead*!" Gus said, voice cracking.

The voice spoke and laughed again, and entered the clearing. They heard it plain as day, but saw nothing. It crossed the clearing on a random course, whispering and giggling the while, and exited into a dense clump of brush and trees. The mutterings faded, and finally even the laughs were no longer heard.

"Ole Joe's ghost," the Parker said, awed, almost in a whisper.

"Yeah," said the sheriff, equally awed. He had taken his hat off, and the grizzled hairs at his temple glowed in a shaft of sunlight. He looked at Parker. "He never had a enemy while he was alive, but he never had a friend, either. So now he's got nobody to talk to but hisself."

"Poor ole Joe," said Gus, solemn.

"Yeah," said Parker. He cleared his throat. "Same

as when he was alive." The ghost of an old song went through his mind. He heard the voice of Hank Williams, senior. "Goodbye Joe, me gotta go," he sang, not badly. "I'll see ya on the by-oh."

"Pore guy." The sheriff looked down at the shattered geode, put his hat on. "That's that," he said, kicking at the pieces. "I hope things are quieter in this county with it gone, whatever the hell it was."

"You think that thing"—Parker indicated the shattered crystals—"was the cause of all these walking corpses and like that, this summer?"

"Maybe not all, but I suspect it made things worse. Kind of like an echo making a fight sound worse."

"Yeah," Parker said musingly. "Maybe things'll taper off after a bit." He sighed. "Now we got a couple stiffs to deal with."

Gus gulped, looked at the bodies and back at them, and retreated. It ain't much like cop shows on TV, Parker thought in sympathy, trying not to smell the gangrene, the thick bloody smell of Clothilde.

The sheriff said, "Look at this, Parker."

He pried the monster's mouth open with the barrel of the rifle. The teeth inside looked perfectly human. Parker bent down, jumped.

"They got fillings! Silver."

He looked the monster over critically. It had a brutish look, it was black with a hint of dark green and brown, its back had a green-brown pattern that reminded him of a lizard, it had a stumpy tail. But it had human teeth, a human-shaped skull under the curious ridges that went from brow to nape, and its eyes, staring open in death, looked human also.

"It's a man that's been changed into a monster," he said slowly. The arms, the legs were human—only the claws and talons were different.

"Yeah. And somewhere there's a dentist who'll recognize those teeth," Evelyn Anderson said. "Wonder what happened to 'im?"

"Maybe it was just his natural personality coming out," Parker said, wiping sweat.

Chapter Ten:

Rum and Coca Cola

1

Jody "Hat" Stetson was stretched at his ease on the riverbank down the backside of his mother's property. The Osage was at low stage, a muddy-looking stream. This late in the afternoon, the fish were not biting, but Hat was not fishing, despite the rod. He was merely here to kill time. His plans were maturing nicely. The hunting party was set up for Saturday night, tomorrow; a goodly number of young men and dogs were engaged, and the location for the start was suitably close to Nona Martens's trailer. That wasn't far from Waley's house. Afterward, he'd follow the hounds and park close, run and rejoin the hunt.

No sweat, no sweat at all. . . .

He must've dozed off . . . into a dream or daydream of Nona nude with her hands cuffed above her head, eyes big and staring. Across this pleasing vision like a photomontage came a thin woman with crazy eyes in a worn face, attacking him with a corn knife . . . no, not him, she was hacking wildly at a wet black man, shit, no it was one of the creatures from the black lagoon. A weird black monster fighting with the thin woman, that was it. . . . The images faded and Hat stirred uneasily, trying to get back to Nona or at least Waley. For reassurance he reached up to touch the medallion with his right hand and felt again, half asleep, the familiar miracle of life returning to the hand.

I'll wash it with Waley's blood and grip the charm, he thought sleepily; that'll cure it. . . .

Then he saw the face of Evelyn Anderson, the sheriff, vividly close and clear, sweating and pale, and behind him Deputy Parker looking grim with that big lowering head. Then the sheriff put a double-barreled shotgun to Hat's head—the barrels looked big as tunnels—and fired both of them. Hat felt his head explode and go shrieking away in a million shards of jewels across night.

"Hurrrk!"

Hat's feet flew up and he rolled over, clutching his head, almost shitting his pants. All his muscles were water and his bones were noodles. For a few moments he lay, shivering, panting, cradling his head. Finally he sighed wonderingly (*What the hell was that?*) and rolled over reflexively to seek the comfort of his medallion.

He couldn't find it. His right hand didn't come alive. Panicky, Hat looked down, felt for it with his left, and found his right hand rubbing over it.

The medallion had gone dead. His right hand remained numb, no matter how tightly he gripped it. "What in hell happened?" he whispered, looking around wildly in the cool dimness of the trees along the riverbank.

There was no one in sight. The shotgun blast that

had leveled his internal landscape had made no impression on the birds lazily calling amid the treetops. Hat sat up painfully, touched his head again. It was no dream, he told himself, hushed. Somehow, somewhere, the sheriff and Parker had put a shotgun to his, Hat's, head, and blown him away. Or maybe they hadn't done it yet, but would. Proof was, the medallion was just a hunk of brass, no good any more.

Clutching it, right or left hand, gave him no longer the old feeling of certainty, no longer the assurance that he'd have his revenge, and get the gold, and live happily ever after. Somehow, they'd taken it from him. Again. All the time he was getting screwed.

"Bastards!" he roared, raising his fists. The birds ignored him. "It won't work this time! I'll still do it— I'll still git it—find the gold, git back at alla you! You watch! I'll teach you, I'll fuck you all over good! I'll—"

His voice echoed away and the birds were still not impressed. Doesn't matter, he thought grimly. I'll still do it. Start tomorra night, git back at that asshole Waley, and that bitch Nona. Make *her* crawl for sure!

After that, he'd see about the gold. It had to be *somewhere*. Maybe that girl Parker was with, that Judith Lammers, might know something. Be fun finding out, anyway, and do Parker one in the eye, besides. . . .

2

Deputy Rod Parker sighed. "Aw, Ma," he said.

"Don't you 'Aw' me," said his stepmother. Her hag's face was twisted into a perpetual grimace of displeasure. "I know you weren't workin' late last night! Where were you? Off with those rotten friends of yours? Your place is here! Not off gaddin' around!"

"I had to *work*, damn it!"

Parker slammed out onto the porch, wishing he could bring beer home. He sure-God needed something. But with Ma on the warpath about last night, he'd never hear the end of it if he slipped off for a beer, let alone a visit to Judith Lamour. Saturday night and he was grounded like a damn high school kid.

He looked mournfully out into the dusk. Back in school his English teacher, Miz Watson, would have called it "gloaming," he thought. Was it gloaming? Something like that.

It was a melancholy thought. He hadn't enjoyed school, but now he looked back on it wistfully. Then, his older stepbrothers were home and Ma mostly left him alone. Then, he'd thought he had friends. He'd run with a gang much like the Stetson-Deutscher-Dubret bunch, only younger. The gang fell apart after school. And then he realized that he'd been the butt of their cruel humor.

He'd blinded himself to that for years, in his desperate need for friends.

The phone rang inside, rang again. His mother stumped slowly over to it, grumbling half beneath her breath.

In consequence of that discovery, Parker had never sought out new friends. Been afraid to. He'd thrown himself into a few jobs that bored him, saved his money with a rather grim intentness, finally lucked into the deputy post. It was the first thing he'd ever done in his life that he'd felt proud of. Not that it had really brought him friends, though he thought that the sheriff genuinely respected him. That was a warming feeling.

And then, Judith Lamour brightly announcing that she liked him! Judith going out with him! Judith finding him interesting! Parker shook his head, awed and a

little frightened. He felt somehow that when she *found
out* about him, she'd drop him like everybody did. He
knew he wasn't worth it all—wasn't worth nothing. . . .

"Yeah, hello, who is it?" his stepmother bellowed.

Parker frowned in at her, sighed. It'd been a crowded
week. Hat Stetson's return. One more troublemaker
to watch out for. The monster killing Clothilde Smigly
and dying. The monster—the dentist they'd called in
had said those teeth had been done thirty-forty years
ago, judging by the materials and workmanship. No
identification, but the sheriff figured it was some guy
who'd worked out some occult way of living a long
time. If you called living underwater and only coming
out at night living.

Funny. Rod had expected that the tabloids would
eat it up, but some werewolf went on a rampage in
Barrington, Illinois, and nobody noticed this country
monster.

"Rod! It's f'you!"

3

Hat Stetson grinned. As soon as the dogs were loosed,
they lunged forward, baying, quartering the woods at
a run, sniffing for scent. Hat followed Greathouse,
who ran after them waving his flashlight wildly. Hat's
chrome-plated automatic was heavy in his waistband.
For tonight he'd traded his cheap white cowboy hat
for a green and yellow John Deere gimme cap, to look
like the others, despite his new-found loathing for John
Deere caps. Fortunately or un-, he had several of them.

"They smell sumpin' awready!" Greathouse said.

Half a dozen young men ran into the brush, yelling,
laughing, waving flashlights. In the dimness, one figure

looked much like another—blue jeans and various blue or olive-drab shirts despite the heat, long-sleeved against the brush. In the dimness it might be hours before they realized Hat was gone. Likely he wouldn't be missed at all, he thought.

He dropped out quickly, sloped back to his pickup and started it up. It was pretty well muffled, and furthermore started with only a short whine, though that brought his heart into his mouth. But the hunters were making far too much noise to hear it.

And he was off, careful not to turn on his lights till he was well away. He made time to Nona Martens's trailer. The hunt might go on till long after midnight, but he had to be quick and reinsert himself into it soon. Pity he didn't have time for a really artistic job on Nona and Waley.

Oh well, he'd crowd a lot into his hour or two!

It was just barely dark when his pickup crawled up the long drive to Nona's trailer. There was a light on inside the trailer, he observed. He had turned his lights off when he left the road, and except for the crunching of tires on gravel and the faint sound of his engine, there was no warning of his arrival. He opened his door quietly and did not close it. He was already wearing rubber gloves.

Walking as softly as his boots would allow, he went up to the narrow metal house. The handcuffs were heavy in his back pocket. Rock music booming out reassured him. Peering through the windows told him nothing; they were too high. He knocked decorously on the door.

"Come in!" came Waley's well-remembered baritone.

He's here! Hat thought in glee. Gripping his automatic in his left, he fumbled the door open with his numb right hand. He slid his gun and his grin around the doorjamb. "Hi, honey, I'm home!" he said.

The narrow place was full of cardboard boxes; they were packing up her things. Dumbfounded, they stared at him, tall thin Waley with his beak, and Nona in her tight jeans with all the wrinkles heading straight for her cunt.

"Hat!" Nona said faintly.

"Yep, it's me, back again," he said cheerfully, coming on in. He couldn't stop grinning; that asshole Waley just stood staring at him, with a handful of Nona's clothes in his hand. He couldn't think of a goddamned thing to say. He didn't look so tough without his fucking sword. "Hey, Waley, you gonna say hello to your old friend?"

"No."

Waley's voice was cold, hard, and controlled. The tall thin man wasn't just staring stupidly at Hat; he was *studying* him like he was some damn kind of bug. For the first time Hat felt a faint chill and reached reflexively for his shirtfront where he still wore the now-dead medallion. It was still dead, and so was his right hand. But Hat rallied, grinned tightly and gestured with the pistol.

"Here," he said, fumbling the cuffs out of his back pocket. "Put these on—both of you—or I start puttin' bullets into you in painful places, get me?" He tossed the cuffs to them.

Waley dropped the clothes and caught his cuffs automatically, still *studying* Hat. "Maybe we prefer that," he said coldly. "They can trace your bullets to your gun."

"Justin," Nona said anxiously. "Please, Hat—"

"He's going to kill us both, Nona," Waley said logically. "We can't stop that. But we don't have to be impressed by the little bastard."

Hat grinned savagely at him. "Oh, so you're not

impressed, mister sword-swinging lover boy? It don't impress you that I can kill you?"

"Any ape could do that, and wouldn't need a gun." Waley's voice was as cold and controlled as if he was making some damn business deal. "But apes get no respect, and neither do you, Stetson. You can't name anyone who respects you. You're a born loser. You fuck up everything you try to do, you've fucked up your whole life. You'll fuck this up, too, and spend the rest of your life in the pen, begging them not to execute you."

Hat felt his superior smile become a snarl, felt his face go pale, his eyes bug out; he quivered with fury. "Oh, yeah, you fucking asshole? Not this time! I got it all planned. Now, put those cuffs on! Or I start by shooting up Nona; got it, fuckhead?" He pointed the trembling barrel of the pistol at her.

She looked nervously at Waley, not at Hat; it was still Waley who decided for her, even when Hat had a gun on her. Hat thought he would explode from sheer rage. He took a step forward, teeth bared, making a weird *Uurrrr* sound. That scared her; she took a step back, but still looked at Waley numbly. Waley didn't look at her; he studied Hat coolly for another moment before speaking.

"Do as he says, Nona." He spoke calmly, and took his own sweet time about clicking the handcuffs around his own wrists.

Trembling, Nona did what Waley said. Shit, Hat had meant to tell them to put them on behind their backs. Still, their hands were fastened, so he could breath a little easier. The next stage was the same as he'd planned it, only now he'd be taking both of them to Waley's house instead of just her.

He stepped forward and deliberately kicked at

Waley's crotch. Waley jerked his hands down and partly doubled up, to protect himself, and Hat slapped him across the face with the pistol. He grinned hatefully as Waley fell back, glaring. He'd shaken the beanpole up, got a rise out of the cold bastard; and nothing had ever felt so good as that jolt back up through his wrist.

"Yeah," he said softly. "We're gonna have a lotta fun, all three of us. Guess what, Waley—me 'n' Nona 're gonna let you watch. Several times!" He wished he had time to give it to her now—he could barely wait—but he had to get them to Waley's quickly. No telling what might go wrong if he got off the plan.

Waley glared at him. "Do you expect *that* to impress me, or Nona? More likely make us both laugh."

Hat snarled. The bastard, he always was on top. But just wait, time he got done with Nona, the son of a bitch would be laughing another tune. Hat started to hit him again, and Waley grinned slightly. Hat paused.

Waley had it figured, he cautioned himself. He couldn't afford to shoot either one of them, especially not here, or even beat them badly, or his setup wouldn't look right. He mustn't let Waley goad him into shooting. Even that bruise on his face might make the coroner wonder.

"All right, outside," he said sullenly, and crowded back to let them precede him. He grabbed Nona's ass as she went by, but his right was numb and he had the pistol in his left hand. Still, the way she jumped and the frightened look she gave him was worth it. He was getting really turned on.

He haw-hawed loudly and said, "You gotta great ass, kid." But Waley didn't do nothing.

Outside, his plan started to go wrong. Nona's car wasn't here; instead there was a shiny black one; Waley's he supposed. Damn, he thought. He'd intended to drive her to Waley's house in his pickup. Her car still being at her own house wouldn't signify; Waley might've driven her to his place, people would think. But he couldn't leave Waley's car here if Waley and Nona were going to be found dead at his house.

Hat thought anxiously for a moment, but felt the passing of time; in the distance he could hear hounds, receding.

"Awright, everybody into the car. Waley, you can drive a automatic with your hands cuffed. Move it." He got into the back seat, sat tensely while Waley dug awkwardly into his pocket for the keys.

He'd figure out later how to get back here. The important thing was to keep moving, stay on the plan. Still, Hat was tense all the way to Waley's. The tall man drove slowly and every now and then Hat caught his beaky profile against the headlight glow. Thinking, always thinking. Damn him, Hat had expected him to be crawling and begging, not *scheming*.

When they pulled into Waley's drive, Hat exhaled silently in relief. Nona's car was here. He'd drive it back to her place and get his pickup and be home free. He started to tremble, to burn with revengeful fury. He could barely keep his voice level as he said: "Stay in the car till I'm out."

He got out on Nona's side and made Waley stay in till she was out. He had the pistol in his numb right hand and felt her up. She felt real good, tight and young, practically girlish. Waley, damn him, just sat looking straight ahead, his hands on the wheel.

"All right," Hat said softly. "You can get out now, Waley. Me 'n' Nona are gonna walk behind you till we're inside. Then we're gonna make a few changes in the handcuffs, fasten you down good, but with a good view. While we're at it we'll git her clothes off. C'mon, *move!*"

Waley led them slowly to the house, between big lilacs, up across the porch, and opened the door. The light was on, but Hat didn't think anything of that, if they were shuttling loads of her things over. Waley kept a good distance from him and Nona; Hat watched him warily, his pistol poked into Nona's ribs, back in his left hand. He was taking no chances now.

The two separated, and from the door Hat took a quick look around the big comfortable living room, expecting to see the fucking sword on the mantel or someplace like that. And found himself looking into the stunned gaze of Billy Martens.

Damn! Hat thought. A look of utter astonishment crossed the Martens kid's face. After a moment of dismay Hat's feeling became anger at his bad luck. Furious, he took a step forward, pointing his gun.

"Hands up!"

The kid's face went the color of new cream at sight of the automatic, Hat observed with satisfaction, though his hands stayed near his wide sloping Western belt.

"Now, get your hands—"

The kid's right hand blurred, then flashed. Hat was struck a violent blow in the chest and his observations interrupted. The thunder of a gunshot seemed distant, irrelevant. His automatic flew out of his hand and he staggered back, clawing at the doorjamb with his left. His right hand leaped instantly for the pistol's gleaming arc, as if possessing a mind of its own.

Another flash, boom, and another blow to the chest knocked him back out of reach of it. Hat was astonished and felt like a fool, lurching backward across the porch. *Wait, wait*— he thought. The big pale house with its pillared porch tilted away from him. *Wait*— Blankly he realized he must be falling down the three steps.

Wait, wait— Hat had the sickening hollow feeling that he'd fucked up his big scene, mistake, should've shot the kid minute he saw him—

Impact with the ground brought pain, a hideous pain through his chest, and a sudden shortness of breath. He was conscious of a mouthful of fluid, a choking sensation. He struggled to take it in, staring dully up at the bar of yellow light that lanced out of the door over him and illuminated the densely leaved lilacs by the steps.

He shot me, Hat thought. He shot me. I never even seen his hand move, but he shot me. When I even had a gun pointed at him. He shot . . . .

Distantly he began to realize that he'd really fucked up bad, lost his one and only, his precious life— Fear came, but it and the choking sensations, and the pain, all receded together, faded into intense pleasure. He had a feeling of immense well-being in which all tribulations and trials and self-doubts alike melted into nothing, a warm dark nothing. Beyond, a light. . . .

Dying was the high that Hat had searched for all his life.

4

"Bill! You all right?" Justin Waley cried, as the boy stood staring in shock at the empty doorway, the smoking pistol in his hand.

"No, he never had time to git off a shot," Bill Martens said numbly.

"Oh, Billy!" Nona said.

"Never had time—!" Justin choked off hysterical laughter. The boy had been practicing his fast draw for a couple of weeks. Justin started to put his arm around Nona's shoulder—she was sobbing in equally hysterical relief—and was reminded again that his hands were cuffed. With an effort he got a grip on himself, went over and toed Hat's pistol, where it had fallen. He was still stunned by the sudden reversal of their fortune. He took a deep breath and peered into the night.

Hat's boots were visible under the bar of light from the door. Warily Justin started forward, then checked, as Bill came to life and brushed him aside. The young man was shorter but heavier than he. Bill pointed his Western-style pistol grimly, crossed the porch, and stood looking down.

"How is he?" Justin asked, joining him. Nona peered fearfully out the door.

"He's dead," said Bill, sounding numb.

Justin heard Nona catch her breath, in fear or relief, he didn't know. "Call the sheriff's office," he said over his shoulder to her.

He went down the steps. Bill hurriedly followed, menaced the still figure in the dusk with his weapon. But Hat was past menace, giving or receiving. Blood was soaking into the khaki shirt he wore; his John Deere gimme cap had fallen off. He stared blindly up at the light.

Where's his fake Stetson, Justin wondered.

Repressing distaste, he squatted and patted the body's breast pockets, shocked at the sweaty warmth it still retained. No keys. A string around the neck proved only to support a cheap brass luck charm. Awkwardly Justin patted the pockets, found keys. He dug into the pocket, obscurely embarrassed at this intimacy with the corpse—avoiding looking at the uncaring face.

With a grunt of relief he pulled out a fistful of keys

and sorted them. A bundle of four fell out, on a separate ring. They looked different from the others.

"Here, lemme help," said Bill. He took the keys and made to insert one into the cuffs in the dim light. Then he jumped wildly. "Damn! Nerves in his hands 're twitching."

"Probably your imagination," Justin said, ignoring the frightened clamor of his own heart. "Come on up into the light," he added.

He didn't stop till he was inside, where Nona's drawn face greeted him.

"Is he——?" she asked, gulping.

"Dead," Justin said. "Thank God—and Bill. We think these are the keys. You got the sheriff?"

"I got the office; there's a deputy on duty." Nona's voice wavered but she was otherwise fine, Justin observed. "He promised to have someone come right out. Keys to the handcuffs?"

Billy's hands had started to shake, but he holstered his pistol and helped them unlock the cuffs. Afterward they went nervously into the old parlor, which he'd refitted as a library, and stood around waiting for the sheriff's cruiser. The wait seemed to last forever. When they finally saw the headlights of the sheriff's car, Justin led them out the other door onto the porch, where they wouldn't have to step over the body. Or even see it, hidden behind the lilacs and spruce along the front of the house.

The cruiser stopped at the part of driveway circle nearest to them and a heavy deputy rolled out, stomped toward them. It was Deputy Parker, Justin thought with pleasure. He was not wearing his regulation deputy clothes, not even the peaked hat; off-duty, no doubt. His face looked cadaverous in the yellow-green yardlight.

"Deputy Parker!" Justin said. "Good to see you. It's—"

"Who 're you?" the deputy demanded. He stopped short and put his hand on his pistol when Bill stepped from behind Justin—the boy was wearing his gunbelt.

"I'm Justin Waley; this is my fiancee, Nona Martens. This is her son, Bill. Bill shot Hat Stetson. Stetson had kidnapped us from her trailer and brought us here."

"Waley." The deputy nodded. "Kidnapped you, huh? What for?"

Justin shrugged wearily; now that the worst was over, he was letting down. There was a tremor in his legs and he felt a great tiredness. "Rape, torture, and murder. Revenge," he said shortly.

"Figures," Parker said musingly.

It occurred to Justin that the sheriff's department had never bought his story about the fight, when he'd cut off Stetson's hand. They'd known Hat was after Nona.

The deputy peered at Nona; the light was behind her. "That the way you figure it, Miss Martens?"

Nona nodded emphatically; Justin heard her panting breaths. He looked over at the other door, but the shrubs and flowering bushes blocked the view. "The body's over there," he said.

"Right. I'll take the gun, boy," said Parker.

"He's over there by the door," Bill cried, his voice cracking. He handed over the pistol.

"Yeah," said the deputy. He pulled a powerful flashlight out of his car and led the way. When they came around the lilacs, Justin felt himself pale—the spot Hat had occupied was empty.

He heard Bill gasp in shock. "He was layin' on his back, at the foot of the steps—"

"There he is!" Justin said. He saw the boots on the

porch, protruding through the door they'd been too stunned to close. Justin and Parker hurried up the steps, Bill trailing behind.

"Jesus!" the deputy said.

Justin jumped back with a croak. Nona and Bill echoed his shock. They all looked in awe at the dead man's hand.

The right hand slipped and skidded on the smooth floor, scritching and scratching as it clawed toward the chromium-gleaming automatic. Its fingertips were bloody with the effort of turning the dead body over and dragging it up the steps, across the porch, and partway into the house.

Justin and Parker looked blankly at each other. After a moment Parker spoke: "That's the hand you cut off, right, Waley?"

Justin started to speak, had to clear his throat. "Yes," he said. Nona had her arms around him tightly.

Gingerly, the deputy stepped past the legs of the motionless body into the room, his pistol aimed at the hand. Justin disengaged himself and followed as delicately, and Nona caught her breath, followed them. Bill stared from beyond the door. The hand ignored them, straining toward the pistol.

Parker shook his head in awe and toed the fallen automatic lightly aside. Alertly, the hand attempted to follow, skitching and scratching on the floor. The dead arm was a heavy drag on it. Parker tiptoed back and toed the prone man's face more to the light. Justin hadn't had a lot of experience with corpses, but Stetson looked very dead to him—all but the eerily moving hand he had once cut off.

Justin stepped forward uneasily to move the pistol farther away, and the hand jerked itself toward him with eager, skritching haste, the fingers drumming on the floor. All of them jumped back, staring in horror, Parker aiming his gun again. The hand strained and scratched and tugged toward Justin, active as a spider.

"He must've rilly hated Miss Nona and you," said Parker, awed. "All that's left alive of him's still tryin' to git at you."

He stepped forward gingerly and kicked at the scrabbling hand, causing Nona to gasp and grip Justin's arm tightly. The hand ignored the insult, went on straining toward Justin and Nona.

Parker holstered his weapon and bent fascinated over the ceaselessly moving hand. "It's weak, and it's runnin' down," he concluded. "Don't reckon you got all that much to worry about from it, long's Culter don't cut it off when he embombs the body."

Justin's arm was tightly around Nona. He looked at the hopelessly scrabbling hand. "I'll have a few words with Culter," he said dryly.

He reached his toe out toward it, teasingly. It redoubled its efforts, but got nowhere. He added, "For persistence, Stetson, if not for brains, I have to hand it to you."

5

The following Wednesday, Deputy Rod Parker was driving nervously through the countryside in the gloaming. He'd looked it up. Judith Lamour sat close to him, and one side of his heart shouted with glad alarms. He didn't know how it had happened, exactly, but he was committed to shacking up with her—and potentially marriage. "If it works out," she had said radiantly, clearly expecting that it would.

They were on their way to see his stepmother.

"Why so nervous? She's just your stepmother, right? You don't even like her—I can tell by the way you talk!"

"Yeah, well, my Ma— She got used to me bein' there, now that her natural sons are gone. Maybe she kind of takes advantage of me. It didn't matter so much, when I didn't have a girlfriend, or any other friends to run around with. I just as well set at home and watch TV. And I was savin' my money all that time. I got a good bit stuck in the bank."

"Really! I had no idea. How much?"

"Not enough to buy a house. I been talkin' to White Bird Hadley, you know him—"

"Yes."

"Well, his job's no better'n mine and he's married and got a kid, and he's buyin' a house. Saves his money, budgets and all. I been doin' that just because I didn't have anything to spend it on, except cars. I wasted a lot there." He shook his head. "Anyway, I got maybe enough to make a down payment on a house, but the upkeep would kill me, and the furnishings, and all. So I just stayed with Ma."

She squeezed his hand in delight. "I never believed I'd meet a man who had enough money squirreled away to make a down payment on a house! Oh, Rod, you're something else!"

Parker's eyes stung; he was so happy. "I still can't believe you'd really m-marry a guy like me. I'm, I'm fat and ignerant and I don't know how to talk or behave, and, and—"

He felt Judith vibrating with suppressed laughter next to him. "Oh, Rod, I know, you told me—you think you're a troll. Well, I don't! You're a nice guy, you don't show off, you don't drink, I can just tell you'd never slap a girl around, like some guys I've been out with, and . . ." she paused, her voice went lower. She peered into his eyes in the gloaming. "You're just a good guy to spend the rest of my life with, that's what you are."

Parker avoided going in the ditch. "Well," he said, and cleared his throat. "I'm game to try, if you are. I hope you don't regret it, but I'll do my best. . . ."

They drove on, sharing delight: Each other, the winding two-lane blacktop road with its deep ditches, the fields alternating with forests thickly leafed in the high summer, dim in the dusk. Presently they turned off onto a narrower graveled road, presently pulled into a rutted iron-hard dirt driveway. An unpainted shanty farmhouse sat back from the road, shaded by maples and lapped by lilacs, like an old, old lady in nineteenth century finery.

Parker sighed, his pleasure gone. His stomach felt nervous. "Well," he said, and got out slowly.

Questioningly Judith followed him, onto the porch, into the house. He heard her catch her breath at the smell. Ma stood up from her upholstered throne and turned to face them: a smallish, shapeless, woman whose complexion had sallowed and darkened over the years. Blotches had appeared here and there on her skin, and her hair, though still more gray than white, was very thin and always untidy. Her soiled dress looked like a sack, and she hadn't tried to put shoes on her swollen, shapeless feet in years. Her mouth was a wrinkled cavern with a few stalactites and stalagmites, not matching.

At sight of Judith her expression went instantly from disapproving to hatred.

"Who's this? What are you doing, bringing a hussy into *my* home? Rod Parker, you git that slut out of here right now—"

"Ma!"

Momentarily checked, she took a breath for further shrillness. Dickie popped out of the kitchen to enjoy the scene, but his expression altered when he saw Judith—and Parker's expression.

"I'm leaving," Parker shouted, before she could start in again. "Me 'n' Judith is movin' in together. We're gonna git married. I come for my things."

Everything but fear drained out of his stepmother; she shrank inside her clothes, inside her skin, turning into a frost-bitten persimmon, all wrinkles. "No! Rod, you can't leave me!" She clutched at her heart. "What'll I do without you? I need you to take care of me!"

"Oh, Dickie'll look after you," he said, feeling a spurt of malicious joy at the dismayed expression on Dickie's face. "You'll still git your Social Security, and I can send you a little money. Dickie'll give you some of his, won't you, Dickie? And I'll stop by every now and then for a visit. Anyway, I'm goin'."

He took Judith's arm and tugged; after a moment she responded, stiff with shock, walking like a wooden doll to the bedroom.

Ma's voice chased them: "You'll stop by and visit! You ungrateful little bastard! You're off with your hussy slut, you'll never think 'a' your ole Ma ag'in—" She went off into hysterical sobs.

Parker closed the bedroom door behind them. Judith had the drained, blotchy complexion of shock; her expression was that of someone not breathing. "This won't take long," he told her apologetically, and she nodded, gamely.

He'd never been allowed to scatter his things about the house, so everything he owned was in here. It wasn't much. They filled a suitcase and a couple of cardboard boxes, working quickly. He was glad to see how well Judith'd taken the shock; a damn brave

kid, he thought, and touched her hand. She looked
at him gratefully. Behind them, they could hear his
stepmother, alternating yells and shrieks with sobs
and entreaties. Dickie's voice came occasionally, and
the sound of glugging whiskey.

When they came out of the bedroom Dickie glared
at them. Ma flung her arms out tragically and sank
onto the couch.

"Bye, Ma," Parker said casually. "I'll be by to see
you someday."

"To see me! Rod Parker, if you walk out that door,
you'll never see me again! You'll just find me laying
here on the floor—!" pointing dramatically at the exact
spot. "I'll go to pieces without you, Rod, you're all I
got—"

"Well, you done your share," he said tolerantly, and
to his surprise Parker felt a twinge of regret. "You done
the best you could, you raised me up," he said gently.
"Now I'm a grown-up man and I got to go. Dickie'll
look after you." He turned to his stepbrother with a
touch of malice. "Your turn, Dickie boy."

Money couldn't buy pleasure like Dickie's expression,
he thought gleefully.

Outside, ignoring her renewed shrieks, they loaded
the things into the trunk and got into the car. Judith
looked at the house as if she expected Ma to come
out on the porch, but of course she didn't.

"Wow," said Judith, hushed. "How long has your
stepmother been dead?"

"Long's I can remember," he said, starting the engine.
"I think my Dad killed her; I hope he did. She sure-
god had it comin'."

"Yeah, I bet. So she raised you like that?"

"Yeah. I think it was partly to apologize to Dad for
the way she treated him. She wasn't a very good mother

even then, too self-centered, but she done her best. 'Course, after she was strangled she lost all interest in other men."

"How did she get by? Does anyone know?"

"I think some of the neighbors know, or suspect, and some of the women she used to go to church with. When she stopped goin' out, people must've started wonderin'. But she fixed up her Social Security so it went direct into her bank, and her own sons is older'n me, so they was able to do the shoppin' an' all till I was big enough. Then they all took off."

"Except Dickie Rodabaugh?"

"Him too, only he got busted and spent time in jail, and lost his job, so he come back to sponge off us."

"You should've left, yourself. Did you think you owed it to her?"

"Not much, even if she did do her best. She wasn't much of a mother; about the only thing she taught me was not to drink. 'Course, she has to drink, or she'll rot. It don't affect her much. And she only eats a little, stuff she don't have to chew."

"She's right, she'll probably fall apart without you. That's probably the only reason she didn't stop moving."

"Yeah. I suppose the whole story'll come out," he said, anxiously but trying to sound resigned. He looked at her. "Whatta you think?"

Judith put her hand on his big knee, smiling slightly but fondly. "I think you turned out very well, for a boy who had to raise himself."

"Aw, Judith," he said thickly, his eyes stinging. "You're too good for me."

"Pull over!" she said. "—Here's a wide spot. Let's cuddle for a minute."

Subdued, he said, against her hair, "I always felt different. If people knew, I knew they'd despise me.

I guess they will, when they learn. And I always knew I wasn't good enough for *you*. If I only had ole Albert Smithers' gold or somethin'. . . ."

"Forget that; he took it with him." That was the town's saying on the Smithers gold. She kissed him tenderly. "We don't need it, dear. I hope you know by now that *I* will never despise you, no matter what some people may think."

Holding her desperately, he said, "I'm just scared people will despise you. God! If only I was rich."

"Oh, Rod, Rod, dear. . . ."

And even as she kissed him again his mind feverishly sought for some way out, the Smithers gold or something. When she pulled away and started to speak, he said, "Shh!" staring past her at . . . the Smithers gold.

"Judith," he said, very very quietly, not to scare off the idea. "Do you have a key to the funeral home?"

Judith had him park behind the funeral home. Smiling and shaking her head doubtfully, she unlocked the back door.

"Here it is, for what it's worth!"

He entered the place uneasily behind her, taking his hat off. "This scares me worse than graveyards," he said, looking quickly around the workroom.

"Silly," she said teasingly. "Funeral homes are almost never haunted—they never meant anything to the dead people, before they died. A nice quiet place for necking—there's even a padded table—" She indicated it.

Parker winced. "How many stiffs you got on the premises right now?"

"Two," she said. "That old guy from out past Iukey Hill. And Hat Stetson. They're both in the freezer, so don't worry."

Parker glanced at the heavy locker door, nodded. "Showroom's over here?"

"Right." She led the way into a large room crammed with coffins, most of them metal. "This one is fake copper—that's just enamel. Funny how it looks even brighter than the real thing, isn't it? Here's the one Mr. McKay got for Mr. Smithers."

Parker looked at it with interest. It had been caked with sandy clay when he saw it last, but they'd cleaned it up. The backhoe's teeth had scarred its top in three bright copper lines.

"I suppose those scratches made it harder for him to sell it," he said, running his hand over the lid.

"That, and the fact that it's used! We don't sell copper ones every month, anyway, you know." Judith slid the latch and raised the lid.

Eagerly he peered in, saw nothing but the "bedding."

"This lifts out," Judith said. "Mr. Culter used to lift it out to show customers that it was real copper." She demonstrated and they looked into the dim interior. "The light's poor, but in daylight you can see the bottom's just this brushed copper look, not polished like the outside—"

Parker reached in to feel of it; his gasp checked her. Judith duplicated his motion and frowned her cute frown, her face less than a foot from his own.

"What's this?" she said. "This isn't the bottom!"

Something tough but not hard. Tar, maybe, Parker thought. He frowned in puzzlement, brought out his massive pocket knife. A twist of his wrist brought out a gouge of the stuff: white, almost translucent, with a faint, familiar odor.

"Elmer's Glue!" they said simultaneously.

"He's covered the bottom of it with glue!"

"Wisht I had my flashlight," Parker said. He gouged

again, and brought out a smallish round yellow object, brighter than a new penny but definitely not copper. "Gold," he said, awed.

"Gold," she breathed.

It was smaller than he had expected. A Krugerrand, one ounce of "fyn" gold—it felt like about an ounce. Parker handed it to Judith, who examined it solemnly but with a glorious excitement visibly building in her.

"You've found it!" was all she said, though.

"Yeah. Must be pounds of 'em all over the bottom. No telling how much glue he poured over 'em when he had the coffin that week. How're we gonna git the glue off 'em?"

Judith thought for a moment. "Boil them," she said. "Scrape them out—there's a box of trash bags, we can put 'em in that—and boil them clean. Won't hurt the gold."

"Right."

Suddenly Judith smiled, so warmly it hurt his stomach. "Oh, Rod, I'm so happy!" She kissed him. "I never believed it was real—I never thought anyone would ever find it, if it was real—and it was, and you did find it!" She flung her arms around him and the conversation lagged for some time.

Then, womanlike, she became suddenly all business. "What will we do with the gold when we have it cleaned up?"

It took Parker several seconds to get back on the same track as she, but she was patient. "We got to tell everybody that we found the gold, and where, so's to establish legal claim to it. Since the previous owners have disclaimed it—is that right?"

"Uh—yes."

"Anyway, they don't want it. So it's legally ours, unless Mr. Culter wants to put in a claim."

"We could offer him ten percent. He doesn't really have a claim, since it was left to whoever found it. And then what do we do?"

"We invest it and live off the pro-ceeds, unless there's not enough. In that case we let it build up and retire on it." Parker turned a massive little coin over in his fingers. He would always afterward associate the smell of Elmer's with wealth and joy. "We'll have a talk with Justin Waley tuhmorra. He'll invest it for us. Tonight, we got to git the gold out of here."

"What'll your stepmother say, Rod?" she asked mischievously, bending over the coffin with him while he scraped.

He looked up at her and for the first time, probably, in his life, the thought of Ma's reaction made him grin. "How about we give her one of the coins?"

7

Justin Waley coughed hollowly. Other coughs echoed, here and there, in the hollow room.

"Ah-men," the Reverend Hallowell intoned, and a relieved rustle went through the mourners in Culter's Funeral Home. Justin raised his head. Taking a breath and repressing his boredom, he looked toward the coffin—no, "casket"—on the trestle. Beside him, a plump young woman who'd introduced herself as "Sadie" dabbed at her eyes, sniffing conventionally. The relatives in the first row, then those in the second, filed out for the Viewing of the Remains. They were a slatternly lot who slouched forward with sullen rather than sad expressions. Murmuring, shuffling, the mourners filed forward.

"Sir?" The discreet usher, Eddie what's-his-face, his

mouth empty for once, speaking to him because Justin
sat at the end of the pew. "If you will, sir."

Justin stood, taking a relieved breath as he stretched
his long legs, and led Sadie slowly out between the
pews and up the aisle. Slowly, slowly, in the "funeral
march" rhythm, half a dozen slovenly friends shambling
sheepishly after him. It was a very small funeral. The
casket grew before him, a gleaming black trap with a
satiny bed in its maw, a more expensive bed than its
occupant had ever slept in before. On this bed,
incongruously dressed in a tan suit, white shirtfront,
and tie, lay a dead man.

Jody "Hat" Stetson, dead at last, if not quite at rest.

Hat's relatives and friends looked at Justin with
curiosity and interest, but without evident hostility.
That had surprised him; he was the man who'd cut
off Hat's hand, and whose fiancee's son had shot him,
after all. But they knew Hat Stetson too well to blame
the enemies he had so painstakingly made.

Justin paused before the casket, his head bowed, a
hypocritical expression on his face, cynicism in his
heart, calculating the minimum time he need pause.
And then his stomach lurched, despite himself.

A scrabble and a knock came from inside the coffin.

"Oh, no," moaned Reverend Hallowell. Culter rolled
his eyes up.

Scrabbling at the starchy shirtfront, Hat's undead
left hand clawed its way grimly up, dragging the dead
and embalmed left arm after it. Its raw-tipped fingers
dug and tugged at the fabric, trying to get at him, but
it was checked by the funereal briefcase caught in the
crook of the elbow.

With a gasp and a silent rush, the friends and
relatives craned to see, some looking at him to see
how he took it. The story of the undead hand had

gone around, though nothing had been printed in the local paper. Justin watched the hand's desperate, ineffective struggle, fighting to keep amusement off his face. Some of the friends weren't so capable; he heard a snort, a couple of giggles, and a muffled guffaw. Reverend Hallowell wrung his hands and bleated in dismay.

Just what you'd expect of Hat Stetson.

The hand made one last frantic effort and paused, as if panting. Then it turned over on its back and gave him the finger. A deliciously shocked murmur ran through the room.

Justin responded with a slight, ironic bow and passed on, the other mourners making way for him, some amused, some shocked, some half-drunk. Justin wondered how much effort the preacher had put into Hat's funeral brief. With mock solemnity, he retreated slowly down the aisle, returned to his place. The mourners followed his example and order was restored.

Culter closed the lid, pretending not to notice the fingering hand. The pallbearers stepped forward, heaved the metal box up, brought it down the aisle.

As it passed Justin the faint knockings became more frantic. A face or two was turned toward him in awe or just curiosity, but everybody pretended not to hear. Precisely as if Hat had farted in church, Justin thought, keeping his face straight.

Hat Stetson had given his last finger.

Justin wasn't going to the cemetery. When the three-car procession pulled out, he crossed the street and walked two blocks to Bracher's, went in on the bar side. To the inevitable question, he responded, "Bacardi and Coke—easy on the rum."

Someone crossed over from the restaurant side and

stood half behind him where he sat on the stool. Justin looked, said, "Rod. Have one on me."

"No thanks, uh, Justin. I don't drink; it's the one thing I owe to my Ma."

Justin nodded; the deputy's stepmother had been found dead the day before. Rumor was that she'd been dead quite some time, but Justin discounted that; the town was full of macabre stories this summer. The news about Parker's finding of the gold had drowned out such minor gossip.

"You just come from the funeral? How'd it go?"

Justin grinned and explained briefly.

Parker shook his head. "Well, too bad they didn't go for cremation."

Justin had no fears of Hat's hand pursuing him through the night. "Not necessary," he said. "It's already seriously weakened, it's locked inside a metal box with the latch outside, and will be buried the full six feet under—I personally arranged with Culter for that. Besides, it's attached to a heavy stiff. No way."

"If you say so," dubiously.

"Yes. And," he added with grim amusement, "the coffin's far too cheap to be worth digging up."

"Well, if you don't worry, I shouldn't. See you—I got to go enforce some law somewheres."

The tough fat man grinned and went back into the restaurant, slapped a skinny black boy on the back. The boy punched his arm. They went out. Justin looked out through the tinted glass at them in the blazing sunshine.

Parker's quarter-million might mean the difference between failure and success for Red Bud and him. And to think I owe it all to Hat Stetson. It was Hat who'd brought him and Parker together, and him and Nona too. Thanks, Hat.

His rum and Coca-Cola was set before him. Justin Waley lifted his dark drink in toast to Hat Stetson and whatever animated his restless hand. May all such enemies of that which lives, fester harmlessly in warm darkness black as blood.

To Read About
Great Characters Having
Incredible Adventures
You Should Try